ALWAYS HAVE, ALWAYS WILL

Other **queer**as**folk** titles

a **queer**as**folk**
novel

ALWAYS HAVE, ALWAYS WILL

Quinn Brockton

POCKET BOOKS
New York   London   Toronto   Sydney

POCKET BOOKS, a division of Simon & Schuster, Inc.
1230 Avenue of the Americas, New York, NY 10020

Library of Congress Control Number: 2004044711

ISBN: 0-7434-7614-X

First Pocket Books trade paperback edition June 2004

10 9 8 7 6 5 4 3 2 1

POCKET and colophon are registered trademarks of
Simon & Schuster, Inc.

Manufactured in the United States of America

For information regarding special discounts for bulk purchases,
please contact Simon & Schuster Special Sales at 1-800-456-6798
or business@simonandschuster.com

chapter one

6:57.

Three minutes left. The big red numerals still glowed despite the gray-blue frost that leaked into the room around the cheap plastic Levolor-look-alike miniblinds Michael had gotten for next to nothing with his employee discount at the Big Q store. He had three minutes. Then the alarm would go off and it would all start again. He closed his eyes and debated whether to wait for the alarm, or turn it off and get up, or just turn it off and try for a few extra minutes.

"The party," he sighed as he remembered. He'd have to get up; too much to do to start the day behind. If he started out fifteen minutes behind schedule, the whole day would run fifteen minutes behind schedule, and there would be too many people jamming his minuscule apartment at eightish to spare fifteen minutes. He peeked.

6:58.

He still had two minutes. He squeezed his eyes shut and

ground his morning erection into the pillow he'd wrapped his legs around. He pulled it to his chest and pretended he wasn't alone in the bed. The thought made him sad.

"It's just another day without you," the DJ's voice cut into the blue darkness of Michael's bedroom from the speaker in the radio alarm. "The latest from Jon Secada here at BZZ 93.7 FM just our way of saying good morning, Pittsburgh, it's seven o'clock."

"*Morning alone,*" Jon sang into the hazy blue room. Michael put the pillow over his head as much to dry the tears suddenly on his face as to block out the way-too-apropos sound track that was beginning his day.

"*I breathe a little faster, every time we're together,*" Mr. Secada managed to interject into Michael's morning before Michael hit the snooze button and shut him off.

He put his feet on the cool wooden floor and his face in his hands. He yawned violently and ruffled his hair ferociously as if to force the sleep from his body.

"Great," Michael sighed, and fell back onto the bed, his feet still on the floor. "I'll be singing that in my head all day now," he said out loud in an effort to dispel the haunting lyric from the room.

"*Don't want to hold on to never, I'm not that strong,*" Jon sang in his head.

7:02. It had all started again.

"Oh God, oh God, oh gaaaaaaaaaaaaaaaa . . ." The strangled cry trailed off as Brian put a pillow over the face of the guy who was doing the screaming. It was too early, and the guy's bedroom technique had mainly consisted of reciting the dialogue from *Powertool.* I gotta find another place to crash tonight, Brian thought, his mind wandering as he continued to plow the porn star wannabe moaning into the pillow beneath him.

Brian's dorm privileges had ended three weeks earlier following graduation, and he had been in no mood to return to the arms of the family he had neither seen nor spoken to since the sophomore-year Christmas-tree incident. He smiled thinking about the looks of horror on the faces of those present when the tree went up like a torch as Brian touched it with the tip of the flame from his Zippo.

His father had been in a drunken rage, and after smashing all the still-wrapped presents, he had shoved his son into the tree, nearly toppling it, so that he could slap his wife, a frequent enough holiday occurrence to be a Kinney Christmas Eve tradition. Brian had felt foolish saving the tree from falling as the blow landed on his mother's left cheek and knocked her backward into her favorite chair.

"I know you don't appreciate it, you little bastard," Brian's father had said, gesturing grandly, raising his half-filled glass of whiskey. "There may be no presents under the tree for you today, you ungrateful son of a bitch," he went on, turning to direct the word *bitch* directly at Brian's mother. "But I've worked all my life so that someday, someday, all this will be yours."

Setting fire to the Christmas tree had seemed the only possible response to that, it being his house and all. He lit the tree and then a cigarette and headed for the door.

"Brian, please don't smoke in the house," his mother had said, the last words any member of his family had spoken to him, though some colorful phrases did follow the blazing tree thrown out the front window onto the lawn as Brian made his way to his muscley little Nova wedged into the heap of snow-plow leavings at the curb.

"What's so funny?" asked Wannabe, making Brian aware that he was not only laughing out loud but that he'd stopped what he'd been doing.

"Christmas," Brian snarled, slamming himself back into Wannabe and eliciting yet another porn star quote. "Better—watch—out—Santa's—coming," Brian grunted, punctuating each word with another thrust as he tried in vain to fuck the guy hard enough to get him to shut up or ask Brian to stop, neither of which happened.

"Oh, fuck me, yeah, that's it. I love that big cock," Wannabe aspirated, trying to catch his own reflection in a nearby mirror.

Brian began to run through the names or, in some cases, just the faces of possible new temporary hosts to distract himself from the constant inane stream of obscenity. His mind drifted. Thoughts of staying at Michael's reminded him of Michael's face at graduation.

Brian had refused to participate in the commencement ceremony at Carnegie Mellon in part because he was afraid that his family would find out and attend. Michael and his mom had been disappointed but understanding when Brian had informed them of his decision. "I've gotten what I wanted and so have they. I played soccer on that field for them for four years, and now I can put their name and the words *cum laude* on my résumé. I can't see putting on a silk gown that doesn't fit well enough to show off my body and standing in line for two hours to pick up an empty leather folder, 'cause they mail you the diploma, you know? Why is it that people always need a ceremony to prove what they already know?"

That's what he'd said was his reason anyway.

And he'd completely fallen for it when Michael had asked to meet him at Gesling Stadium where the commencement had taken place several days before. Michael, his mom, and his uncle Vic were waiting for Brian on the empty field with a boom box blaring "Pomp and Circumstance" and a diploma cut in the shape of a sheepskin that they'd made themselves proclaiming that they the undersigned, Deb, Vic, and Michael, were "hereby officially way fucking impressed."

That had been all that really mattered; they were the family that counted. He remembered the pride on Michael's face and the celebratory kiss they'd shared unabashedly in the middle of the soccer pitch where Brian had been the star for four solid years.

He found himself kissing Wannabe with an intensity that surprised them both and which, Brian was thankful, had finally gotten the guy to shut up. He was hot, but he was really only a means to an end—more so than usual. Brian had spent the two weeks following his dorm departure with Michael, Deb, and Vic at their summer rental on Lake Harmony in the Poconos. After that he'd not really had any place to go. He could have stayed at either Novotny's—Michael's apartment or Deb's house—and both had offered, but their old friend Emmett was on the way to stay with Michael, and Vic had been living with Deb since his HIV had turned south two and a half years earlier. Both still had room for him, but Brian had grown accustomed to coming and going when and with whom he chose and was not ready to live with anyone. For that reason, he'd avoided the roommate question with Michael as well as several others from school. So, he'd dropped his stuff at Michael's and proceeded to do what he'd have been doing anyway.

"Yes, yes, yes," Wannabe said, sounding for all the world like Meg Ryan's fake orgasm in the deli in *When Harry Met Sally*. Did he have any original material? Brian wondered as he rolled off.

"What about you?" Wannabe asked. "You didn't finish."

"Oh, yes, I did," Brian said, reaching for the cigarette he'd wanted since he'd first been awakened by Wannabe's persistent but uninspired blow job.

"Oh, come on," Wannabe began, grabbing for the prize and licking a nearby nipple.

The phone rang. They exchanged a look and Brian took the opportunity to light his cigarette. Wannabe sighed wistfully, then turned to get the phone. Brian exhaled a cloud of smoke and a sigh of relief and mentally began to narrow his list of possible new residences.

"It's for you," Wannabe said, thrusting the phone irritably at Brian.

"Hello?" Brian asked.

"Brian, it's Michael."

"Michael," Brian said, visibly relaxing. The smile that spread across his face accomplished what Brian had been trying to achieve all morning. Wannabe shut up and fucked off, flouncing into the bathroom, closing the door a little harder than necessary. Brian heard the shower come on.

"Listen, Brian," Michael said, his voice pinched in a way that Brian knew meant he had the phone tucked between his ear and his shoulder while doing three other things. "I need a favor."

"Name it," Brian said.

"Could you pick up Uncle Vic for Emmett's welcome-home party tonight?"

"Isn't he coming with Deb?" Brian asked, idly drying himself with a corner of the sheet.

"She's got a PFLAG committee thing and he's in vocational therapy at the center. I'd do it but I've only got three hours from the minute I get off at the Q to hit the bakery, get the hot stuff in the oven, lay out the food, and get a cab out to meet Em at the airport. I'll probably still be wearing my work smock and name tag as it is."

"Well, I love a man in uniform, but how about if I pick up Vic and Emmett?" Brian said, blowing smoke at the ceiling as he lay back on the strange bed.

"That'd be great but the airport—"

"I don't have anything after the interview at Inverness/Muir and I have a car," Brian interrupted.

"Right." Michael's voice lit up. "The apprenticeship. That's today? Good luck. Anything I can do to help?"

"Paid internship," Brian corrected. "Thanks, I've got it covered. Leave the door open, would you? I've got to stop by your place—I need my suit."

"It's in the closet in the little hall behind the Captain Astro cutout," Michael said, tossing hot toast onto a plate and licking a scorched fingertip. "I don't know why you don't just stay here."

"Because I'd never leave," Brian said.

"Find the right lines, to make you stay forever," Jon Secada sang in Michael's head during the longish pause that followed.

"You stayed here half the time while you were still in school," Michael said quietly as much to shut Jon off as to make his case again with Brian.

"That's different," Brian said. "It was just a dorm room, but I had a place to go then."

"So, you could stay here if you had a place of your own?" Michael asked with a snort of laughter as he poured his coffee.

"Count on it," Brian said, smiling at the welcome and familiar laugh.

"When do we start apartment shopping?"

"Right after I land this job," Brian said.

"This weekend then."

"It's a plan."

"I gotta eat breakfast," Michael said. "I'll write out the time and address for Vic's class and Emmett's plane and leave them on the fridge for you."

"Perfect. Big wet one."

"I want mine in person," Michael said primly.

"Later then," Brian said, hanging up.

"How's your boyfriend?" Wannabe asked, taking a playful cut at Brian with the wet towel he'd had around his waist. The tip of the rat tail snapped harmlessly in the air too near Brian's face to be truly playful. Brian put his cigarette out in a plant on the nightstand.

They exchanged a look.

"I've got to go to work," Wannabe stated by way of indicating that it was time for Brian to leave. "What are you going to do all day?"

"Job interview," Brian said, peeling back the sheets and looking idly around for his clothes.

"The Art Department at Pitt is hiring life models if you're looking," Wannabe suggested, toweling his hair so vigorously that his cock flopped around crazily. "A friend of mine does it part-time."

"Nude models you mean?" Brian asked, pulling on the underwear he'd only just untangled from the bedclothes.

"Mmmm," Wannabe said, tossing the towel over the back of a chair. "It's actually a state job. Like *The Naked Civil Servant.*"

Brian gave him a blank look.

"Don't they teach anything at college?"

"How to be a nude model apparently," Brian said, pulling on one shoe as he scanned the room for the other.

They finished dressing in relative silence. It was over, like a seventy-two-hour flu. Both knew it. Wannabe cared only in so much as it meant that he'd have to find a new infection. Brian cared not at all.

"Will I see you tonight?" Wannabe asked, making it final.

"Probably not," Brian said. "I've got a party, friends, may be out."

"Something to eat?"

"Meeting a friend for breakfast."

"See you around then."

"You bet," Brian said, pulling his backpack over his shoulder and making for the door.

Lindsay paused at the gallery window as she made her way up Liberty Avenue to the diner. She knew the artist. A woman just her age who'd skipped college to get a head start on her "real" work. Assemblage—high-concept collage. It was crap, Lindsay thought to herself with a rueful smile. Just a lot of wood scraps and typeface glued together and daubed with acrylic paint to evoke clichés.

"She any good?" Brian asked, suddenly behind her.

Lindsay's focus shifted and she saw instead of the trivial art her reflection in the plate-glass window of the gallery and Brian's where he stood looking over her shoulder.

"Like Louise Nevelson with no talent. But her work is in a gallery."

She smoothed her hair unconsciously and turned to move toward the diner and away from the reminder that not only was her work not hanging in a gallery, but that she'd devoted the two years since graduation to working as an itinerant elementary-school art teacher.

"Bitter party of one," Brian teased, following her.

"You smell like your last trick," Lindsay said.

"So do you," Brian laughed, trotting playfully around her. "And Rebecca dumped you two years ago."

"Did you come specifically to ruin my day?" Lindsay demanded, getting a little heated.

"I think you beat me to it," Brian continued, teasing her.

Lindsay smiled despite herself and took a playful cut at Brian, who caught her hand and turned it into a hug. "Good morning, grouchy."

"Morning, slut," Lindsay said.

"So, what brought on this mood?" Brian asked, making to open the diner door for her. "The Miss No Talent installation at the Who Cares? gallery in the heart of beautiful downtown Palookaville?"

"A little yeah."

"Hey, kids," Deb called, looking up from her side work. "Grab a seat; I'll be right with you. Coffee?"

"At least," Lindsay sighed, throwing herself into the nearest booth.

"So, what's the deal?"

"I don't know what you're—"

"What did Mr. and Mrs. Peterson do this time?"

Lindsay smiled sadly more for Brian's insight than the answer to his question.

"Lynette is getting married and Mom and Dad are footing the bill for a big wedding, a reception, and the honeymoon."

"Those bastards," Brian said playfully. "Wait a minute, not the guy I . . ." Brian trailed off with an expressive hand gesture.

"The one you fucked on the kitchen counter at my parents' beach house, that New Year's? The same."

"She's marrying him?" Brian asked, incredulous.

Lindsay nodded.

"Where are they going on their honeymoon? Da Nile?"

Lindsay laughed again despite her determination to be in a bad mood. When Brian wasn't the cause of her mood, he could always be counted on to pick up her spirits. Their brief and inadvertent affair in college had blossomed into a strange friendship that bore even stranger fruit. He'd become her gay mentor in as much as that was possible. Setting her up for her first girl sex and then sponsoring her as she came out. He was even there to hold her hand as she inadvertently came out to her parents and to cheer her up in his own unique way when she'd broken up with her first lady love, Rebecca Tucci. He could be quite nice when he wasn't being a total bastard.

"Straight people are so weird," Brian muttered, shaking his head in disbelief.

"Watch it, buster," Deb said, giving him a playful pop on the back of the head as she leaned in to pour their coffee. "There wouldn't be any new gay boys for you to boink if it weren't for us weird old straight people."

"And for that I'm truly grateful," Brian said, rubbing his head. "But Lindsay's sister is marrying one of my former boinkees, and her good old mumsy and dadsy are underwriting the wedding, reception, and honeymoon cruise down Da Nile while pleading poverty when it comes to helping Linds with the rent money so she can get under way as an artist. Which they had previously promised to do. A promise they forgot as soon as they found out she prefers cleaning rugs to polishing knobs."

Lindsay cuffed him mildly.

"God, straight people really are weird," Deb said, sitting beside Lindsay and putting a reassuring arm around her. "Cheer up, hon. Not all parents feel that way and lots come around over time. My PFLAG group has some former hard cases who march with us every year in the Pride Parade."

"Thanks, Deb," Lindsay said with a small, sad smile.

"You need some French toast," Deb declared, pounding the table and chattering the cups and setups.

"Oh, I don't think so," Lindsay began, trying to wave off the big meal. "I think just some Special K and skim—"

"It's on me and you're having it," Deb said, rising.

"But, Deb, I'm trying to—"

"Listen to your mom," Deb said with a wink. "I know what's good for you."

"There's no point in arguing," Brian said. "What am I having, Mother Novotny?"

"Cornflakes, whole milk, bananas, and a short stack," Deb said, writing it down as she spoke.

"Pancakes?"

"Carbo-loading. You'll need the extra energy for your big interview today." Deb smirked.

"You remembered," Brian said, tugging Deb down to sit on his knee.

"It must have been that ad in the paper or maybe the fact that you talked about it the whole time we were at Lake Harmony," she said, pinching his face in one hand and giving him fish lips, which she kissed. "Good luck."

"Thanks." Brian grinned, releasing her, trying not to let on how much it meant.

"I'll be back in a jiffy," Deb said, sailing back toward the kitchen, topping off coffees along the way.

"I feel like such a big baby." Lindsay frowned. "I'm jealous of Lynette. I'd planned to get married all my life and now it's never going to happen. And I don't mind the working. I just feel like maybe I'd have done things differently if I'd known they weren't going to be there for me. I can hardly make ends meet as it is, let alone having the extra time for my work."

"Well, I heard about a great part-time job this morning," Brian said with an evil grin. "Working in the Art Department at Pitt."

"Michael Novotny," the intercom echoed through the store, and startled Michael back to reality. "Michael Novotny, call the operator." Michael stuffed his pricing gun into the pocket of the blue, polished cotton Big Q flak jacket he wore and crossed the few feet of harshly lit terrazzo to pick up the wall phone, mounted on the poorly disguised steel girder that was also holding up the roof. There were no dials on the floor phones, and it began ringing the switchboard as soon as he picked it up.

"Big Q."

"This is Michael," he said when the store operator picked up.

"Oh, hey, Michael," the operator said, recognizing. "There's a supplier calling about the big Kotex order? He specifically asked for you."

"Oh, he did, did he?" Michael said suspiciously. "Well, then, I'd better talk to him about it, hadn't I?"

"Well, duh," the operator said, switching the call.

"Allo?" the voice crackled through in a stilted French accent. "Is zis zee beeg Q in need of zee Kotex Grand Deluxe?"

"This is Michael Novotny. Can I help you?"

"Are you zee beeg Q who needs zee beeg Kotex?"

"I work at the Big Q." Michael nodded, pricing the back of his hand idly with the pricing gun.

"Oh, zis beeg Q is a place?" the caller guffawed. "I

thought you were just having a really bad day because your *ami*, how you say, friend Emmett, she was coming to visit and stay with you."

"No." Michael smiled. "He's not coming until next week and by then I can be in Canada or New Jersey even."

"Oh my God, Michael, I'm already at the airport in L.A.," Emmett wailed. "Is it next week?"

"What happened to your accent?"

"Cut it out, Michael, I'm serious. One time back in Mississippi I showed up in drag at the Royal Ambassador's hall for a friend's wedding, but I came on the wrong night and spent the most excruciating evening at a funeral for a Baptist minister who'd accidentally drowned in this bizarre baptism accident. It was tragic. Though I did meet that cute deacon who took me to dinner a couple of times."

"A baptism accident?" Michael found this more dubious than the French accent.

"Michael," Emmett shrieked. "Don't change the subject."

"But I didn't change the—" Michael began, but thought better of it and cut himself off. "Sorry. No, you're right on time. Tonight's the night. All Pittsburgh is aflutter with nervous excitement in anticipation of your return."

"Whew," Emmett sighed. "That's a relief. I'm sorry to schiz out on you but it's been quite a week what with getting the new line delivered and preparing for the fall show. It's the dead of summer and I'm already planning what people will be wearing in winter in a city where there are no seasons at all. I don't know what time it is anymore."

"It's June," Michael said flatly. "Still."

"Bridal season," Emmett moaned. "Don't get me started."

"I'll try not to," Michael said, trying not to sound as edgy as the conversation was making him feel. He was glad for

Emmett. He'd finished his associate's degree in fashion merchandising at Allegheny and parlayed it into a job with In
Gear, one of the hottest and gayest clothing lines since International Male applied for a passport. There were catalogs as
well as showrooms, and the company was growing as fast as
Gap and taking Emmett with them. From a small job with
promotional in-store merchandising, Emmett had rocketed
into a position in charge of fashion styling for all In Gear pro-
motions. A fact Emmett never missed an opportunity to work
into the conversation. And Michael was glad for him. Most of
the time. When he didn't think about it.

"So, you called me, missy, I'm just returning," Emmett
said with a gaspy little laugh that sounded more like he was
fighting for breath than laughing.

"Oh, right," Michael said. "I'm getting as bad as you. It
must be the suntan-lotion display I set up earlier throwing me
off where I really am."

Emmett made the gasping sound again.

"Brian and Uncle Vic are picking you up at the airport,"
Michael said, fighting off the negative thoughts that the pretentious little laugh evoked. "Just so you know who to look
for. I have to work right up until the last minute, so I'll meet
you at the house."

"Oh, honey, I can just take a cab. I don't want to be any
trouble."

"It's no trouble," Michael cut him off. "Especially since
Brian is free after his interview today and he's picking up
Uncle Vic anyway."

"How is he doing?"

"Brian's great, cum laude from Carnegie Mellon,"
Michael said ruefully.

"No, I meant your uncle."

"Uncle Vic's fine. I mean, he's too thin and frail. But he's still fighting."

"Is he well enough that your mom could help you get back to school?"

"Listen, Emmett, I really do have to get back to the sales floor; it's kind of busy here," Michael said, looking around at the vast and largely abandoned store. "We'll catch up tonight."

"I'm looking forward to it," Emmett said with a sigh of relief. "See you for cocktails."

"The gimlets are already chilled," Michael said.

"Tah." Emmett was gone.

Michael held the receiver for a minute and tried to breathe. More and more lately he was having the feeling that everyone around him was passing him by at high speed. He loved his uncle Vic and his mom, and so he had been more than willing to quit school after only a year and a half to help out, which turned out to be mostly just supporting himself. He was living on his own in his own place, but despite all his hard work the burdens and reasons not to go back to school seemed to grow each year, rather than lighten. He'd completely stopped writing more than a year prior, and the dream seemed only that, fleeting and ephemeral when it had seemed within his grasp only two and half years before.

"Trying to find exactly what I miss," the Jon Secada song came back to him.

"Michael? Hello?" the operator said, coming back on the line, chasing the song away and waking Michael from his daymare. "Are you still there?"

"Oh, sorry," Michael managed.

"What do you need, Michael? An outside line?"

*   *   *

Michael took a minute to survey the apartment. He'd come to love the place even though he'd only moved in because it was such a great deal so he could still give Deb a big chunk of his income and get the breathing room from her that he needed. He didn't know it then and he hadn't realized it at the time he'd signed the lease just after his twentieth birthday, but he'd still be living under the same roof when he turned thirty.

Everything looked great. The candles were lit. The discs were shuffling a nice mix of house favorites, and everything but the hot food was laid out. He reached to straighten the In Gear catalog he'd worked into the centerpiece along with a couple of pairs of brightly colored In Gear underwear among the white glads. The place looked great. He wrapped his arms around himself and held on tightly, imagining that someone was behind him, with him, that he was not there alone. He could almost see that someone's reflection in the window, mirrored against the night outside.

"Michael," Deb called, easing the door to Michael's apartment open a crack. "Are you here?"

"Yeah, Ma, I'm right here," Michael said, looking back into the room.

"How are you, sweetie?" she asked, steaming in and mauling him. "The place looks great. Oh, there are underwear in the flower arrangement. Fabulous."

"It's In Gear, in Emmett's honor," Michael said, fussing with the arrangement.

"Em Gear," Deb said with a little laugh. "I brought some of those lemon bars he loves."

"Great, thanks, Ma." Michael took the white paper bag from her. "Fix yourself something to drink; I set up the bar on the console behind the couch."

"Thanks, hon." Deb moved to take him up on it. "What can I fix you?"

"Nothing now," Michael said, banging around in the cabinet to try to find a nice dish that wasn't already in use. "I'll get something in a minute. Thanks though."

"You have to have something to toast me with," Deb said, popping a beer. "We're celebrating. You are in the company of a PFLAG committee chairperson."

"Chairperson?" Michael said solemnly, emerging from the cabinet under the sink with a metal Rolling Rock beer tray Brian had given him to clean pot on when they rolled joints. "Good luck."

"Aren't you happy for me?" Deb demanded.

"I am, and I am not being on your committee," Michael said in one breath.

"And why not?" Deb slumped into one of the mismatched dining chairs Michael had lined up opposite the couch for extra seating.

"I'm busy that night," Michael said, wiping the tray down.

"You don't even know what night it is," Deb pouted. "You just don't want to have anything to do with my PFLAG group."

"Ma," Michael sighed. "We've been over this before. Everything you guys do is always so public, and I have to work at the Big Q, where, despite the name, they don't exactly welcome Big Qs with open arms. I'm sorry, but I just can't."

"And you'd be so good at decorations," Deb said, trying to tempt him.

"Oh, yeah, you'll have such a tough time rounding up people to help decorate in your line of work," Michael snorted as he arranged the lemon bars on the tray.

"I just thought it would be fun to do together."

"So, what's the event?" Michael asked, not going for it.

"It's called the Red Dress Ball. It's near Halloween and the idea is that everyone who comes to the party has to wear a red dress."

"Yeah, it's gonna be tough getting queens on board to do decorations for that," Michael said with a fake sigh. He added the tray to the table with a self-satisfied little "There. Now I'm ready for that drink."

"Too late," Deb said, taking a pull on her beer.

"Well, we've done guilt and seduction," Michael said, crossing to the bar. "I guess punishment had to be next."

"Oh, Michael," Deb said, giving it up. "I just want you to be as proud to be my gay son as I am that you are my gay son."

"Thanks, Ma," Michael said with a conciliatory smirk.

"Hi, honey, I'm home," Emmett called from the door. "What is all this?"

"Emmett," Deb bellowed, charging him.

"Hi, Deb," Emmett said, nonplussed. "Michael? It looks like there's going to be a party."

"Surprise," Vic and Brian called from the door, bringing up the rear as they struggled up the stairs.

Vic was pushing the wheelchair he should have been riding in. Balanced across the arms was an enormous cake designed to look like the Hollywood sign in the hills above Los Angeles.

"Oh my God, Vic?" Emmett said. "Did you make that?"

"Yep," Vic said. "I'm honing my skills as a chef in classes in my vocational therapy program at the center during my sabbatical from the world of haute cuisine. But the tricky part was hiding it from you in that tiny car."

"It's beautiful," Emmett said again without much enthusiasm. "Michael, can you help me put my bags away?"

"Sure, Em," Michael said. "Where are they?"

"Here you go," Brian said, thrusting the heavy bags he'd been dragging up the stairs onto Michael, who dropped several of them in the transfer. "The rest are in the car."

"The rest?" Michael said, trying not to make a face. "Okay, well, right through here. I put a bed in my old office a while back so Brian could have overnight guests without my having to sleep on the sofa."

"There's a sales pitch." Emmett shuddered as he followed Michael through the archway.

"Here you go," Michael said, more or less dropping the overloaded bags he was struggling with.

"Michael, darling," Emmett said with a retail smile. "You didn't tell me there was going to be a party."

"It's halfway a surprise," Michael explained, unsure of how to respond to Emmett's odd behavior. "We all wanted to celebrate you home. No one's seen you since the big promotion, and I'm not sure how long you'll be here, so I figured this way everyone would get to see you at once."

"Great," Emmett said, still not sounding very pleased, the smile not moving.

"I'm sorry, Em," Michael said, unable to think of anything else. "I thought you'd be pleased."

"Emmett," Deb called. "Come out here. The guests are arriving.

Despite his initial trepidations about the party, once he got rolling, Emmett had an insufferably good time.

"And so I said to her, 'Honey, Cindy Crawford doesn't have a beard that heavy!' " Emmett said, howling at his own wit. "And she said, 'Well, not since he lost all that weight to do *Pretty Woman*!' "

Michael smiled patiently and effected his escape to the kitchen shielded by a tray of hors d'oeuvres that didn't really need to be freshened. It had been a funny story three tellings earlier that evening, but it was growing old.

"So, Emmett, what celebrities have you met out in Hollywood?" Vic asked, perched in his wheelchair as if on a throne. "And by that I mean, who's gay that we don't know about?"

"Well, there's only one celebrity I know about for sure," Emmett said, putting a hand over his mouth.

"From personal experience?" someone asked. The laughter mercifully covered his answer as Michael began trading warm for tepid chicken-asparagus tarts. He felt almost invisible, like a cater waiter at his own party. Most of the guests were Emmett's friends from the small world of Pittsburgh fashion and from the black book of Emmett's mentor, the notorious drag queen Godiva, whose belated arrival promised to be the event of the evening.

"Darling, you'll be faaaaaaaaaaaaabulous," Deb's voice rose above the din as did her very vocal Italian hands. She was holding forth about the Red Dress Ball and gathering recruits from among Emmett's fashion schoolmates to help out as well as to attend modeling their own original creations. She was aided and abetted by Brian, drawing them into Deb's evil plan like Elizabeth Taylor in *Suddenly, Last Summer*. Michael had barely been able to get two words out of him about the interview.

"Lindsay," Brian called, spotting her sneaking in the door. "Over here."

She closed the door and squeezed through the crowded apartment as Brian squeezed to meet her midway, just outside the kitchen.

"So, how was the interview?" she said, giving him a little

hug and taking his drink to get a sip. This familiar gesture made Michael's blood run green, and he was not sorry when she began coughing violently.

"Jesus," she gasped as she regained her breath. "What's in that?"

"Everything." Brian smiled. "You want a Shirley Temple?" he went on, reaching into the nearby refrigerator to get her a beer, inadvertently knocking Michael out of the way.

"And a stomach pump," she said hoarsely. "So, are you celebrating?"

"Always," Brian answered with a little grin.

"It went well then?" she prodded, sipping her beer gently as she began to breathe more normally.

"The interview?" Brian shrugged. "It was just a prelim with the HR lady, but it must have gone pretty well."

"What makes you say that?" Lindsay continued the interrogation. It was always like this with Brian, she thought. He'd make you work for every shred of information, and even then it was like salad for dinner: you always wanted more than you got for your trouble.

"Mmmm," Brian went on as if trying to figure out the riddle of the Sphinx. "They had me call in this afternoon, and I've got an appointment with the creative director tomorrow."

"Brian, that's wonderful," Lindsay said, giving him a hug.

Michael was stung that Brian hadn't shared the news with him.

"We'll see," Brian said. "Now on to the important business. There's a dyke over here you've got to meet. She's an industrial designer who came with one of Emmett's gaggle of girlie boys."

"Oh, Brian, give it a rest, will you?"

"Linds," Brian said sotto voce. "We were both still in college when you broke up with Rebecca. It'll grow back together if you don't get a girlfriend soon."

"Brian, gross," Lindsay said, striking him on the shoulder.

"Sorry, I'm not really sure how girl things work." Brian grinned sheepishly.

"That's not how I remember it," Lindsay chuckled nastily.

The hors d'oeuvres tray shattered as it hit the floor.

"You okay?" Brian said, turning to look at Michael, then back to Lindsay. "Did you get any on you?" he asked, guiding her away from the kitchen.

"I'm fine, thanks," Michael said genially as he walked out the door of the apartment unnoticed.

Woody's was never crowded on Tuesdays. It was karaoke night at Pistol and dollar margaritas at Boy Toy. It wasn't that no one was there, but the yuppies, the twinkies, and their cream-filling fans were otherwise occupied and so you got a truer Woody's crowd on Tuesdays.

That Tuesday was no exception. Michael sipped his light beer and regarded the sparse room's reflection in the mirror behind the bar. He liked Woody's. It was his *Cheers* bar. He knew the crowd. His mom and his uncle were regulars as were most of his friends. It was between the diner and Babylon and so it made a perfect stopping-off place between the two. You couldn't be early for Babylon without looking desperate, and Woody's was close enough to allow for a perfectly timed entrance; it was the greenroom for some. And for plenty of others, it's more established older crowd, it was a final destination. With shows on the weekends, Godiva worked as both the bouncer and an entertainer, depending on which drag she wore.

"It'd never be the same, if you're not here. How can you

stay away so long," Jon Secada's voice pumped out of the speakers.

Michael put his face on the bar. Isn't this where I came in? he thought as he tapped his forehead lightly on the bar ledge.

"That's attractive," a familiar voice said.

"Is that working for you, Mikey?" another friendly voice said.

Michael looked up. "Emmett? Brian? What are you guys doing here? The party . . ."

"It's at your house, dude," Emmett pointed out.

"We didn't invite all those people." Brian shrugged, signaling the bartender.

"Yeah, we only came to see you," Emmett said, sliding onto the stool beside Michael. "So, once you left, we figured there was no reason to be at the party."

"But we don't want to cramp your style," Brian said, pointing to Michael's beer and writing on his palm. "I mean, pounding your face on the bar looked pretty hot." The bartender nodded at Brian and gave him the thumbs-up as he caught the gesture and added Michael's beer to Brian's tab.

"I'm sure it was just a matter of time before Mr. Right came running across the room to get some of that," Emmett giggled.

"Wait a minute," Brian said, holding up a hand to his ear. "I think I, yes, I do, it's our song, Mikey." He grabbed one of Michael's arms and Emmett grabbed the other as the two dragged him out of the bar.

"But my beer," Michael protested. "I haven't paid . . ."

"Your money's no good here, Michael." The bartender grinned as he waved at the three. "Good to see you, Em. Sorry I missed the party."

*   *   *

It's just like old times, Michael thought with a grin as he leaned against the glowing neon backlit bar at Babylon flanked by his most constant companions. It had been a while since Emmett had been a part of the posse, but judging from the fixed look on Brian's face, one of the reasons Michael missed Emmett the most was just about to happen.

"I'll see you guys in a few minutes," Brian said, knocking back the last of his drink. "I think I see someone I don't know yet."

He plowed onto the dance floor with the focus and certainty that made him Brian Kinney, Big Fish, Pittsburgh, PA.

Emmett laughed. "Some things never change."

"More like nothing."

"Okay, Miss Crawford, what's the arthropod in your posterior?" Emmett demanded, turning Michael to face him. "And so help me, if you say nothing, I'll fill your closets with wire hangers."

"No, not that," Michael said, making a cross with his two index fingers and thrusting them at Emmett.

"Seriously," Emmett said, grabbing the two fingers and bending them back toward Michael, not enough to hurt but enough to get his attention. "What's the deal, Lucille?"

"That's Miss Leseur to you," Michael said, dusting himself off. "I'm sorry; I didn't mean to wear my heart on my sleeve. It's just been one of those days I guess."

"Nice try, very convincing, not buying it," Emmett said, stacking arms and shaking his head. "You've sounded like a Cher ballad every time we've talked for months, dude."

"Well, you've sounded like Mary Hart at a Hollywood premiere," Michael said. "I mean I'm glad for you. And I'm glad for Brian. And I'm doing my best to be glad for Mom and to help out with Uncle Vic. But I'm not very glad about me."

Emmett regarded Michael a moment before putting his arms around him. He rocked Michael back and forth for a minute before Michael realized that Emmett was crying.

"Jeez, Em," Michael sighed, holding Emmett at arm's length when he realized. "I'm sorry, I didn't mean it. I really am glad for you. It just reminds me that I haven't done much with my life."

"No, it's not that," Emmett managed, laughing a little even though he was still crying. "It's me who should apologize. I try to do the right thing and get the wrong result every time. All that stuff about L.A.? Bullshit, all of it. I made it up. Well, not that part about the straight movie star at the bathhouse, but most of the rest of it, because I didn't want you to feel bad. I worked at the In Gear store for a few months doing window displays, and then when I wouldn't sleep with the troll manager, I got canned. Well, that and the spandex snafu. If he'd only been cute, but darned my heart. Anyway, I've been shelving tapes at Video West for a year and a half and making up good news for you and Godiva. I finally couldn't take it anymore so I came home—well, here, anyway, I think it's too late to go back to Mississippi. I'm really glad I have a place that feels like home. Thank you, Michael."

"God, Emmett," Michael said finally. He felt enormous relief though he'd never admit it. "You made the whole thing up?"

"Well, they did hire me and put me into their training program." Emmett shrugged. "But that apparently consisted of blowing senior management. And while I do have some experience and genuine skill in that area, fashion is in my blood. Well, that and a fair amount of lime juice. Waiter, could I get another gimlet?"

"So nobody knows?"

"No," Emmett said. "Touch pearls and nobody better find out. I'm only telling you 'cause I can't stand for you to be hurt by lies I only made up to please you."

"So, what are you going to do?" Michael asked, his own troubles temporarily forgotten.

Emmett leaned in with a confidential air, looked both ways, put an arm around Michael's shoulder, and inclined his head right next to Michael's ear. "I have no idea."

Michael lost it. "God, I've missed you," he said, putting an arm around Emmett's shoulder. "I tell you what. One, this will be our secret and I'll take it to the grave with me. Two, you can stay at my place until you're back on your feet. My life may be depressing as all hell, but it's stable. And three, I think that we need to get really stinking, throw-up-in-the-cab-on-the-way-home drunk."

"Here's to hurling with old friends," Emmett said, raising his new gimlet and toasting Michael's light beer.

chapter two

Brian checked his reflection in the oversize brass bezel that covered the wall surrounding the elevators at Fifth Avenue Place. His hair, the Hermès tie, the Armani suit, and—a quick but not so flattering grin revealed that—even his teeth were perfect and in no need of adjustment. He tucked the leather portfolio Michael and Deb had given him for graduation under his arm and boarded the elevator.

He'd never been in the building before. It was relatively new to the Pittsburgh skyline. He'd never liked it. The ground-floor mall was lame and the architecture was eighties faux-Memphis in *Miami Vice* pastels and not in keeping with the other more timeless structures in what was called Pittsburgh's Golden Triangle.

It was a prestige address, but for Brian the most impressive aspect of the building was that it was on the corner of Fifth and Liberty and he could be at Woody's or the diner or the fountain in Point Park in a few minutes' walk from his potential new offices, even if they were pink and green.

The doors opened onto the twenty-third floor and Brian stepped off.

There was no hallway, only an elevator lobby and the door to the floor's only occupant.

He wanted to be excited about this. He was trying to be. Inverness/Muir was the local office of the prestigious Madison Avenue agency of the same name. It was a great start, the right thing to do, and it looked good on paper. Brian was one of a very few even being considered, but for Brian it felt anticlimactic. He had set his classes on fire in both business administration and the j—short for "journalism"—school's advertising track. He could talk money and creative, finance and art, with equal ease. Going to work for the "Big" firm seemed like a sellout at the very least if not missing the boat entirely.

"You never get rich working for someone else," Brian said often enough, and yet here he was at the Big Blue of ad agencies. Brian wanted to be Andrew Inverness, the often quoted and published founder of I/M, whose quick wit and great good fortune had created the international firm while he and a handful of other men invented modern advertising. Brian didn't give a shit for inventing advertising or being quoted, but he did want to be as rich as Andrew Inverness.

"I'm Brian Kinney," he said to the striking young woman seated behind the massive block of marble that served as the reception desk. "I've got an eleven o'clock with Evan Steele."

"You're the one," she said. "Hope there are Band-Aids and Mercurochrome in your clutch."

"No, just my sharp wit," Brian said, making light of it. He gave the portfolio a pat.

"A gun would have been more helpful." She shrugged. "Have a seat. He'll be with you eventually."

Brian took a place on a big clubby leather sofa and picked

up a copy of *Adweek*. Rather than fearful, the receptionist's warning had only made him irritable. Unable to focus on the inane puffery of the most sold-out trade publication in history, he looked around at his ironic surroundings.

Despite the belatedly trendy exterior stone-and-brass facade of Fifth Avenue Place, the agency's interior was all hardwood, Persian rugs, and classical-come-lately. He sighed. It was all a fake. The offices and an interview with some self-important regional director of a big publicly held company sounded more Kafkaesque comedy than awe-inspiring.

"Mr. Kinney," Angie Howell, the HR woman he'd met the day before, addressed him from the oak-paneled archway beside the receptionist's station.

"Ms. Howell," Brian said, pronouncing it *miz* since he didn't know which it was and "Hey, Angie" seemed a bit too presumptuous. He rose and crossed to her, extending his hand. "Didn't know I'd be seeing you again."

"Just wanted to make the introduction," she said, smiling. "This was my recommendation. Walk with me."

He nodded and followed as she struck a brisk pace down the grass-cloth-and-oak paneled hallway littered with hunting prints and enough Chinese Chippendale reproductions to open a branch of Ethan Allen.

"You see," she went on, leading him through the mahogany maze, "I'm not recommending you for the paid internship. I think you're overqualified for that. I'm actually recommending you for an opening in the creative director's office. You'll be an assistant creative account manager with a more substantial salary, full benefits, an office, the works."

"But?" Brian prompted, sensing that there was in fact a but.

Angie stopped so suddenly that he almost ran into her. She

turned to face him. "The position has been open for a while. Evan Steele, our creative director, doesn't feel that we've found anyone qualified for this position so it's gone unfilled. He's like that. You've got the internship if this doesn't work out, but I think you're too good for it and that you'd be great in this job."

"But it's up to Evan," Brian concluded for her.

"Right," she said, turning and walking. "So, either way, congratulations, you got a job today, which one is up to you."

The parquet flooring, faux Oriental runners, and Gainsborough knockoffs ended abruptly and were replaced by a two-story gymnasium, bare brick walls, and a basketball court with a remarkable view of Pittsburgh, Point Park, and the rivers. The room extended into at least one upper floor to accommodate the regulation-size structure, and the other two sides of the enormous space were galleries lined with glass-walled offices, design spaces, editing suites, meeting rooms, and, among other things, a pinball arcade.

"Welcome to my kingdom," a man's voice echoed down from the top of the cast-iron spiral staircase where he stood. "Abandon all hope ye who enter here."

"Where are the Oompa Loompas?" Brian asked.

"They're at lunch," Evan said with a little smirk as he descended the stairs to meet them, regarding Brian suspiciously.

"Evan, this is Brian Kinney, the young man I was telling you about," Angie said by way of introduction. "Brian, this is Evan—"

"The one you've been warned about," Evan said, reaching them and extending a hand.

"Nice court," Brian said, taking Evan's hand and withstanding the bone-rattling handshake administered by the above-average male specimen barely contained in the jeans and T-shirt and apparently trying to break Brian's fingers.

"You play?"

"A little." Brian shrugged.

"Game of horse?" Evan asked, turning to retrieve a ball from a nearby metal rack. "Spot you five points."

"Evan," Angie chided. "He's here for an interview not a ball game . . ."

"If he can't play basketball, I don't want him," Evan said, throwing the ball at Brian's chest with great force and little or no warning. Brian caught the ball as his portfolio fell to the floor and immediately sank a basket flat-footed without so much as taking a step or disturbing the net.

"Do you want me to let you win?" Brian asked.

"I'm not looking to hire experienced losers," Evan said, dashing to rebound the ball and make the layup, his Adidas squeaking on the hardwood.

"Then you might want to reconsider the five points," Brian said, removing his coat and handing it to Angie. "Because I don't have any experience with losing."

Lindsay took a deep breath, made sure the sheet was tucked in securely and flatteringly as she opened the door.

"Miss Peterson?"

"Professor Johns?" Lindsay asked, trying to sound formal and official despite her circumstances.

"Good to meet you," the professor said, extending his hand.

Lindsay tried to extend her hand without unclenching her arms from her sides but decided that it made her look rather like a T. rex and gave it up, only to have the sheet slip away. As she grabbed for it, she snatched her hand away from the professor again.

"Nervous?" Professor Johns asked with a gentle smile. A genial man in his late fifties, he wore an ill-fitting, old tweed coat that spent so much time on the hook behind the door in his office that there was a small peak between the shoulder blades where the hook usually supported it until it was demanded for faculty meetings or, as at that moment, interviews.

"A little." Lindsay nodded shyly.

"Ever done this before?" he asked, taking her elbow elegantly and guiding her toward the door that adjoined his classroom as if he were escorting her to the dance floor at a rather formal cotillion.

"Not officially," Lindsay said, then regretted it at once.

"Yes, of course," Professor Johns said easily, as though her meaning were perfectly clear and her scarlet blush invisible. "Everyone is a bit nervous at first. Today will be just a simple session with the faculty members for whose classes you'll be posing. We'll talk with you and sketch you for an hour, and you'll be paid the standard rate for the day whether or not we hire you on a regular basis. Don't want folks accusing us of anything improper. So, not to worry. Not that you'd have any reason, you're a lovely young woman with more reason to be proud than nervous. Shall we go in?" He presented his arm.

He was so dear and charming that, save for the slight chill, Lindsay forgot that she was standing naked save for the modesty drape she'd been provided to take her from dressing room to classroom. She smiled and took his arm as much at ease as it was possible as he swept open the door to the room.

"Good evening, everyone," he said, raising his voice slightly as they entered the nearly empty classroom. He set a steady pace for Lindsay as he led her to the posing bench on a slightly raised platform at the center of the room and surrounded on all sides by chairs, desks, and easels—her latest place of employment. "This is Lindsay, our model for the evening."

There were nods and murmured greetings directed toward her. She allowed her gaze to sweep over the small group; there were women as well as men, and their ages ranged from steely gray to middle-aged to quite youthful. She smiled a greeting in return as the professor helped her up the step onto the platform. She held the drape where she'd tucked it just over her breast and sat as ladylike as possible on the low, padded bench.

"Ready?" he asked so quietly that only the two of them could hear.

She blushed a bit and nodded. "As I'll ever be."

"Then open the drape and allow it to fall so that we can get you comfortable and posed for the session," he said, stepping back and off the platform to allow her space.

With her hand already at the juncture, she undid the tuck and the gauzy muslin material fell away, some just to her side and the remainder over the back of the bench to puddle on the platform. The professor immediately began arranging the fabric, his focus there as the others began setting up their drawing materials.

No one was really looking at her at all. It helped. Her breath became more even.

"The main thing to remember is comfort," Professor Johns said as he fussed with the material, a fold here, a flounce there. "You'll want to find a pose that you can maintain for the better part of an hour or more at a stretch. Certainly we look for models who are beautiful," he said with a glint as he caught her eye. "You're here, aren't you?"

She laughed a bit as she fought with herself over folding

her hands in her lap, not wanting to look prudish or vulgar
and trying to be comfortable or at least to look as if she were.
She'd been in lots of life-drawing classes as an artist, and yet
she'd never considered what it would be like to be on this side
of the equation. It was slightly exciting. A bit exhilarating to
be naked in a room full of fully clothed people, all seated so
that they could get a good look at her. The chill of the air
against her skin tweaked her nipples and she shivered
slightly, not from cold but as if from a fever. She tried to focus
on what Professor Johns was talking about to calm herself
down, but it was a definite challenge. And she smiled broadly
in spite of herself.

"I'll give you a moment to settle," the professor said quietly. "Let us know when you are comfortable so that we may
begin."

They're looking for someone who can hold still, she
thought.

She allowed herself to squeeze her thighs together once,
twice, as if stretching, but it was really a sort of itch that
needed scratching. She had the feeling of getting away with
something and smiled mischievously. She tried to remember
models she had seen and poses that she had enjoyed as an
artist, but thinking about naked women she had seen only
made the "itch" worse. She put an elbow over the one
rounded arm off the end of the bench and extended her legs
the length of the bench. Finally she laid her head on her arm,
allowing her long blond hair to cascade over the end of the
bench. She relaxed, and her free hand trailed down and came
to rest, palm up and dangerously close, on her left thigh. The
itch again. She grinned in response. Lindsay Peterson, you
tramp, she thought to herself. She was enjoying this. It was
the most attractive she'd felt since Rebecca had left her.

"I'm ready, Professor," she said in a husky voice that surprised her.

Am I ever, she thought.

"Perfect," Michael said, sounding and meaning exactly the opposite as he made his way to the bus stop after work. It was just starting to piss rain and he had forgotten his umbrella in his sleep-deprived state that morning. He had stayed out late the night before with Emmett ultimately as Brian had gone missing earlier than usual, having found someone to go home with.

Michael stood under the awning at the front of the store and debated whether to go back inside to buy yet another umbrella. Given the Pittsburgh weather and his continued economically enforced commitment to mass transportation, not to mention his propensity to forget, he would soon be able to open his own umbrella stand with the stock he'd amassed.

He was really more irritated with Brian than with the rain or the umbrella or having to ride the bus or work at Big Q or anything else. Once again Brian had opted to spend the night with some trick rather than to stay with Michael. It felt like rejection, whatever the reason. And given how many nights they'd spent together since Michael had gotten the apartment, it was confusing.

Michael decided against the umbrella and braced to walk into the rain to the covered bus stop across Amity Street from the store. The rain felt good on his face, gentle and warm in the way that early-summer rain feels. He didn't rush. He'd always heard that you get wetter if you run in the rain. You could only be so soaked, he figured.

He made it to the bus stop and shelter without giving in to the urge to run, enjoying the feeling of getting wet and not caring. He had nowhere to go and nothing much to do for the rest of the day.

Deb and Vic had stayed late to clean up after the party, though they'd mostly just stayed to fight about Vic helping. Michael had sent Emmett to bed after the third broken serving piece. So, mainly he'd stayed up to get the house clean so that Deb would take his uncle Vic home so that he could get some sleep. As a result Michael had gotten hardly any. On the upside, the house was clean and he could take a long ride on the living room sofa; it was *Murphy Brown* night and he'd have a night alone with the TV.

"Emmett."

He said it aloud.

He wasn't going to have the night alone. He had a houseguest. And he'd agreed to allow him to stay on indefinitely.

The moaning caused the others waiting for the bus to move to the far side of the covered area, just in case.

"Hello?" Emmett said into the phone. "I'm calling about your ad. I was wondering if . . . Oh, yes, actually I have tons of phone experience." He'd never answered the phone for a living, but he'd been talking on the phone practically nonstop since birth, so how hard could it be? "Yes, tomorrow at one would be great. Should I ask for you? . . . Oh, yes, of course. My name is Emmett Honeycutt, and yours? . . . Well, okay, Connie, then I'll see you tomorrow at one."

He smiled to himself as he hung up the phone. One appointment already set and it was only—he checked his watch—God, four thirty already? Well, the appointment he'd already made was to interview for work at a prestigious local law firm. He reasoned that would soften the blow of announcing that he was no longer a mogul in the fashion industry, which he had technically never been—had in fact not been working in the rag trade for all but a brief stint when he'd first arrived in L.A. He picked up the paper and began to scan the want ads again.

"Where's Michael?"

Emmett screamed, leaped from his chair, and hopped on one foot threateningly as he removed a red, silk, paisley, leather-soled bedroom slipper with which to defend himself from the intruder.

"Fuck, Emmett," Brian said, raising an arm to ward off a possible blow from the deadly slipper. "Calm down. Do you suppose a lot of would-be rapists break in and ask who's at home by name?"

"You shouldn't sneak up on people like that," Emmett said, clutching at the vee in the front of the matching silk robe he wore.

"I did not sneak in. The door is only ten feet away and I said hello as soon as I saw you."

"You did not say hello," Emmett went on grandly. "You asked where Michael is."

"Hello, Princess," Brian said with a rude little bow as he headed for the fridge. "Did I wake you?"

"No," Emmett sang, making it more than one syllable. "I'm just still on Pacific time."

"So," Brian said, twisting the top off a beer with a little hiss, "you're usually still in your nightgown at one thirty in the afternoon out in Los An-hel-eez?"

"Really, Brian," Emmett said, rising and snatching up his teacup noisily as he moved to the kitchen to make himself some more. "Anyone would think you're not glad to see me."

"So, where is Michael?" Brian asked pointedly.

"You know, Brian, you are the rudest man I know."

Emmett turned on the kettle. "Is it a Yankee thing, 'cause I don't see it in Michael or Deb. Where did you learn to talk so mean to people? It's like you don't care about anybody at all."

"Why you looking at the want ads?" Brian poked at the paper spread across the small, green-velvet-covered dining table.

"I was not," Emmett lied coyly. "I was just looking to see what the market was like here for retail fashion. You would be surprised how much you can tell about a business from the want ads. Lots of job openings means lots of business. Get it?"

"So, how are they doing?" Brian asked, raising his leg over the back of one of the dining chairs as he sat on it backward.

"Not so well," Emmett answered ruefully. The truth was he'd had to call for office jobs because so few retail jobs were advertised.

"Well, it's a good thing you're not looking for a job then," Brian said with a piercing gaze.

"No, yes, it's not. Very glad." Thankfully the whistle on the kettle removed Emmett from the conversation. He turned and began fussing with the tea.

"What's everybody doing here?" Michael said, regarding the two of them.

Emmett screamed and dropped and broke his teacup.

"Oh, Michael, you scared me," Emmett said with a coquettish little laugh. "I had no idea. I'm going to owe you a whole set of dishes by the time I *git.*"

"Michael," Brian bellowed, rising and riding over whatever it was Emmett was on about. "Come on, little buddy," Brian said, throwing Michael over his shoulder in a fireman's carry. "We're celebrating . . . You're all wet." He turned and carried Michael to his bedroom, setting him down in front of his closet.

"It's raining," Michael volunteered.

"Put on something tight. We're celebrating."

"What are we— Oh, Brian! You got the job?"

"Better."

"You won the lottery, you're taking me away from all this, and I'll never have to work again?"

"Not as good." Brian nodded.

"What happened?"

"Apparently you forgot your umbrella. Again." Brian gave Michael a smack on the ass. "Now put on something cute, I'm taking you out."

"But—"

"I'll tell you what happened when there's champagne in our hands." Brian pulled the French doors closed on Michael's bedroom.

"So, what happened?" Emmett asked, dunking his tea bag in a fresh cup.

"Michael got caught in the rain without an umbrella," Brian said in a broad whisper. "How long are you staying?"

Lindsay sat fully clothed, back in Professor Johns's office, waiting to hear how she'd done. After the sitting, they'd said she could get dressed and that they'd let her know how it had gone. She could hear them talking, though she couldn't make out what they were saying.

The whole interview had been a complete fluke. Brian had only suggested the idea to her the day before. She'd only managed to get up nerve enough to call, and they'd had a cancellation and asked if she'd like to take the appointment. Professor Johns had made it seem more as if she were doing him a favor, and she'd forgotten what she was agreeing to do in substance until she was hanging her clothes in the dressing room.

It was probably for the best. If she'd had a chance to think about it, she'd never have done it. And now it was done, one way or the other, and she'd get the job or she wouldn't.

She was feeling pretty good about herself when the door opened and the professor came back carrying the coat he'd really only worn long enough to say hello at the beginning of the interview. "Here you go." He handed Lindsay a collection of nudes of herself from a variety of perspectives and styles. He turned to return his tweed jacket to the hook on the back of his door.

"Thank you," she said, rising. "I appreciate you taking the time."

"My pleasure," he said, turning to take her hand. "Oh, and you'll need to fill out a W-4 and a couple of other things to get paid for tonight, and as the university's newest employee."

"Oh, Professor," she said with a flush of enthusiasm. "I got the job?"

"You were a marvelous subject," he said, smiling. "And call me August."

"Thanks, August." She gave him a little hug.

"Don't thank me. You got raves out there. Not only are you a lovely subject, but you're a natural at this."

"I guess four years of art studies at Carnegie really paid off," she said with a bitter little laugh.

"Well," Professor Johns said with a conciliatory chuckle, "I can only think that that might lead to something more commensurate with your abilities. And you'll already be here to find out about it when it comes available."

"Thank you." What a gentleman. Whether or not it was the truth, the thought that this might lead to work in the classroom—well, other work in the classroom—took some of the sting out of having to take such a job in the first place. Not to mention that it had really recharged her batteries in a whole variety of ways.

"So, fill these out and we'll see you at three on Monday, Wednesday, and Friday to begin with, and then we'll see where we go from there."

"So, did you get the job?" Michael asked, his patience wearing thin as Brian eased the cork out of the champagne.

"Not exactly," Brian said as the cork came free with a gentle sigh from the bottle.

"What exactly does that mean?" Michael demanded.

"You don't follow instructions well," Brian said, pouring the fizzing amber liquid into two chilled flutes that had been waiting in the fridge at Woody's for quite some time. The bartender had been surprised, though not unprepared for the unusual but not unheard-of request. Brian ground the bottle into the bucket of ice at the side of their table and raised his glass. "A toast."

"To what?" Michael asked, raising his glass.

"To the newest junior assistant creative-account manager at the largest advertising agency office in Pittsburgh."

"What about the apprenticeship?"

"All done." Brian struck his glass against Michael's.

"What do you mean all done?"

"Are you going to drink to me or not?" Brian smirked at Michael over the top of his champagne.

"To you." Michael smiled. "Always."

They drank.

"Okay," Michael said, setting his glass down solidly. "Now, tell me everything or I'll kill you."

Brian laughed and ruffled Michael's hair.

"It's a real break. I got the job that I applied for, the paid internship that you insist on calling an apprenticeship."

"Because a paid internship is an apprenticeship," Michael said with a shrug.

"Whatever."

"So, you got the paid internship," Michael prompted, then took another sip.

"But they had another opening, working for the creative director. So, the personnel lady recommended me for this better post. And I met with the creative director and I got it," Brian said, shrugging it off.

After the basketball, Evan had taken a look at Brian's portfolio, composed almost entirely of prospective pieces with a few summer and quasi-school jobs thrown in. He had shredded Brian's work and his ego, asking scathing questions and offering brutal criticism for each piece and idea.

Then he had gone through a variety of ads from trade magazines and off sample video reels, grilling Brian on his thoughts and ideas on copy, design, production value, film quality, art direction, execution, typefaces—they'd even gotten into a heated discussion on architecture.

"Mr. Kinney," Evan had said in the end, shoving Brian's portfolio at him with an air of finality. "You're a hack. You've no experience, you've no taste or style that I can see, and you're not remotely qualified. Why should I hire you?"

"Because I'm only as good as the teachers I've had so far; in fact I'm better. I have the talent whether you're willing to admit it or not, and I'm smarter than anyone else you're going to interview. The only thing I don't have is experience, and that's what I need from you. Hire me for six months; if you don't like me, fire me. You don't have anyone to fill the job now anyway," Brian said with a shrug, gathering his portfolio and moving to the door. "And I beat you twenty-one to eleven at basketball. If you don't hire me now, you'll never get another chance at me."

He'd stormed down the hallway. He didn't even know why he wanted the job except to show that asshole that he didn't know what he was talking about.

Brian had been on his way out the front door when the receptionist had run around the block of marble to stop him.

"Wait. Brian, isn't it?"

"Yeah?" He turned back.

"I'm Trish, by the way. What did you do, steal his watch?"

"He wasn't wearing one," Brian said flatly. "Why? Did he say I did?"

"No. He said I was to stop you from leaving before Angie could sign you up."

"Sign me up for what?"

"You got the job," Trish said, taking her seat again. "Why do you think I introduced myself?"

"So, that's it?" Michael asked incredulously. "You just showed up and this fabulous job opportunity fell in your lap? Your luck. Everything always goes your way. I wish you had bought a lottery ticket."

"Yeah," Brian said with a sheepish smile. "Well, it's not a lot more, but it's a better job. So apartment shopping starts Saturday?"

The smile on Michael's face was worth the whole hideous afternoon.

chapter three

"Bernhardt, Clark, Hunsaker, Epstein and Regan-strife. This is Emmett, how may I help you?" Emmett said, wrapping his mouth around the required phone greeting.

"That's correct," Connie, a well-heeled Young Republican explained as she led Emmett on a tour of the offices, which would be Emmett's new place of employment. "And this will be your work area."

"It's beautiful," Emmett said as though he'd not seen the reception area when he'd first arrived. In truth, it was stunning. Located in the US Steel Tower, Pittsburgh's tallest, the sleek, modern offices looked more like an art gallery than law offices due in part to the remarkable art collection of Bernhardt, the most senior partner, and to the cunning decorator, whose design it was to make the offices look as little like law offices as possible. Light and airy and not a book in sight had been the charge. Cold and lifeless had come at no extra cost.

"I'll tell you the truth," Connie said in a confidential tone, taking Emmett's arms and drawing him in close. "The main reason I decided to hire you was because I thought your clothes would go with the artwork."

Emmett jumped when she let out a laugh in response to her own joke that was part donkey-braying and part tropical-bird call. "Thanks," he said with his best retail smile as he scanned the blotchy splatter paintings that brought the only color into the otherwise black-and-white room.

"Don't mention it," she said with a dismissive wave. "You'll be among the first things that people see when they walk into our offices. Why don't you go ahead and take a seat and we'll review the phone system. Do you have experience with the Phonatron 2000?"

"Um, not as such," Emmett said, attempting to take a seat on the misshapen black, rolling chair, which kept getting away from him each time he attempted to actually sit on it.

"Well, it's much more hands-on than the Codaphone or even the Lutech," she said as though real people spoke to one another in such a fashion.

"Do tell," Emmett said distractedly as he wrestled the unruly chair into the leg well of the desk, barking his knee smartly.

"It is, but once you get the hang of it, you'll never want to go back to code keys again," she confided, leaning over his shoulder to lift the black plastic drape from the massive panel of buttons, most of which were already flashing angrily.

Emmett froze when he saw it and the chair got away from him again, ejecting him onto the floor in front of the switch-board. "Isn't this what Lieutenant Uhura used on *Star Trek*," he asked to cover as he attempted to regain his seat.

"Haw, haw, haw," came the laugh again, and Connie

accompanied it with a good, sound smack this time. "I like you," she declared. "Now let's go over this to get you acquainted before I have the phones switched back to you here. Thank God you've got a history with heavy phones, 'cause this is not an easy system. The good news with the Phonatron is there are no codes. The flip side is there is a button for every single solitary function. The trick is to remember which button."

Emmett looked at the hundreds of flashing buttons on the console before them and slid off the chair again.

"Any ideas, Kinney?" Evan demanded, storming into the break room in search of Calistoga water. "I thought not. Have you ever had an original thought?"

Brian looked up from his papers and sketches spread across the lemon-slice Formica table that served as his desk as well as the lunch table.

"I've got some real cutting-edge thoughts on murder," Brian answered, pursing his lips as he arched his left brow.

"I doubt it," Evan snorted, rooting around in the refrigerator. "There is nothing original about murder. Revenge, there's the opportunity for originality. How about Calistoga water? Any ideas there? There is no black cherry in here. I don't really expect you to be able to come up with anything helpful in the way of advertising, but I had hoped that you'd be able to keep the fridge stocked, or is that too much—"

"Crisper," Brian said, returning to his sketches.

"What?"

Brian sighed, looked up, and as though indulging a dull-witted child, said again, though more slowly, "Crisper."

"What is?"

Brian sighed deeply, pushed his chair back from the table,

crossed the room to the refrigerator, opened the door, leaned down, pulled the crisper drawer open, took out a black cherry sparkling water, thrust it into Evan's hands, kicked the drawer shut, closed the door, and returned to his work.

"That's more like it," Evan said, opening the water and crossing to look over Brian's shoulder. "Hmmm," he intoned, taking a red pen from his shirt pocket with which he began to mark on Brian's presentation board, rendering it useless. "This will reduce readership by about twenty-five percent, and this is a rip-off from the Nike campaign. Good idea about putting my waters in the drawer though. It is much crisper."

And he turned and walked out the door, leaving Brian alone.

"Bernhardt, Hunsaker, Epstein and Reganstrife, this is Emmett, how may I help—oh, sh—I mean shoot. I forgot Clark. Wait, let me start over. Hold please," Emmett said, disconnecting the call and pressing a flashing button on the massive console that caused his voice to be broadcast throughout the entire office. "Heartburn, Clark, Epstein, Hunsaker and Reganstrife, this is Emmett, may I help you? Hello? His voice echoed throughout the expansive suite. Damnation," he said with an exasperated snort to the entire legal staff. "That is the third fucking time that's happened this morning."

And then, as he'd done the other two times after he'd first activated the office intercom, he put the intercom back on hold, which caused classical music to play throughout the offices until his next outburst.

The console beeped and he pressed another flashing button, which connected him to a conference call two of the partners were having with a translator and the principal officers of a Chilean mining concern they were representing in a federal antitrust action filed against the U.S.-based conglomerate that owned the Chilean mines.

"Front desk, this is Emmett," he broke in.

"*Qué?*" one of the clients asked.

"I'm sorry, I don't know a Kay. Do you have a last name?"

"*Qué es eso?*" another inquired.

"That's middle initial *S?*" Emmett asked, looking over the company phone directory.

"Who is this?" demanded Epstein, the lead partner on the call.

"I'm sorry, this is Emmett from the front desk. And you were looking for Kay?"

"Who the hell is Kay?" Epstein shouted.

"You'll forgive me, but that is exactly my question," Emmett chuckled. "I don't know who the hell she is. I can't find her anywhere on the directory. Could you hold on a minute?" Emmett pushed a button to answer the now ringing switchboard, but really only reconnecting to the conference call through the line of a junior partner who was also sitting in. "Bernhardt, Clark, Hunsaker, Epstein and Reganstrife, this is Emmett, how may I help you?"

"Well, for starters you can get my name right," Epstein snarled. "It's *steen*, not *stine.*"

"Yes, Mr. Epstine, I mean *steen*. Sorry, sir, it's my first day. How can I help you?" Emmett stammered.

"You can hang up this phone and stop breaking in on my conference call," Epstein shouted.

"Very good, sir," Emmett said efficiently as he hit the disconnect button and cut off everyone on the call except himself.

Michael was striping new Corning Ware into the gondola, which meant he was lining up boxes one above the next one of the Big Q's built-in shelving units. He smiled, thinking of how much money probably went into renaming everything in the store to make it sound as though the marketing people were actually earning their salaries.

As he reached for another box, he looked up and found himself staring directly into the face of one of the best-looking guys he'd seen in a while. He was still smiling from his contemptuous ruminations on the overpaid MBAs who had never set foot in the store but were deciding how he should restock the cookware aisles from their home offices in Cincinnati.

The customer returned the smile and did not look away.

Michael was a second away from offering a bright Big Q "May I help you?" when the man stepped more fully into the aisle and ran the back of his index and middle fingers along the top of a rather sizable erection pointed northwest where it lay plastered across the front of his trousers.

Instead of speaking, Michael drew in a sharp little breath and began to cough. The shopper looked around and then retreated down the aisle out of housewares and into the domestics department. As Michael regained his breath and stopped coughing, the shopper turned back from where he stood quite some distance away to look at Michael again. He licked his lips, turned his head to face down the aisle where he stood, and then back at Michael. He smiled and turned down the aisle to his right, disappearing from Michael's line of sight.

Intrigued, Michael followed.

By the time he turned the corner in the domestics department, there was nothing but an aisle lined with sheets and pillowcases, which dead-ended into a cross aisle that ran along the back of the store and was filled to the ceiling with draperies and drapery displays. Directly ahead was a small alcove with a water fountain in the center and doors to the men's and ladies' on either side. Michael walked to the end of the aisle and then turned to look both ways down each side of the cross aisle. Nothing but café curtains to the left and box pleated drapes and traverse rods to the right.

He looked around a bit, trying to be inconspicuous, but there was no sign of his phantom. He was just about to return to his Corning Ware striping when he paused to lean down for a quick pull of cool water from the fountain. He turned his head to take a drink and saw the men's room door.

The thought occurred to him and it was irresistible. He was at work. He was not "out" at work even a little bit to anyone. But he had to find out. A quick look revealed no one around and he ducked into the men's room. There were two doors to the room. One opened into a modest vestibule; the second was at a sharp right angle to the first, opening into the room itself and creating a buffer to the view from the outside.

It also created a warning to those inside that someone was coming as the vacuum created when the first door was opened sucked the second door into the facing with a small bang. Michael had never been so keenly aware of the bath-room doors to the customer restrooms before.

His breath was short as he slowly opened the second door and stepped cautiously inside. At first there was nothing unexpected. The sound of dripping water. The cloying cherry smell of the deodorizer. The aqua blue tiles and Formica counters and stalls. He stood frozen for a moment taking in the room, and then he heard it, a small shuffling sound. Michael stepped past the sinks and down the aisle that ran between the stalls and the urinals. His footsteps echoed on the tile as he made his way toward the sound.

It stopped.

He paused at the end of the aisle.

No sound. He was undeniably excited and a bit disappointed, though also quite relieved. Just as he turned to leave, the stall door nearest him swung open, revealing the handsome young man from cookware on his knees in front of a middle-aged businessman, still wearing his tie and suit coat, though his dress trousers were in a pool around his wing tips. The young man turned to look at Michael. The older man stroked himself and, with the other hand, motioned for Michael to come into the stall.

Michael was so startled and excited by the proximity of sex that he felt the small spasms of imminent orgasm though he had not so much as touched himself. He looked into the businessman's eyes, into the shopper's eyes, at the hand on the erection, and then the younger man turned and took the older man in his mouth. Michael began coughing again and turned quickly away from the scene if for no other reason than because he did not have a spare pair of pants to get him through the rest of the day.

He splashed cold water on his face, then paused to hear the small squishy sounds he was not unfamiliar with and the unsteady breathing that meant it would soon be over. Michael left before he too lost control.

It seemed unreal as he stepped back into the harsh fluorescent lighting of the store and made his way back to the half-uncrated cases of Corning Ware. It took him a few minutes to get his breath to steady and his hands to stop shaking. The idea of public restroom sex had never appealed to him, but the effects of what he'd seen were undeniable.

As he returned to the task at hand, he fell back into the comforting routine of his dreary job, turning over the event in his mind. He smiled thinking of the scorching moment. He turned to get the next box for the stripe and found himself once again face-to-face with the handsome young man he'd followed like Alice's rabbit, through the looking glass.

The young man smiled at Michael, gave him a wink, then turned and headed for the front of the store.

"Clarkbern, Hartsaker, Epsteen-stine and Reganstrife, this is Emmett, how may I help you?"

"Um, yes," the caller said doubtfully. "I need to speak to Mr. Bernhardt."

"I'm sorry. Mr. Bernhardt is on a conference call with Mr. Reganstrife just now. May I take a message or have him call you?"

"This is Mr. Reganstrife," the caller identified himself hotly. "And I was on a conference call with Mr. Bernhardt and then there was this clicking and then I was on with the catalog switchboard for Conran's."

"Really?" Emmett said, discreetly shoving the Conran's catalog into the trash bin by his desk and looking around sweatily to make sure he'd not been observed. "So, are you in the office?"

"No, I'm representing a client at a hearing in Washington, D.C.," Reganstrife replied defensively. "And I need to speak with Mr. Bernhardt before we go back into session."

"Right away, sir. Hold please." Emmett pushed the hold button and pushed a button to transfer the call. "Hello, Mr. Bernhardt?"

"No, this is Conran's," said an irritable woman on the other end of the line.

"Oh, thank God." Emmett retrieved the catalog from the bin. "I thought for a moment I'd lost you."

*   *   *

"Kinney," Brian heard his name being called, shouted really, for about the thirtieth time that day.

"Yes," he answered in a normal tone, rising to go to see what it was this time. He made his way down the second-level gallery walk above the basketball court along to Evan's office.

"Kinney," Evan screamed again.

"Yes, Mr. Steele?" Brian asked genially, leaning around the door into Evan's breathtaking office. It wasn't a corner office because there were no corners on that floor of the building or the one above it. In fact, an indentation where the corner of the building would have been created a terrace onto which the office opened. So, in addition to the enormous space, the multiple-screen bank of televisions, the showroom quantity of leather furniture, the artwork, the awards, the chrome and steel and glass, there was an impressive fountain, a greenhouse-load of plant life, and a private patio garden overlooking the park below.

"What are you doing about lunch?" Evan asked, looking up from photographs he was sorting through on his desk.

"Not sure," Brian said. "I'd thought I might pick something up from one of the vendors in the park."

Evan stared at Brian with a mix of bewildered irritation. "Are you really that stupid?" he asked at last, breaking the silence.

"I, um," Brian answered adroitly, unsure of the question, or the conversation or his footing or anything else.

"Cripes," Evan aspirated, hurling his reading glasses across the show-window-sized sheet of plate glass that made up the surface of his vast desk. "Brian, I don't give a shit what you're having for lunch. I want to know what I'm having for lunch! When I don't have lunch plans, you are to see to it that

I have lunch in the office. Or is that concept too tough for you?"

"No, sorry," Brian said easily. "I didn't realize that you didn't have lunch plans. I'll bring you back something from the park." He turned to leave a very much surprised and still quite vocal Evan shouting expletives at him as he made his way back to the table in the break room where he'd been forced to work.

"Clarksaker . . . No, that's Hunsaker, Clark, Ep-Steen and Strife," Emmett struggled to pronounce the tongue twister that he was rapidly realizing was his new job. He sighed rather than trying to correct the latest mangling. "Who would you like to speak to?"

"Young man," a rather operatic female voice chided, "you should never end your sentences, even your questions, with a preposition."

"Is this the grammar police?" Emmett asked politely.

"Do you have any idea to whom you are speaking?"

"I sure don't," Emmett answered brightly. "Especially since you didn't have the good manners to identify yourself when I first answered your call."

"But you answered improperly, young man. You are the voice of Bernhardt, Clark, Hunsaker, Epstein and Regan-strife, and as such, your answer reflects on the entire firm. Can you see how important your job is?"

"I have to say I think I've had a bead on the importance of my job pretty much since I got here," Emmett said as ambiguously as he could manage without laughing out loud at the crackpot on the phone.

"So, what do you suppose you should have said when you answered this call?" she clucked.

"This call? Well, I've been having some problems with all those names," Emmett said coyly. The phone was beeping madly as the flashing lights multiplied.

"Yes, they are a mouthful," the caller agreed, chuckling.

"But more than getting their names wrong," Emmett mused, "I think I regret most not saying, 'Fuck off, you bossy old cow.' There now, that doesn't end in a preposition, does it?"

She hung up on him before he had the chance to hang up on her.

Lindsay had chosen a charcoal sketch of the Smithfield Street Bridge tacked haphazardly to a corkboard on the far wall of the art studio on which to focus her attention. The life-study class was small, but still, there she was naked and surrounded by twenty-five or so strangers, many of them attractive young women pretty much her own age. It made her feel quite differently from the small group of professors she'd sat for in her only other such appearance; more vulnerable somehow.

And it was not that she'd felt exposed. Well, it wasn't only that she felt exposed. There was also something a bit exhilarating about being naked in a room full of people who were clothed; vulnerable and powerful at once.

She stole a quick glance over at the group.

One young woman near the front Lindsay found attractive, which made her predicament even more challenging, and she felt the fevered shiver she'd had the last time she'd posed. Her mind drifted into fantasy over the lithe, little brunette front left as she held her gaze fixed on the crosshatchings of the charcoal bridge.

In her fantasy the handsome little brunette was waiting for Lindsay after class. Her name was Eugenia; she was an

Italian exchange student, smitten not just with Lindsay's beauty but also an admirer of her work as an artist. Over cappuccinos at the nearby Café Latte, Eugenia revealed that she was in fact Italian royalty and had left her Tuscan principality to come to America to study. She was moved by Lindsay's plight: "Such common work for such an uncommon talent." They made mad, passionate love in front of the Cézanne at the Carnegie Museum, a shared favorite. And then, on a romantic walk across the Smithfield Street Bridge, oddly devoid of traffic, the Principessa Eugenia Vermicelli had proposed, asking Lindsay to give up the degradation of the life that had been thrust upon her in favor of a life at court in Tuscany, where Lindsay might devote herself to her art and pose only for Eugenia.

Lindsay was torn. She looked out off the bridge down the Monongahela River toward the hills above Pittsburgh along the Ohio River that had always been her home. How could she leave this all behind? "Sometimes we only know what is valuable when we lose it," Eugenia said in her soft, husky Italian accent. Lindsay ran across the bridge toward the South Slopes. "Lindsay? Lindsay?" Eugenia's voice called over the high piercing wail of the fire alarm.

"Lindsay?" What was Professor Johns doing standing in the middle of the Smithfield Street Bridge?

And then she was naked in the University of Pittsburgh life-drawing studio in the middle of a fire drill.

"Leave your things where they are and follow me out," Professor Johns said, raising his voice only loud enough to be heard. "I'm sure it's just a drill, and the faster we get out there, the sooner we can come back. And better yet, the sooner they turn off this dad-blamed racket. Lindsay, sorry about all this. Pull the drape around yourself and come on.

I'll grab my coat, but I think it's warm enough you won't need it for anything but coverage."

In a daze Lindsay followed. The large swath of muslin gauze, pleated with wrinkles, trailed grandly behind her as she attempted to follow the group and maintain her dignity. The Principessa Eugenia had met up with a young prince and was holding fast to his arm so that he might protect her from the imaginary fire.

"Looks like the engagement's off," Lindsay sighed. The class wandered out onto the lawn in front of the Frick Fine Arts Building to join the other evacuees as much to get away from the deafening alarm as to follow directions and wait for the all clear. Lindsay made to keep herself aloof from the class, preferring her air of mystery, or belief in it at least, rather than letting them know she was just another artist, down on her luck and in need of a few extra bucks. Clutching the unruly fabric with as much dignity as she could marshal, she took up a place on the opposite side of the fountain nearest the parking lot that the Italianate Fine Arts Building shared with the library and the museum.

She was just about to take a seat on the broad lip of the fountain when the wind got wedged in between the three buildings, licked the back of Lindsay's wrap skyward, and began flapping it into the air and down again, like a sail off the mast. Lindsay did her best to hold the helm on her capricious vessel, satisfied that most of her potential spectators had already seen what the animated fabric was supposed to conceal. She did not hear the motorcycle as anything more than traffic on busy nearby Forbes Avenue or the Schenley Park Bridge. But the wolf whistle was unmistakable, coming in direct accompaniment to a particularly revealing updraft on the back of Lindsay's drape.

Lindsay reeled instinctively to glare down the violator.

She didn't see him at first. Then she spotted him getting off his motorcycle. Lindsay wouldn't have known the whistle was his but for the solid thumbs-up. She was just about to raise a finger of her own in response when the motorcyclist took off his helmet.

"Thanks for the show," the young woman called to Lindsay as she transformed herself from a leather-clad guy on a motorbike into a young woman on her way to class. And not too hard to look at either, Lindsay had to admit.

"Well . . . I . . . really," Lindsay said, her bluster and invective dissolved into a stammering blush as she continued to fight for control of the billowing fabric that surrounded her at its own will. She clutched more tightly across her breasts and at the join of her legs. Strangely, the presumption that Lindsay would welcome the attentions of another woman made Lindsay feel more exposed than the wind's continuing efforts to denude her.

The young woman slung her backpack over her shoulder and paused to give Lindsay a deafening smile. "You look like Venus rising. Raphael? Right?"

"Botticelli," Lindsay corrected sharply, maintaining her grasp all the while.

"Okay, Botticelli," the young woman said. "I gotta get to class, but I hope I get to see more of you."

"Very funny," Lindsay said crossly. "I can hardly wait."

"You know," the motorcyclist said as she turned to face Lindsay and began walking backward toward the library and the law school buildings, "two tips. If you don't want this kind of attention, you might want to consider a pair of jeans and a T-shirt. And two, you really shouldn't have stood so close to the fountain."

Lindsay turned to see that her train was submerged in the

murky waters of the huge pool surrounding the fountain and pulling more behind it as the soaked material gained weight. She let out a cry and threw an accusatory glare in the direction of the whistler, only to find that the only view available of Lindsay's assailant was of her back.

"Oh my God!" Emmett shrieked into the phone, his voice ricocheting off the stark white walls and gleaming parquet floors of his office. "A tea room? At the Big Q? You have got to be kidding me."

"No," Michael said. "I don't know. Maybe it was just someone else he met in the store."

"No, not that fast. They wouldn't have had time to hook up so quickly unless it was a regular thing or was some kind of code they both knew."

"I guess," Michael allowed.

"So, did you go into the stall?" Emmett asked, actually leaning in closer to the console, which began beeping wildly. "Oh, hold on," he said, exasperated as he cut Michael off. "Heartburn, Cocksucker, Steenstine . . ." He trailed off as he realized. "Who do you want?" Emmett asked, squinting his eyes and hoping that he'd gone fast enough that the caller wouldn't notice his Freudian faux pas.

"What? What did you . . . Emmett?" Connie's voice was trembling. "Did you just call Mr. Heartburn's—I mean, Mr. Bernhardt's wife a bossy old cow?"

"I'm not entirely sure," Emmett admitted honestly, as he'd never been on a first- or last-name basis with the old cow in question.

"Could you come to my office?"

"Um, sure," Emmett said, grabbing his things and the Conran's catalog, then running for the door.

*　　*　　*

"No, no, no," Evan shouted at one of the creative staff gathered around the huge guitar-shaped conference table. "The target market is young men eighteen to twenty-four, not geeks in training."

"But the focus group said . . ." Benny, the young man who was currently the object of Evan's wrath, began.

"Fuck the focus group," Evan said, throwing the presentation board against the wall. "The only thing anyone ever got out of a focus group was a study in how people interact in a group. They tell you what they think the other people in the group want to hear or will be impressed with. They'll always tell you that what they want is just straight information. If you believed focus groups, we'd all be out of a job because what they'll tell you is they basically just want an announcer and bullet points scrolling by on the screen. But the truth is, if it doesn't have big tits on it or drip with sex or one of the other seven deadlys, they'll zap you, turn the page, or buy the exact same thing from someone willing to put tits on it."

It was the first part of the day that Brian had enjoyed and not just because someone besides him was getting yelled at. It was his first real creative session with real professionals having a real discussion about a real campaign for a real product that would really be produced and aired with real and measurable results. He had been playing pretend ad executive—albeit at one of the finest schools in the nation, but pretend nonetheless—for the past four years in anticipation of just this moment.

The other really great part, though he'd die before admitting it, was Evan. Brian had agreed with every hatchet job Evan had done on each presentation board that Evan had reviewed. In fact, the only downside to the meeting for Brian was that he had slipped his own presentation board into the stack with the others when Evan had had him collect them from the staff in preparation for the meeting. All the boards were drawings, designs, storyboards, or a combination, mounted on heavy illustration board and flapped with I/M's standard, heavy gray paper. So, Brian had done the same with his own ideas just to see how Evan would react to the work not knowing in advance it was from Brian.

Unfortunately, Evan had hated everything and was eviscerating each submission as they went along.

"Hmmm, now have a look at this," Evan said, lifting the flap on the next work. "Can you tell me what's wrong with this ad?"

The client was an electronics manufacturer, and in the example being held up, a component stereo system was dripping with chocolate syrup, whipped cream, and dotted with cherries. A woman could be seen, only from mouth to waist, licking a finger she had obviously dipped into the gooey mess.

" 'The only way to make our stereo better,' " Evan read the headline. "Okay, anyone, what's wrong with this ad?"

No one spoke.

Brian raised his hand.

"Jesus, Kinney," Evan sighed. "What is it? Do you need to go to the bathroom?"

"No, sir," Brian managed in a stagy show of respect. "I was going to say that it tells the buyer that their products need improvement."

"No, it doesn't," Evan sighed. "In fact it makes a mockery of the idea that their products could be improved."

"Well, it doesn't take the product very seriously." Brian shrugged.

"The target market is not interested in serious, moron,"

Evan said, throwing a red sharpie in Brian's direction. "This
is the kind of attention-getting non sequitur which will not
only gain the target's attention but drive home the client's
market superiority. In effect, despite the fact that ours is not
the best-selling, this makes the point that it's the best and
positions all the competition as less than the best. And it tells
the moron that the product comes with a sexy girl who gives
great head. The same basic concept can roll out to other market segments by simply changing up the visuals."

"That's what I thought." Brian smiled.

"So, now you agree with me?" Evan asked, giving Brian a
disgusted look.

"I think I've agreed with everything you've said since we
sat down," Brian said politely.

"And you now think this is a good idea?"

"Don't you?"

"I think it's the only good idea I've seen this afternoon,"
Evan said forcefully. "Whose idea is this?" Evan asked, turning to the group.

"Mine." Brian smiled.

Deb had not attended church for quite some time. The poli-
cies of bigotry, discrimination, and hatred and the overtly
political agenda of most denominations had long deterred
her interest or belief in any of what the churches said they
stood for. Actually it wasn't as complicated as all that. All Deb
needed to know was that the church didn't like and wouldn't
accept her brother and now her son, and that was pretty much
all that she needed to know.

She'd been raised a Catholic, which she'd always thought
was the most convenient religion since you could do pretty
much whatever you wanted and then confess, say a few rosaries,

and get off the hook. It had seemed a pretty good deal until it didn't anymore. When her brother, Vic, had come out, everything had changed. The church said Deb had to choose, and Deb chose her brother, unable to believe in a God who'd expect anything less, let alone one who couldn't love her brother.

So, as she crossed Fifth Avenue to the historic old Third Presbyterian Church for her PFLAG committee chairs' meeting, she felt the uneasy pang that always accompanied her visits. The regular PFLAG meetings on the second Sunday afternoon of each month had taken some of the edge off the feeling; even so, just showing up at church gave her the willies. What's more, chairing the committee for the Red Dress Ball meant that she'd be in the church even more often for regular meetings of her decorations committee and twice a month for the meeting of committee chairs she was going to be late for if she didn't get a move on.

"Deborah."

She almost didn't turn to see as no one ever called her that.

"Deb," the man repeated her name genially, rushing a bit to catch up to her.

"Hi, Daniel," she said, lighting up as she recognized one of the other PFLAG parents. "What committee did you get stuck with?"

"Ticket sales."

"Ouch." Deb winced. "Decorations," she volunteered, tapping her chest.

"I'd rather have ticket sales. How's by you?" he asked.

"I'm great really." Deb smiled, giving his shoulder a friendly pat. "My boss is the one not doing so good hearing that I'm not there two nights a month for this."

"You work nights?" Daniel asked as they made their way to the side entrance.

"My boss doesn't seem to think so." Deb smiled. "But I'm there anyways. Liberty Diner, you know it?"

"Yeah." He smiled, holding the heavy wooden door for her. "I used to meet my son there for Sunday brunch a lot."

"I almost never work that shift," she said, pausing at the door.

"Well, it was a while ago," he said with a little shrug.

"Oh, did he move away?" Deb asked as he followed her into the hallway.

"No, he died." Daniel's voice echoed down the empty hallway.

"Oh, God, I'm sorry," Deb said, instantly wishing that she was anywhere else.

"Me too," he said with a gentle smile.

They walked in silence down the hallway to the Sunday school classroom where their meeting was to be held.

"You get a good employee discount?" Daniel asked, breaking the silence.

"A what?" Deb asked, pausing as they reached the open door of the meeting room.

"I just thought if you got a good price for pie and coffee at the diner, I might be able to buy us both a slice?" he said, catching her eye and not letting it go.

"Won't your wife be worried?" Deb asked pointedly.

"I doubt it." He grinned. "But we can call her and her new husband in Ohio and find out."

"I get a great rate on pie."

"If everyone could take a seat," the event chairwoman called over the noise in the room, her voice drifting out to Deb and Daniel in the hall.

"I'll catch up with you after," Daniel said, giving her hand a quick squeeze and then darting inside.

*   *   *

"Get in," Brian said, pushing the car door open without stopping the car as he slowed to match Michael's pace on the sidewalk as they both neared Michael's apartment on Edmond Street.

"Where the hell have you been?" Michael asked as he kept walking.

"At work, hot stuff." Brian sighed, still driving alongside. "What'cha got in those grocery bags? You got daddy's dinner in there?"

"You were supposed to be here two hours ago," Michael said without breaking stride.

"I got your dinner right here," Brian called, grabbing himself as he followed along.

"I've never been that hungry," Michael sniped.

"It is a big meal." Brian grinned. "But the leftovers are just as good the next day."

Michael laughed, but did not stop walking. "You are so vile."

"Are you going to get in my car or do you want a preview?"

"Brian, I live here," Michael scolded.

"It's really big and wide," Brian growled. "And it's got hardwood floors and a view of the river and the old Heinz plant on the north side.

"You found something," Michael said, stopping so abruptly that Brian had to put the car into reverse. "You found a place?"

"I haven't seen it yet," Brian said with an eyebrow wave. "But I think it could be the one we're looking for. Anyways, I didn't want to see it without you."

Michael folded the passenger seat forward and stowed the groceries on the tiny backseat. "I can't wait. Where is it?"

"Fags," one of a couple of teenaged boys lingering on the curb outside a nearby building called over to them.

Michael sighed as he tried not to appear to rush as he rushed to get into the safety of the car. The boys were from the neighborhood and sneaking cigarettes under a nearby streetlight, their bikes leaned together conspiratorially in a nearby driveway.

"You better run, fag," one of the other boys called. "Your boyfriend's waiting and so are we."

"Just ignore—" Michael began evenly, sensing Brian's tension, but that was as far as he got. Brian grabbed him and kissed him as passionately as Michael had ever dared dream.

Their audience screamed in the throes of agony and revulsion, throwing lighted cigarettes and half-empty Budweiser cans in their direction.

At length, Brian broke the kiss. "Thanks, I needed that." He grinned at a slightly overwhelmed Michael. "It's been a hell of a day."

With that, Brian slammed the little muscle car into gear, hopping up onto the curb and neatly taking out all the bicycles nested there.

"Great," Michael groaned, laughing in spite of himself as Brian chased the scattering boys for a bit with the car before laying a nice stripe of rubber down Edmond and heading north. "Now I'm going to have to hire a bodyguard to walk down my own street."

"Sorry, I just needed a little celebration," Brian said, lighting a cigarette as he steered with his knees.

"Well, we haven't seen the place yet," Michael said reasonably as he searched for the seat belt in the dark.

"That's not the celebration." Brian exhaled a gust of smoke as he made a left at full speed onto Penn. "If it is, we can come back and chase them all over Bloomfield if you want."

"No thanks," Michael sighed, trying to sound more exasperated than he was. "So, I give up, what are we celebrating? Your dick grow another inch?"

"Want to find out?" Brian put his hand on the back of Michael's head and pushed suggestively.

"The tweezers and magnifying glass are in my other bag," Michael said, fighting Brian's halfhearted attempts. "So, it's an inch and a half now, huh? That is reason to celebrate."

"I got my first campaign idea picked up today," Brian said, trying to sound more casual about it than he felt.

"Well, that took long enough," Michael said, punching him in the shoulder. "You've been there almost a week. Who's the client?"

"Walden Electronics," Brian said, keeping his eyes on the road trying to find the unfamiliar address.

Michael whistled. "That's big time. You get a raise?"

Brian gave a snorting little laugh. "I got to stay three hours late to have more ideas for my boss to see when he gets in first thing tomorrow morning."

"So, that's where you've been." Michael nodded. "I thought you'd stopped by Woody's or Boy Toy and picked up a quickie."

"Sorry, I should have called. I lost track, and by the time I remembered you'd already gone to the grocery store. How long is Emmett going to be at your place?"

"Oh, not sure." Michael shrugged. "He hasn't been home for a while so he's got a lot of catching up to do."

"Well, I sure hope the fashion empire won't collapse in his absence." Brian slowed to take the turn. "Here we are, Mulberry Way. We're looking for 947."

"Oh my God. There it is. I can't believe it."

"Oh, right." Brian pulled the car to the curb. "I forgot to mention it's above a TV repair place."

"Don't you see it?" Michael asked intently.

"See what?"

"That."

Michael pointed at a sign, painted on the inside of the plate-glass window. " 'Authorized warranty service,' " he read aloud.

" 'Walden Electronics,' " they said together.

"It's a sign," Michael said, thrilled, leaping heedlessly out of the car in the questionable neighborhood.

"Literally."

Brian led the way to a mailbox hanging precariously from the side of the building where the keys were to have been left. "Right this way," he said, jingling the keys in Michael's direction and making his way down the alley to a rusty metal staircase.

Michael followed and stood anxiously by as Brian struggled with the rusty lock on the old industrial fire door. "Kind of odd that they'd just leave a key for you," Michael said. "You'd think they'd be more concerned about security."

"If they were concerned about security, they wouldn't still be in this neighborhood," Brian snorted derisively. There was a deep metallic click, and the door groaned open.

The smell of mildew greeted them on the cloud of dust that the darkened room exhaled. Only the light that could get through the grime-encrusted broad-paned industrial windows illuminated the space.

Brian felt the nearby walls for a light switch. "Ow, fuck," he hissed as he picked up a splinter for his trouble.

In response to Brian's shout, something squeaked and scurried away.

"You got a chair I can stand on?" Michael asked.

"Hold on a second." Brian remembered his lighter and pulled it out.

"There's a light, over at the Frankenstein place," Michael sang as the Zippo sparked and warmed the seemingly impenetrable darkness of the dank space. There was more squeaking and rustling. Brian explored the walls around the door in wider and wider arcs looking for a switch, until the small circle of light fell on an old knife switch standing open, mounted to the wall about fifteen feet from the door where Michael remained.

"Look at this," Brian said with a little laugh. "It really is the Frankenstein place." He took the handle and pulled. The disused metal resisted with a rusty yelp, then gave in, and with an arc and a few sparks came the first the hum of the ballasts, and then a few random fluorescent tube lights scattered throughout the space flickered enough to allow them to see.

The room was filled with heaps of old broken appliances and machinery, covered with tarps and rotting paper and rust and clouds of greasy dust. The wooden floors were unfinished either because they had never been or because whatever finish they'd ever had had simply worn away. Little floor space was available due to the enormous quantity of ancient discarded junk piled, in some places, all the way to the ceiling.

The walls around them were mostly raw, rough-finished brick, held together by oozing and untroweled gobs of mortar. Though in some areas, unfinished two-by-four frames were stuffed with fraying masses of pink fiberglass insulation, which was leaking onto the floor.

Brian extended his hand to Michael, who was still waiting in the relative safety of the doorway. Their eyes met and Michael took a few tentative steps into the space and reached to take Brian's hand.

Silently, they weaved their way through the stacks of detritus and came finally to one of the massive, floor-to-ceiling, metal-framed windows that wasn't completely obscured by the storeroom's contents. Pausing there, Brian dropped Michael's hand and tore off a piece of a nearby tarp and used it to knock off some of the thick coating of dust and cobwebs that were caking the window.

Below them were a few blocks of similarly disused warehouse spaces and the Allegheny River beyond. On the north bank, the red lights at the top of the brick smokestacks at the old Heinz plant blinked on and off like crimson stars burning overhead the distressed and decaying neighborhoods below.

Without speaking, Brian pulled a slim joint he had tucked into his cigarette pack in his inside coat pocket and lit it with the Zippo he still held in his hand. He inhaled the smoke deeply and held it a moment, before popping the joint backward into his mouth and, putting a hand on the back of Michael's head to guide their faces together until their lips almost touched, blowing Michael a shotgun.

Brian left his hand on the back of Michael's head as he turned away and, reversing the joint, took another hit for himself. They held the harsh smoke for a second as they watched a barge pass under the Sixteenth Street Bridge on the river below, then exhaled almost in unison.

"Well?" Brian said at last. Their eyes locked.

"It's the most beautiful thing I've ever seen," Michael said as the grin spread across his face and onto Brian's.

chapter four

Brian made his way down Liberty Avenue. The sights and sounds that were usually all the aphrodisiac that he needed went unnoticed as he made his way to meet Michael at the diner for a little food on Deb's employee discount before they went over to do some more work on the new place. He was in a strange and indefinable mood. It had been yet another hideous day working for the two-headed cyclops, tyrant Steele.

The son of a bitch had rejected an idea Brian had brought him, destroying the boards without ever looking at them. "That's not your best work shithead," Evan had snarled. "You haven't spent nearly enough time on it, and your first ideas always suck."

Brian had spent the rest of the morning redoing the original idea, then waited until after lunch to present it so that it wouldn't seem too soon. By the time he'd been ready to present it, Brian no longer liked the idea or thought it was his best work, but he had to present something.

"So, what do you think of this, Kinney?" Evan had asked after looking it over.

"I think it sucks," Brian sighed, snatching the board off the desk and stalking toward the door.

"So, I was right the first time?" Evan said, freezing Brian in his tracks. "Next time don't waste all morning trying to put one over on me. If the ideas come too easy, it's probably because they're clichés."

Brian did not move and did not turn back to look at Evan. Evan took a phone call, then Brian slowly moved out of the office and down the hall to the break room, where he was still forced to work.

Evan was abusive, unreasonable, unfair, dictatorial, and hypercritical without ever once being constructive. The only thing Brian could say was that Evan was never wrong. Brian had never once disagreed with a single unreasonable, inappropriate remark about the work, Brian's or anyone's. And despite that Brian was sure he would not brake if he saw Evan in a crosswalk, he came in early, worked late, worked weekends, and had even started skipping party nights out to work harder to please him.

Brian hated the guy and he was all Brian could seem to think about.

Should he quit? he was wondering as he opened the door into the diner. The place was dead.

"Brian," Deb called. "Come sit at the bar with me. Michael's going to be a few minutes late."

"It's his turn," Brian grunted, taking a stool.

"You look like shit. Coffee?"

"Thanks, 'cause I feel like shit." Brian upended his preset cup and pushed it toward Deb. "Not shit, exactly, but, I don't know, strange. How about you? You look really hot. And bothered," he added, warranting a smack on the back of the head.

"Smart mouth," Deb said, pouring his coffee.

"I didn't hit you in the back of the head when you said I looked like shit," Brian whined, playing up the injury.

"That's because you do, Blanche, you do," Deb said with a little cackle as she returned the coffee carafe to its warmer.

"That and I'm afraid of that wig," Brian mumbled.

"I heard that," she said, giving the big, red, bushy thing a tug.

They both laughed.

"So, what's up your ass?" Deb asked, leaning on the counter between them as Brian took a slug of coffee and made a face. "It can't be man trouble. I mean, you're usually the trouble."

"Actually it is sort of," Brian gasped. "When was this coffee made?"

"The seventies," Deb answered with a little shrug.

"And still it's so bitter," Brian concluded as if searching for the perfect compliment.

"What do you want for fifty cents?" Deb shrugged. "I'll make a fresh pot."

"People will pay a lot more than that for good coffee. I was just reading about this company out of Seattle who've got something like two hundred and fifty shops that just sell coffee for a couple of bucks a pop and they're making money like they're minting it."

"People on the West Coast are odd," Deb dismissed it. "So, who's the guy?"

"My boss."

"Oh, right," Deb said indulgently, giving his cheek a pinch. "That's so cute. It's your first real job. I forgot. So, don't tell me now, he's supercritical, rude, always finding fault with everything you do, and generally ruining your life?"

Brian nodded.

"That's his job, honey," Deb said, throwing her palms skyward in an expansive gesture. "He's supposed to make you miserable."

"Well, I want his job."

"And I think you'd be great at it," Deb cackled, tearing open a couple of packets of Maxwell House and thumping them into the basket of the Bunn BrewWISE. "But meanwhile you gotta live with it."

"So, what's got you down?" Brian asked, surprised by the message of capitulation coming from give-'em-hell Deb Novotny.

"Oh, I don't know," Deb sighed. "Life? No, that's not it. Don't say anything to Michael or anyone for that matter, or your gonads are mine. I've got enough dirt on you to make you so sorry—"

"Whoa, whoa." Brian waved her off. "Don't tell me if it's that personal. I don't need to know that bad."

"I met this guy," Deb sighed.

That shut him up. Brian grinned. "It's been a while."

"Tell me," she said, wiping the counter nervously.

"I can't remember the last time Michael had an 'uncle,' " Brian said, bursting into lascivious laughter.

"Yeah," Deb snorted. "I had to let that go when Michael started to ask me how many brothers I had."

"He was a late bloomer." Brian gave her a wink.

"But you weren't." Deb popped the dish towel at him and took his coffee cup to empty it.

"No," Brian said, leaning back by pushing off the counter. "I wanted a couple of those uncles to take me camping or out in the woods at least."

"Yeah, I bet you did," Deb chuckled as she rinsed out the cup, then stopped suddenly. "You didn't, did you?"

Brian only grinned in answer.

"Brian Kinney," Deb said, fanning herself with an imaginary fan as she made her way over to cheat the coffeemaker out of a cup before it was done.

"Deb, I'm actually younger than Michael, remember? I was precocious, not a prodigy."

"What? Did you wait till you were twelve?" Deb set the cup in front of him and went back for one for herself.

"I am so not having this conversation with you." Brian took a bit of his fresh coffee.

"And I so don't want to know," she said, shoveling sugar into her cup. "You boys give me the willies now. I don't need to know what I should have been worrying about then."

They sipped in silence for a minute.

"Where'd you meet him?" Brian asked.

"Who?"

"Michael's new uncle," Brian teased.

"Oh, it's nothing like that. In fact it's probably just my imagination, *running away with me,*" she sang.

"What makes you say that?"

"Oh, he's this really nice guy." She shrugged. "College or whatever you need to be an engineer. Big job, nice car, different suit every time I see him. You know the sort."

"Yeah," Brian scowled. "I think the word is *average.* I don't see why that qualifies you for a Rolling Stones blues lyric."

"Just not the kind of guy who'd be interested in someone like me," Deb said, mugging it off.

"What is that supposed to mean?" Brian asked with an edge. "You're from different sides of the tracks so it'll never work out? You'll drink the finger bowl at the formal dinner at the palace and he'll send the wine back at Woody's?"

"Yeah," Deb said, putting her chin up. "That's exactly what I mean."

"That's crap," Brian said irritably. "Those are the kinds of excuses people make when they're afraid to try something."

"God damn it, Brian," Deb started out defensively, then lost steam. "That's pretty much it, yep." She sighed and rolled her eyes at herself. "You're right. I'm just afraid he'll reject me so I'm using a story I saw on *Sisters* as my excuse."

Brian smiled at her.

"You're a smart kid," she said, rubbing the back of his neck. "And you don't let anything like fear stop you. No, sir, you'd hardly be working at that big fancy ad firm in that big fancy building with those big fancy people with your degree from the big fancy college if you could only see yourself as the mascot for the Eastway Kings from your father's bowling-league days."

Brian felt as if someone had walked across his grave. He was no longer listening to Deb, though she went right on talking. She was right. He kept seeing himself as the delinquent from Morningside rather than the cum laude Carnegie graduate who Evan was lucky to get for so little to do so much. He wasn't learning, he was honing his skills. And he was not going anywhere; if anyone was leaving, it would be Evan.

"Brian?" Michael said with that tone that let Brian know he'd said it two or three times already and Brian was in the doghouse for not paying attention the first time.

"Hey, Mikey," Brian said, spinning on his barstool, snatching Michael off the floor and spinning him around in his arms. "Are you ready to come paint the ceiling on the Sistine Toilet?"

"I'm not putting out till you buy me dinner," Michael said, laughing despite his determination to be in a mood as he struggled to escape Brian's grasp.

"That's not what I heard," Brian said, pulling Michael firmly into his lap.

"Well, you would have no way of knowing," Michael answered, moving his ass suggestively enough to get a reaction and then sliding off.

"But I've got a way of finding out." Brian laughed, taking the challenge as he grabbed Michael and pulled him back onto his lap.

"Too late," Deb said, dropping the enormous white paper bag, dappled with just enough grease spots to make it tempting, onto the counter before them. "Dinner's served. I figured if you got it to go, you could get to work sooner."

"Marry me," Brian said, dropping Michael to the floor and making kissy motions as he leaned across the counter toward Deb.

"Fickle," Michael said, rising and dusting himself off indignantly.

"Now you're interested," Brian said, locking his arm around Michael's neck and dragging him and the takeout toward the door.

"There's food involved," Michael explained, awkwardly waving good-bye to his mom from under Brian's arm.

Deb smiled and waved after her two boys. She knew that neither boy would believe that she got way more from the two of them than she ever gave. In a moment of inspiration she set her jaw and marched herself to the phone and dialed. The call had been very much on her mind, and she did not have to look at the number. She listened impatiently to the ringing.

"Daniel? Hi, it's Deb. Just thinking about you. . . . Yeah, I had a great time too. That's kind of why I'm calling. Do you like baseball? . . . Well, I've got these Pirates tickets."

*   *   *

The Al—as the Allegheny was called by those who knew—
looked more glorious than a tattered old river in a rusty old
town had any right to look that night. The moon and the stars
and the lights from the twin brick smokestacks of the old
Heinz plant reflected in the water. If you craned your neck a
bit, you could see the giant ketchup bottle that adorned the
plant. Or, if you really craned, you could see the lights of
Three Rivers Stadium peaking over the two interstate
bridges, not to mention the railroad bridge and the four others between Brian's new home and the brighter lights of the
big city.

The rusty-metal, floor-to-ceiling industrial windows,
intended to provide ventilation to the workers in a time
before air-conditioning was common, made the perfect frame
for the view as Michael and Brian sat on the rough wood floor
and ate their Liberty Diner feast off an upturned tomato
crate that rented with the space.

Formerly storage for the appliance wholesaler who had
had offices downstairs, the space had fallen into disuse as the
operation was replaced by the discount chains that bought
direct from the manufacturer and eliminated yet another
layer of the middle class. As the owners scaled back their
operation to authorized warranty repair for the brands they
used to sell, the space had sat empty until appliances became
disposable and drove them further out of business. What was
left of Mulberry Way Repair Services had put the space up
for rent as a means of augmenting income, never considering
that anyone would want to live in the warehouse space.

Brian had found the place almost by accident. He and
Michael had made themselves sick looking at trumped-up little apartment developments. With names like Allegheny

Mills and Monongahela Run, each was tailored to trumped-up young executives on the go and fitted out with ill-appointed weight rooms, crapulous unused saunas adjacent to obligatory and ubiquitous Olympic pools where bored sun-bathers rinsed off between coats of Coppertone on plastic furniture wedged between uninviting clubhouses and lighted tennis courts that were little more than nets stretched across an enclosed bit of the parking lot. Done up with Tudor lathing and cheaply framed fox-hunt paraphernalia, or faux colonial cupolas and Monticello porticos, they were remarkably identical. Brian was repelled by these bastions of hypocritical posers as much as he was by their residents, to whom he was already subjected each day at the office.

"I'd feel like I was still at work," Brian had groaned. What's more, it was all miles from the life on Liberty Avenue.

In fact it had been on one such night of his real Liberty Avenue life that Brian had discovered his new home.

Michael and he were blowing off a little steam from the week at Babylon, something Brian seemed less and less available to do as Inverness/Muir took more and more of his time and energy and what was left was spent trying to find a place that he could (a) afford and (b) see without hurling. Brian had not been able to drink away a week of Evan and unproductive apartment hunting and yet another night with the trick he'd been imposing on since they'd met midweek, but that hadn't stopped him from trying.

"Brian," Midweek whispered in his ear, sneaking up from behind. "I've got a surprise for you."

"What?" Brian asked, shivering involuntarily as he pulled away and wiped at his ear.

"That," Midweek said, pointing across the dance floor at an enormous tower of ebony flesh, flecked discreetly with bits of torn denim and a white tank top that seemed to glow against the dark flesh.

"How is that a surprise for me?"

"Well, I felt in a generous mood," Midweek hissed as his hands slithered over Brian's shoulders from behind. "We've agreed to split you tonight. It's nice to share." His tongue flicked Brian's ear. Brian shivered again. He scanned the floor for Michael and saw that he was dancing with Emmett to a spirited remix of "Knock on Wood." Was Emmett ever going back to L.A.? he wondered.

Brian felt trapped. It was late. Emmett was staying at Michael's, forever it seemed. Brian had not lined up a new place to stay, and while the prospect of a three-way didn't bother him, the notion of being "shared" did in that it implied an ownership to Midweek Brian didn't want him to infer even tacitly.

"I see you've got my evening all planned out," Brian said quietly and without commitment.

"And most of your morning," Midweek chuckled, waving a tiny Ziploc filled with white powder under Brian's nose.

"You've thought of everything." Brian laughed, pulling himself free. "Wait here for me, okay?" Brian said, giving him a hungry little nip of a kiss.

"Sure, baby." Midweek grinned, motioning his friend over, fait accompli. "We'll be right here."

"You have no idea how much better that makes me feel." Brian turned and headed toward the men's room. At the end of the hall, past the line at the men's room entrance, was an emergency fire door. Do Not Open—Alarm Will Sound. Brian opened the door, as he had hundreds of times, and stepped out into the cool summer night.

His Zippo blazed up to meet the end of the cigarette he'd

pulled from the pack with his teeth as he made his way down the alley. He exhaled the tension with the smoke and began to rethink his options for the evening. As he cast his eye down the alley, he caught a glimpse of one of the club's dancers dressed up for the Fourth of July as GI Joe, with a few fortuitous costume omissions. Brian's dilemma momentarily forgotten, he focused on the object of his intention, who was taking a leak against the stained brick wall farther down the alleyway habitually used by those who knew that the alarm did not sound and that there was never a line, to take a piss at least.

Brian leaned against the brick wall and made it clear that he was looking.

GI Joe looked up and made it clear that he knew and didn't seem to mind. When he was done, he turned to face Brian without zipping up or putting himself away. Brian took a deep, meaningful drag on his cigarette. GI motioned him over and then, just before Brian got to where he was waiting, playfully ducked around the corner. Brian tossed the cigarette aside and gave chase. The game was on.

The main entrance to Babylon was actually on a side street, little more than an alley off the north side of Liberty Avenue. Also to the north of Liberty was an area of Pittsburgh's former warehouse district, an area known as the Strip. Bounded on the north by the Allegheny River, the Strip had not kept pace with the city around it and had been overtaken in its stunted evolution by a sort of twilight existence made up of resident artists too poor to live anywhere else and businesses too bad to find better quarters.

The game of fag tag progressed through the broken glass and boarded-up windows of the Strip until GI Joe had taken a turn into the dead end alley beside Mulberry Way Repair

Services. Realizing his mistake, Joe had turned abruptly only to find that Brian was there to block his escape. Brian stepped Joe off as he jockeyed for a way around Brian. Too many years on the soccer pitch gave Brian the edge, and he slowly herded Joe into the back corner of the dimly lit alley that he did not yet realize would become his driveway less than a week later and onto a rickety metal stairway, held together mainly by rust, which led to Brian's soon-to-be front door.

Joe backed into the staircase, tripping over the first step and falling back partially, balancing on his hands on the third step. Brian stepped between his legs, kicking Joe's feet farther apart with the same soccer skills that had helped him to corner his prey. Joe lost what was left of his balance, almost falling, as Brian took control, guiding him to rest on the third step up as he raised Joe's legs. With Joe's ankles propped on Brian's shoulders, Brian leaned in and made short work of the breakaway military outfit. Brian swallowed the soldier whole and came up for air only to tear open the Trojan packet with his teeth. He spat the foil out of his mouth, dove again, and began to make his way ready, even as he unrolled the condom.

The midsummer night was warm and balmy against their naked skins, and they used their clothes as much as was possible to keep from injury on the unforgiving metal stairs. The soft, warm air of the night, the heated touch of flesh, and the cool, sharp metal of the staircase produced cries of pain and passion as Brian's condom wrapper became a part of the detritus that was the landscape of the place.

Brian finally found escape from the week he was having.

He lay on top of Joe for a moment to enjoy the last embers of the brief flames of shared passion, as quickly extinguished as they were ignited. Joe, being the one pinned to the metal steps, struggled to free himself of the fleshy burden he had welcomed and urged deeper with the same hands and legs only moments before. Ordinarily Brian would have been more sensitive to the moment, always delighted to be done swiftly and without expectation of the postcoital kissing and cuddling that he thought were indicative of a far greater intimacy than sport fucking demanded or required. But he was so distracted that Joe was forced to speak the first words that they had spoken to one another since meeting.

"Get off me, would ya?" he groaned.

Brian lifted himself up in a one-handed push-up off the rusty banister, never breaking his gaze from the sign that so captivated him. Space for Lease, the sign said. Brian climbed up on the railing and tore the sign off the side of the building: a business card to be used during business hours.

He and Michael had looked with only the aid of a couple of ancient and strobing industrial fluorescent shop lights. It was like looking at a silent movie about a storage unit—a really dull but realistic silent movie about a storage unit. Old appliances reduced to little more than rust and grease, old refrigerators waiting to swallow children and choke the life out of them. Spare parts and engines, unrecognizable as the appliances they once were. The room was filled with grease, rusting metal, sheets of plastic, and a flourishing crop of oily dust configuring itself into exotic blossoms and fluffy vines uniting and strangling everything. It was beautiful. They fell into one another's arms and their dance of joy and celebration was lit by fluorescent lightning.

Each night since Brian had gotten the key, they had come and worked tirelessly in the way that only the truly inspired can labor. The junk was carted away; much of it sold for scrap and spare parts, the profits split with the building's owners. They traded some of it for working appliances that they used to make the space more habitable. An old 7-Eleven—styled, glass-doored beer cooler became the apartment's refrigerator. They tried cleaning the place and finally brought in a garden hose with a high-pressure attachment and rented a sand-blaster. Slowly the harsh beauty they had seen from the start began to emerge.

Brian had slept there from the first night, his joy born of freedom and the circumstances of his liberation irrelevant.

The final step was to varnish the bare wood floors. It was the last step before they could begin to decorate the space.

Fortified with the cityscape and Liberty Burgers all the way, they arose from their perch by one of the broad windows, stowed the tomato crate—one of the apartment's only furnishings—and began to apply the stain and varnish to the thirsty old wooden planks that had supported their utilitarian load in common garb and were being dressed up to do more refined work.

A boom box echoed off bare, unfinished walls and tin roof with Z-93 recycled hits in FM stereo. The floors glowed wet under the bright red pendulum warehouse lights they'd gotten at Conran's with Brian's first paycheck. They talked to one another sporadically. Mainly they used the floor-waxers to apply the stain and varnish that were transforming an ugly storeroom into a beautiful apartment. It was a beauty they had both seen instantly on opening the crash-barred commercial door and pulling the lever on the Dr. Frankenstein knife switch that lighted the single large room by turning on the electricity.

Occasionally a really good song would come on the radio and they'd sing "Rain" with Madonna and "Dreamlover" with Mariah and even "Whoomp! There It Is" with Tag Team.

They had zoned into the task, helped along by the over-whelming fumes, mumbling the last of "Ordinary World" with Duran Duran when they backed into one another and realized that they were done.

"Hey, watch where you're going," Brian said, giving Michael a little shove.

"Me?" Michael said, grasping his pearls indignantly. "I'm the guest."

Brian flicked his finger in the nearby pan of mahogany stain, and with a quick flick Michael had a thin mahogany mustache.

"You son of a bitch!" Michael screamed, and turned to run to the drywall cubical with an airline-size sink, a singing toilet, and a jury-rigged shower that, aside from the beer refrigerator, was the only vestige of human habitability the space possessed. He froze as they both realized it at the same moment. They had painted themselves into the corner and had something like eight hours' drying time to kill.

"Oh my God," Michael whispered, overwhelmed by the gravity of the moment.

"Fuck."

"Well, there's only one thing to do," Michael said, nodding sagely.

"What's that?" Brian asked, glad of any sort of rescue as his cigarettes were by the door.

Michael turned, put his hands on Brian's shoulders, leaned in, and kissed him firmly on the mouth. He pulled back and looked into Brian's pleasantly surprised face.

"Mikey," Brian said with a sly laugh. "I didn't know you had it in you."

"Well, I don't know so much about that," Michael said, checking his work. "But I'm sure I've got it on you."

"What?" Brian said with a confused expression that could not obscure the lithographic mustache print Michael had applied to Brian's upper lip.

"It's one of those you won't get until later," Michael said with a little smile that broke into a little laugh. Maybe it was the moment or the fumes or the mahogany mustaches or exhaustion or just being painted into a corner, but Michael lost it.

"What?" Brian asked again, snickering in spite of himself. "What is it?"

Michael couldn't stop laughing and Brian couldn't help it either as the laugh infected him.

It was one of those perfect moments from life you'd never consider perfect at all. The apartment wasn't finished and they really were trapped. Michael was hating life and Brian was stuck in a hateful job working for an SOB, bringing home peanuts and forced to live in the hellhole they were desperately trying to make livable. They both had work the next day and yet sitting on the floor, half-overcome by toxic fumes and laughing in each other's arms, couldn't have been more perfect.

As if in accompaniment the radio began to play the Proclaimers hit "I'm Gonna Be," and the two joined in the chorus:

If I get drunk well I know I'm gonna be
I'm gonna be the man who gets drunk next to you
And if I haver yeah I know I'm gonna be
I'm gonna be the man who's havering to you

Naturally they were up and marching around to the irresistible cadence.

But I would walk 500 miles
And I would walk 500 more
Just to be the man who walked 1,000 miles
To fall down at your door

And they threw themselves to the floor in keeping with the lyric.

"What the fuck is 'havering'!" Brian said, cracking them both up once again.

chapter five

"Hello and welcome to Kaufmann's," Emmett said, beaming from behind the small, navy-skirted demonstration table on the aisle beside housewares at Kaufmann's Department Store. "Could I ask what you had for breakfast today?"

Emmett loved his new job. The timing was reasonably in keeping with his after-hours schedule—not in too early and there late enough that he was earning money almost right up until bar time. Kaufmann's was a Pittsburgh institution, and the downtown flagship store was the jewel in a sizable chain. He got an employee discount that he was already applying to clothes and trinkets he had been secreting in the stockroom for payday. But best of all, all he did all day was make omelets and talk.

The Fold-N-Serve omelet company had developed a non-stick, electric omelet pan, and they paid a sizable portion of Emmett's salary at Kaufmann's in exchange for the retailer's commitment to maintain an in-store Fold-N-Serve omelet station through the end of 1993, with an option to extend into the new year.

After the disastrous, if brief, engagement at Heartburn, Cocksucker and Strife, as Emmett had referred to the law firm since the breakup, he had fallen into the job at Kaufmann's by chance. Well, chance and Michael's threat to throw "you and all your feathers" into the street if Emmett didn't start at least bringing home groceries once in a while.

What else was Emmett to do but go shopping? And Kaufmann's was having a sale. He'd made a wrong turn on the way to the little boys' room and inadvertently walked into the personnel offices. And just like that, the idea hit him. He actually had retail experience so he didn't even have to lie on the application.

They hired him and had even paid him for the brief training period at Omelet College in the Fold-N-Serve home offices in Canton, where Emmett had graduated at the top of his class in folding, presentation, and garni. And he had become a star in a housewares department already crowded with demonstration booths.

"What did you have for breakfast this morning?" was Emmett's patented invention. Usually people couldn't remember, or if they did, it was cereal or a doughnut or toast. And if they'd had something better, it invariably took longer and cost more. He couldn't lose, no matter what their answer. "Could I make you an omelet?" he'd ask them. "It'll only take me three minutes." And they were off. The smell of the first omelet got people interested, and Emmett used the three minutes not only to make the most perfect omelet but also to explain how a high-protein, low-carb—that is, omelet-rich, toast-and-doughnut free—diet would improve muscle tone and take off unwanted pounds. The Fold-N-Serves were just flying off the shelves.

He had sold all they had the first day and had orders for a quarter of their next scheduled shipment. Of course the home office was only too happy to ship over backup supplies of Fold-N-Serves that very day, Canton being practically a suburb of Pittsburgh.

It had seemed only natural what with his success that the self-sharpening-cutlery consultant was moved from the department's prime demonstration location in favor of the new Fold-N-Serve star.

Much to her consternation, the Ginsu lady's star status and location in the seasonal alcove was usurped by Emmett's omelet operation. Emmett was to spend his days on the island of parquet that gleamed softly under the incandescent lighting along with the holiday decorations and serving ware and other impulse buys—all of which were marked up 100 percent or more.

Lady Ginsu and her Benihana blade work were relegated to the mercury vapor and terrazzo of the common kitchen-wares demonstration aisle from which Emmett had graduated with such distinction. She was not only irritated, she was armed, and Emmett gave her a wide berth as he took up the place of honor to begin brunching the Kaufmann's shopper.

Things went as planned. Not only were the Fold-N-Serves leaping into customers' shopping bags, but so were the dried-flower centerpieces, the holiday tea towels, and the jack-o'-lantern hot mitts.

One of the most amazing parts of Emmett's demonstration and one of his biggest draws was his offer to prepare an omelet for the customer in three minutes. Because the Fold-N-Serve cooked at incredibly high temperatures, had a no-stick surface, and actually folded the cooked eggs into the traditional omelet pocket, Emmett could put the finished product on the plate in record time.

Em had it down to a science. His fillings and garni were all preminced into attractive shapes and sizes, and all he had to do was keep moving to produce perfect omelets. The main trick to it was paying attention, which is what made Emmett perfect for the job. Not that his focus was all that much better than that of mere mortals, but he could carry on a conversation without paying the least attention to what he was saying. Since he couldn't have cared less about the omelet maker or Kaufmann's or the frumpy hausfraus he was hustling, he never once paused to think, and the omelets just kept on coming.

Tragedy came center stage that first day in the seasonal spotlight in the form of Thomas Henneghan. Emmett had looked up from his culinary curriculum to behold a vision in Tommy Hilfiger, the new designer who was like Ralph Lauren but in color. Thomas would have been a vision in nothing at all, but for Emmett fashion sense only improved the package.

"So, you just flip it over, count to ten. One, two, three . . ." Emmett trailed off as he followed Thomas mentally down the gadget aisle. Fortunately the eleven-year-old daughter of his current mark, a young mom from Penn Hills, had been keeping count with him.

"Ten," she shrieked, bringing Emmett back to the demonstration table. "Ten!"

"Oh," Emmett said, snapping out of it. "Merci for keeping count for me and voilà." The perfect omelet slid out of the pan and onto the plate. "A couple of berries," he said, adding them. "A dollop of sugarless marmalade"—he gave the flick of the wrist. "And salsa, cream cheese"—two more spoonfuls added artfully to the mix. "And there you have the perfect breakfast, in under three minutes every morning for less than you'd pay for a single breakfast out. Taste." He sliced the omelet into perfect little wedges with one of the knives that used to be sold on the exact same spot. The Ginsu lady ground her teeth as she always did at that point in Em's presentation.

By the time he had time to look, Thomas was gone.

"Ah, well," he sighed, and began again. "Excuse me, ma'am, what did you have for breakfast this morning?"

Time whisked passed in a flurry of omelets and Thomas was soon forgotten. Emmett had just served his latest. "And there you have the perfect breakfast, in under three minutes every morning for less than you'd pay for a single breakfast out. Taste," he said by rote, passing the perfectly sliced omelet as the Ginsu lady ground the edge off her incisors.

"What did you have for breakfast?" the warm male voice queried, from just behind Emmett and just out of sight, startling him slightly. He spun to see who had stepped on his next line. It was Thomas.

"Well, I had an omelet." Emmett blushed, spilling a bit of the olive oil he was daubing the pan with, delighted that the interloper had been paying enough attention to know that that was the next line in Emmett's endless pitch.

"What do you like in your omelet?" Thomas asked, jumping ahead but still using Em's lines to advance the conversation.

"Ham, Swiss, and mushrooms," Emmett answered dreamily, whisking a couple of eggs into the preheated pan and oil.

"Who made your breakfast this morning?" Thomas asked with a little leer, departing from the script.

"I did," Emmett answered, sprinkling ham and grated cheese along the future fold of the rapidly congealing eggs.

"That's too bad." Thomas closed what little distance there was between them.

"You think?" Emmett said, folding the pan over idly.

"I think having someone else to make your breakfast would make the perfect omelet even better."

"Do you make good omelets?"

"I think so, but I've never had an expert opinion." Thomas shrugged.

"I'm an expert," Emmett volunteered with a flirtatious little laugh.

"I'm Thomas." He extended his hand. "Thomas Henneghan."

"Emmett Honeycutt." Em took the hand and held it in his own. "And as it happens, I'm free for breakfast tomorrow."

"What time is good?" Thomas asked, not letting go of Emmett's hand.

"Whenever we wake up?"

"That works." Thomas nodded. "What time do you get off tonight?"

Thomas never got to hear Emmett's answer to that leading question as the screams drowned out their conversation.

"It was like it was in slow motion," Emmett said when he recounted the horrific story. "There were just suddenly flames everywhere. I can only guess there was an explosion of some sort."

What had in fact happened was far less pyro-spectacular. The superheated omelet pan had reduced the omelet to a quick-burning cinder. Flaming grease from the ham caught the olive-oil-soaked navy-blue tablecloth, and from there it was but a short leap to the dried-flower arrangements, tea towels, holiday linens, and wreaths. Even the jack-o'-lantern oven mitts burned brightly.

Perhaps more chilling than the conflagration in a store filled with shoppers was the hideous and triumphant laugh of the Ginsu lady, which rose above the panicked screams of fleeing customers.

Emmett was, of course, torn. On the one hand there was the fire. But on the other was Thomas, who had been holding on since their introduction. As Emmett stared at the fire, he felt Thomas's grip loosening, but before he could turn back to answer the question still poised between them, the store sprinklers went off and Thomas joined the ranks of shoppers running from the department and indeed the store and Emmett's life.

"Nine," Emmett screamed in vain, his voice lost, the moment gone forever. "I get off at nine," he repeated more quietly to himself.

"Because it sucks," Evan said through threateningly clenched teeth.

"That is not an answer," Brian snapped.

"But it is the truth," Evan said, trembling, clearly fighting to control himself.

The rest of the staff was once again seated around the guitar-shaped conference table for the afternoon creative-staff meeting, frozen in fear as both men stood, only a fret's width apart, fists clenched at their sides, vibrating with anger.

"No, it's only your opinion," Brian said, leaning on the oversize fingerboard.

There was an audible collective gasp in the room as those present waited for the inevitable explosion.

"Everybody, get out," Evan screamed, the dam bursting, never breaking eye contact with Brian.

People ran from the room, leaving notebooks, presentations, and, in one case, lunch behind in their panic.

The door slammed and neither man moved.

Brian's new resolve not to forget who he was and what he was doing there had improved the quality of his life in direct proportion to a noticeable decline in office tranquillity. There were a few dustups initially, such as when Brian suggested a new possible storage space for Evan's black cherry Calistoga. Evan had allowed rather loudly that such a location would not keep them cool and might in fact have the opposite effect.

"Only to ninety-eight point six, if it turns out you're human." Brian shrugged, returning to his work.

But Evan never asked again and Brian was still employed there.

Voices had also been raised over Evan's lunch order when Brian ventured a prediction of the weather in hell on the date and time that he'd fetch Evan a sandwich. There had been a lot of screaming and door slamming, but Evan had made other arrangements for his lunch order from then on. And the staff became afraid to go into the break room where Brian continued to work.

But no one had ever dared to take Evan on in the afternoon creative-staff meeting, and given the apparent outcome, it didn't look as if it would ever happen again.

"Brian Kinney," Evan erupted as the door closed behind the last refugee. "Did you smoke crack at lunch?"

"I'm all out," Brian said with withering calm.

"Why is not a question you get to ask at staff meetings," Evan shouted, hurling whatever he could immediately lay hands on.

"Dictatorship does not foster creativity," Brian answered, dodging a couple of presentation boards and a handful of colored pencils.

"Of course it does," Evan bellowed. "The power of a single author is present in every great work, creative success, and worthy human endeavor. Even when it is a collaborative effort. Nothing good ever came out of a committee."

"Like the Declaration of Independence?" Brian asked smugly.

"And you see how that's turning out." Evan threw himself into a chair.

"Evan," Brian said with frightening quiet, "why are you so hard on me?"

"What? More questions?" Evan seethed.

"Meeting's over." Brian shrugged.

"You stupid git," Evan chuckled, shaking his head. "Don't you know?"

"So, I'm right?" Brian said, shocked at how easily the admission had come.

"This once," Evan retorted, almost jovial suddenly. He had the upper hand and he knew it. "It's really never occurred to you?"

"Yes, but I just thought I was being paranoid and you were just an asshole to everyone," Brian said, lost suddenly in the large, empty room.

"Well, of course I am," Evan said with an impish shrug of his shoulders. "That's part of my charm. But I am obviously much harder and much more unreasonable with you. Can't you guess why?"

"Because you didn't pick me for this job?"

"Are you out of your mind?" Evan said with a shriek of near hysterical laughter. "Do you imagine that you are not my choice? Or rather that there is anyone alive on the earth who could cause me to do anything I don't want to do, let alone work with someone I don't want to work with?"

"I guess not," Brian admitted, sliding his hands into his pockets. The two men regarded one another for a moment.

"Well?" Evan demanded.

"Well?" Brian questioned.

"Have you no clue?"

"Not one."

"That's really not worthy of you. I just assumed you knew, that you'd figured it out, given the past couple of weeks. Ninety-eight point six." Evan laughed out loud, remembering the moment with the fizzy water.

"You're trying to get rid of me?" Brian ventured.

"Oh, you're just guessing," Evan said almost gleefully. "I think this is the first time that I have truly and completely had the upper hand with you. I almost hate to end it."

Brian looked at him blankly.

"Oh, well," Evan sighed. "Too much work to do to wait for the cretin to catch up to the rest of the class. Follow me." Evan rose and moved purposefully toward the doors that linked his office directly with the conference room. Brian followed as Evan flung the doors open and moved across his office to another door on the other side that Brian had never seen open. Evan paused at the second door and turned to face Brian. "There." He gestured like a spokesmodel. "There's your answer."

"What is it, a twenty-three-story drop to the pavement?" Brian asked sheepishly, reluctant to open the door.

"Sadly no." Evan sighed, stepping away. "Labor laws or something. They were also quite firm about a trapdoor leading to the basement in front of my desk. Too bad really."

"So, I should open the door?" Brian asked, still completely put off by Evan's odd and unexpected almost cheerful behavior. It was like Ebenezer Scrooge on that fateful Christmas morning after the three ghosts had paid a call.

"When you're ready." Evan shrugged it off and returned to his desk and began to leaf through the presentation that had started the row.

Brian turned back to the doors. What a strange turn this conversation had taken. How could this be an answer? he thought. "Now or never," he said to himself, opening the doors. It was an office. Actually it was quite a nice office. It opened onto the same terrace as Evan's office, though the view was not quite as spectacular. And of course it was nowhere near as big as Evan's office. How small was Evan's penis? Brian wondered, chuckling to himself. "How is this an answer?" Brian called back across the vast room.

Evan sighed irritably but went on with his work.

Brian stepped into the office and looked around for some sort of clue, then saw the outer door to the office, the one that opened into the hallway outside. It was frosted glass, but Brian could still make out the dark outline of the name painted there.

Brian Kinney

It took him a moment. He stood transfixed, staring. He opened the door and looked at it from the hall side and found that it opened into the same anteroom that Evan's office opened into.

"Hi, Brian," Evan's assistant said with a smile, looking up. "You need anything?"

"No," Brian said shortly, almost as though he'd been caught. He withdrew back into the office abruptly.

"You figured it out yet?" Evan asked, suddenly there and

startling Brian, who closed the door a little harder than necessary, rattling the glass.

"Jeez," Brian gasped.

"Scare you?" Evan grinned.

"No," Brian lied.

"I think you're really good," Evan said finally. "I think you're a talented young man. I hired you because I liked your work and your attitude. This business requires a stainless-steel ego and yours is titanium. I wondered how long you were going to fetch me sparkling water and sandwiches."

"You asked me to do that intentionally?" Brian asked, the idea dawning but still not fully realized.

"Well, I was really thirsty," Evan said, sitting on the edge of Brian's desk.

"So, this has all been some kind of sick test?" Brian demanded, his voice climbing yet again.

"Most jobs begin with a trial period." Evan smiled. "And believe me, yours is far from over. But you can also believe me that I would not waste time arguing with you if I didn't think you were worth it. So, yes, I am especially hard on you. The sharpest blades get the most punishment. That's in fact what keeps them the sharpest. But you were already Toledo Steel when I found you, a wonder since you came directly out of the Pittsburgh mills. I'm only putting an edge on what I found."

Brian said nothing as he looked around the office—*his* office.

"How long has this office been here?"

"You're from Pittsburgh." Evan shrugged. "When did they build this building?"

"Okay." Brian smirked. "How long has my name been on this door?"

"A couple of weeks."

"I've only worked here a couple of weeks."

"Yes." Evan nodded. "I hope you're not going to be this dense about everything."

"Thanks," Brian said, a bit overcome by the moment and still more impressed with the man.

"Oh, don't muddy it up with a lot of sentiment," Evan snarled, turning away. "You won't get anything you didn't earn from me or anyone else. In fact you won't often get even that. Back to work."

"What is it now?"

"There's the sullen and defiant attitude I love," Evan said with a long-suffering sigh. "Go get your miserable boards out of the conference room so I can show you what's wrong with them."

"There's nothing wrong with them," Brian said, recrossing Evan's office to collect the boards that Evan had thrown at him earlier.

"That's only your opinion," Evan shouted after him.

"It happens to be the truth," Brian shouted back, managing to hide most of his laughter.

Melanie Marcus had first met Ted Schmidt when she was still an undergraduate at Pitt. Ted had been walking across the Sutherland Hall Cafeteria when a group of more than typically sophomoric sophomores decided that it would be fun to relive their good old days as high school bullies and knock the lunch tray out of his hands.

What the bully wannabes had not counted on was Ms. Melanie Marcus, who was approaching in the opposite direction on her way to grab a much needed coffee to get her through her hangover and her biology lab.

The three brave sophomores were still moving forward but looking back over their shoulders in Ted's direction to admire their work when one of them had the great misfortune to say out loud in Melanie's hearing, "Sorry, faggot."

"What did you say?" Melanie demanded of the rather surprised young man.

"I wasn't talking to you," the young man said, trying to go around her.

"Did you just call somebody a faggot?" Melanie demanded loudly, stepping into his path again.

"Yeah, what of it?" he answered irritably.

"This guy?" Melanie said, taking Ted's arm mostly to prevent him from leaving. "Are you flirting with him?"

The bullies laughed.

"Are you crazy, lady?" the now rather embarrassed bully demanded, really only attracting more attention to himself. "I hate fags."

Again he tried to go around her.

Again Melanie stepped fearlessly into his path, dragging Ted with her.

"And you think this guy's a fag?"

"I know it."

"Really?" Melanie said. "'Cause I got to tell you, the only guys who spend time looking for and thinking about fags are fags."

Ted and a growing cafeteria crowd looking on were hanging on Melanie's words.

"Are you calling me a fag?" the enraged young man snarled threateningly.

"All I'm saying is you've come into a cafeteria filled with beautiful college coeds, and you've gone out of your way to find and flirt with another guy who you're sure is a fag, and you start flirting with him like a schoolboy." Melanie shrugged. "That sounds pretty gay to me. What's next? You gonna dip his pigtails in the inkwell? Why don't you just ask him out? There's a big dance Saturday," she called after him over the laughter of the crowd as the little trio of former bullies fled.

She and Ted had lunch together that day: hers a glass of V8 and some black coffee, and his a replacement mac and cheese, vegetable soup, and garlic bread of what he'd originally chosen.

The memorable first meeting had defined their relationship. Melanie, always a fierce defender of those she loved, took Ted under her little wing, even though he was the older of the two, she a mere freshman at the time. It was the same sense of advocacy for those who needed defending that had led her into the law.

Ted had left Pitt and was still in school and concluding a rather protracted MBA as Mel wrapped up law school. But she still helped him through the tough spots and talked him in off the ledges he was forever crawling out onto as life overwhelmed him.

And that day was no exception.

He was having a particularly tough time with his thesis committee over the development of a macroeconomic model to support his theories of predicting the emerging economies of post-Communist Eastern Europe. The debate was technical, but the point was that Ted was unable to compile a model of Western economic development from which to predict Eastern growth that was acceptable to all the professors on his committee.

"The point is, they're all theorists," Ted wailed to Melanie over drinks at one of the tall tables at Woody's. "We're all theorists. Nobody actually knows how economics works. There is no right answer. It's all just somebody's best guess. So, trying to get a room full of theorists to agree to one descriptive theory is like herding cats."

"Ted," she said, shaking her head and laughing a bit, "are you sure you want to do your thesis in economics? I mean, why not just take the CPA exam and get to work and leave the theory where it belongs. Who care's if you got a degree or not?"

"I do," Ted said, taking the debate she had laid out for him. "It's very important. A CPA is something I definitely want to pick up along the way, but that only qualifies me to do one thing. The MBA opens doors and possibilities for a lifetime. I don't just want to be a CPA for the rest of my life. Sure it's a good start and solid foundation, but I plan to be retired from it by the time I'm forty and to move on to more entrepreneurial opportunities, to make a difference."

She smiled as he launched into a very Tedesque description of why he should finish his MBA before making any decisions about career direction, completely convincing himself to stay the course, follow the plan, and deal with his committee. It was a plan she'd heard him repeat hundreds of times in their friendship. Melanie didn't stick with Ted because he was weak. She stuck around because he was strong. He was a man of convictions. She had never known Ted not to do what he said he was going to do, unless it involved men. All she really had to do in their friendship, besides enjoying his company, was to remind him of his own plans and convictions and he took care of the rest.

He'd helped her to find creative ways to finance her education so that she wasn't going to graduate from law school with a crushing debt and she was not going to have to spend her inheritance. Instead, with Ted's guidance, that money was earning the money that was paying for her law school as she went. He'd even showed her how to depreciate her beloved motorcycle.

"And so if they can't get on board, I may just have to get myself a new committee," Ted declared as he concluded his latest rediscovery of what had been his plan all along.

"I'm convinced," Melanie said with a shrug.

Ted caught her eye and the small smile and they both broke up.

"How do you put up with me?" Ted chuckled at his own expense.

"Oh, please." Melanie rolled her eyes and raised her Rolling Rock. "Enough of these and I could eat dinner with Jesse Helms."

They enjoyed the laugh.

Ted had always been the more surprised of the two of them by their friendship. They seemed to have absolutely nothing in common. He was all about numbers. She was all about ideas. He was very much in the closet in a lot of areas of his life. She headed up the Pride Parade each year with Dykes on Bikes. He was about solid, quiet persistence. She was about solid frontal assault.

What they had in common was a deep and abiding belief in family, in hard work, and in surprisingly traditional and even conservative values. Civil libertarianism was at the heart of what the country was founded on. And money was the heart of what the country was founded on. So, you'd have been hard-pressed to find two more conservative people despite outward appearances.

"Oh my God," Melanie said, breaking off so abruptly in midlaugh that Ted wheeled to see what gun-wielding Aryan supremacist had burst in the door. "Don't look, don't look," she warned, grabbing his shoulder and turning him back, terrifying him even more.

"What is it?" he hissed. "Are we all going to die?"

"No, just me," Melanie said, putting her face on the table inconspicuously.

"You remember that girl I told you about?" Melanie asked a marginally relieved Ted. Some of Melanie's "girl" friends were every bit as terrifying as any skinhead Ted had ever seen. Hell, some of her more politically militant women friends were skinheads.

"You know, Venus rising by the fountain outside of Frick Hall?" Melanie said, not lifting her face from the table.

"The one you said gave you a hard-on?" Ted asked, turning.

"Don't look, don't look," Melanie said without looking up to see him looking.

"Oh my God," Lindsay said to Brian, spotting Melanie from where they stood near the entrance to Woody's looking for a place to sit.

"What's up?" Brian asked, not losing eye contact with the young Sly Stallone look-alike planted like a fireplug next to the popcorn machine.

"It's that woman," Lindsay said sharply.

"That really narrows it down," Brian said, almost looking at her. "Do you still know any women? Or is this someone out of your past?"

"Over there," Lindsay said, trying to get Brian's attention. "At that table by the Boys Will Be Boys pinball machine. It's her from the fountain."

"The one who called you Botticelli?" Brian asked, turning to look, his interest piqued. "The one passed out on the table?" he groaned. "You know the expression *live one* is not entirely a euphemism."

"She's hiding," Lindsey snapped.

"Is she an ostrich?" Brian made his way across the room to introduce himself.

"Brian don't," Lindsay said forcefully as she followed him.

"Okay, Mel, what's the worst-case scenario here?" Ted asked, amused at Melanie's uncharacteristically girlish behavior, but still trying to help. "That she'll sic her cherubs on you?"

"No, that she might recognize me," Melanie said, still facedown in their cocktail napkins.

"Does she see me?" Melanie hissed.

"I really can't tell if I don't look. And even then, I don't actually know which one she is."

"Okay, you can look," Melanie told Ted.

"Okay, is she a tall, good-looking blond woman?"

"Yes," Melanie said into the tabletop.

"And is she with a dark-haired man about her height wearing a gray Armani suit?"

"I think so. I didn't really look at him, but she was . . . standing right in front of me watching me make a fool of myself," Melanie said, looking up to discover Brian and Lindsay standing at their table.

"It was my turn," Lindsay said.

"Botticelli," Melanie said, raising her green beer bottle in toast and greeting and then downing the contents.

"Butthead," Lindsay sniped.

There was a moment's sweaty silence as the two women regarded one another.

"I'm Brian Kinney." He extended his hand. "I'm a friend of Botticelli's."

"Ted Schmidt." Ted took Brian's hand. "I'm here with Butthead."

"Butthead, good to meet you." Brian extended his hand. "Let me introduce Lindsay Peterson-Venus-Rising, it's hyphenated."

"Hi, I'm Melanie Marcus Butthead." Melanie extended her hand to Lindsay. "It's really more a part-time hobby than a hyphenate. Though you, I see, are Venus full-time."

Lindsay was so charmed and surprised by the unexpected compliment from her former heckler that she extended her own hand in greeting.

"Even with your clothes on," Melanie said as she took Lindsay's hand for the first time.

Lindsay tossed her white wine on Melanie and departed without saying good-bye.

"Impressive," Brian said, regarding Melanie. "You ever heard the expression *less is more?*"

Melanie put her face back on the table.

"I'll do what I can," Brian said, giving her shoulder a reassuring little punch. "You got her attention, that's more than you know. Not tonight but better luck next time. Ed," Brian said with an inconsequential nod to Ted as he departed.

"That went well, Ed," Mel said into the black Formica tabletop she was becoming overly familiar with.

"Yeah," Ted said, then took a hit off his beer. "You never get a second chance to make a first impression." And then dissolved into fits of laughter.

chapter six

"Because it's your mother's drag ball," Brian called over his shoulder to Michael, who was neatly folded into Brian's Nova's impossibly small backseat.

"How often do you suppose that phrase gets said in real life?" Michael argued.

"Is it really drag if I go in a dress?" Lindsay further clouded the issue.

"Linds," Brian said, batting his eyes sweetly. "It's drag when I put on a suit to go to work in the morning. We're all just getting into costume for one event or another."

"So, it's the uniform that makes the soldier?" Michael scoffed.

"It's what makes 'em hot." Brian laughed, flicking the lid and lighting his Zippo, touching the flame to his cigarette in a single well-rehearsed move.

"And there's the gun," Lindsay added helpfully.

"I just don't think I can risk it," Michael said with a tone of finality as Brian pulled up in front of the Second Hand Rose, a fashionably shabby, Squirrel Hill thrift store.

"What's this?" Lindsay asked. "Castoffs of the rich and famous?"

"We have to start somewhere." Brian shrugged, slamming the car into reverse and simultaneously flipping off the horns behind him as he swept the little car into a space along Murray Avenue near the shop.

"I'm not doing this," Michael reiterated for the hundredth time since Brian had dragged him down to the car and stuffed him into the backseat.

"Michael, I don't think you can afford not to," Brian reasoned, opening the door and holding the seat forward as he forcibly pulled Michael out of the backseat.

"Shotgun on the way home," Michael said in Lindsay's direction.

"Like hell," Lindsay said, closing her door and looking through her bag for change for the meter.

"One," Brian went on with his proposition, not releasing Michael's hand as he guided him toward the store, "this is important to your mom. She's been there for all of us, you especially, what with pregnancy and labor and raising you and stuff. Two, no one from Big Q is going to be there, except maybe a couple of the fairies from the tea room." Brian giggled and almost lost his grip on Michael as they neared the door with the huge rose painted on the glass.

"There's a tea room at Big Q?" Lindsay asked, incredulous.

"Not those kinds of teapots," Michael said, waving off the topic as he continued to struggle.

"And three," Brian concluded, lifting Michael's face kissing close to his own, "she'll fucking kill you if you don't go."

"There's that," Michael conceded, the fight going out of him.

Brian set Michael down while reaching behind him to hold the door, making sure to block any means of escape.

"What kind of teapots are they?" Lindsay asked, completely stumped.

"Public bathrooms where men can have sex with one another are called tea rooms," Brian said as they walked into the store, attracting the attention of pretty much everyone there. "What?" Brian said, addressing the room. "You never heard of sex before?" The other shoppers pretended to turn away but kept an eye out.

"No, darling," said an elderly woman among the group who did not look away but beamed at them and answered. "It's just so old-fashioned to call glory holes tea rooms." She sighed. "Can I help you find anything?"

"Even when there are no actual glory holes?" Brian asked, genuinely curious.

"Oh, you work here?" Lindsay asked, punching him in the arm.

"I'm Rose." She extended her hand palm down as if to have it kissed.

Brian obliged and was rewarded with a little giggle. "We're looking for red dresses," he explained. "Do you have anything in our size?"

"Oh, yes, indeed," Rose said, turning to lead the way. "Why Godiva herself shops here so I make it my business to keep well stocked in the plus sizes."

"I didn't see Godiva at Emmett's welcome-home party," Lindsay observed.

"She had a drag show at Woody's that night," Michael explained. "She came late."

"Michael has to take the words of others for that fact since he walked out on that party, even though it was at his house," Brian said as he began leafing through the rack that Rose had pointed out to them, pulling out possibilities.

"Here you go," Rose said to Brian. "And you'd be about an eight," she said to Michael, pointing toward the regular women's racks. "But I expect a pretty little thing like you would already know that."

Brian and Lindsay lost it.

"You see, Mikey," he croaked. "You're a natural."

"I have never done drag before," Michael made the mistake of saying out loud and with just enough indignity to make it a challenge.

Rose lit up. "A virgin. Well, my darling, for your first time then, you get the full treatment."

Michael was horrified as she took him by the arm and led him to the slaughter.

Brian gave Michael an arched eyebrow over the tops of the dress racks as Rose took charge of the fitting.

"This one," she said, tossing a crimson and marabou number over his arm, hanger and all. "And this one, and this one. Oh, and definitely this one."

She loaded him up with their scarlet quarry.

"This is too many," Michael complained.

"Dresses are like men, you never know which is going to be the right one, so you have to try them all on for size," Rose said, waving a wrinkled finger at him.

"Hear, hear," Brian said, holding up a red, sequined frock to himself as he stood in front of the mirror.

"Shoes," Rose continued, leading Michael to the racks at the back of the store and having a look at his feet. "What delicate little feet you have. Here, try these on."

Brian guffawed but pretended that he was making fun of Lindsay's choice when Michael shot him a look.

"I don't think—" Michael began.

"Now, darling," Rose said, "I know. We can't really pick out the final shoes until we know which dress, but you're wearing flats, and since we're looking at gowns, we'll need an idea of how the dress will look with heels."

As Brian and Lindsay and everyone else in the store pretended not to watch, Michael put on a pair of simple black heels and attempted to stand. He went down as soon as he was up. Michael's complete inability to stand in heels revealed him as the novice he was, and the other shoppers began to take part, the ladies bringing possible shoes, if only to see him fall, as well as accessories and other possibilities, and even a couple of the men lingered just to rubberneck as the fashion show began.

Brian tried to help out by putting on a particularly challenging pair of stilettos and walking around in them. And he and Lindsay had tried on several possibilities by the time Rose gave Michael a dress, some platforms he could manage to stay up in, and packed him off to the dressing room.

"Michael," she called in after a reasonable amount of time had elapsed. "How are you?"

"Great," Michael said in a way that sounded not so great.

"Does it fit?"

"Yes."

"I knew I was right," Rose sang to the other nodding coconspirators. "A perfect eight. Come out and let us see."

"Mmm, that's all right," Michael deferred.

"Do you want me to come in there to—"

"No, no," Michael said, grabbing for the handle to stop her, though nothing else he'd done had stopped her.

"Well, come on out then," Rose said in a sweet scold. "Let us see."

"Don't the other shoppers have something else to do?" Michael said in a less than gracious tone of voice.

"Michael, Michael, Michael," Brian began chanting, and soon everyone in the store was chanting with him.

"Oh, God, why couldn't I have an intolerant, homophobic mom like the other fags?" Michael sighed to himself as he threw the bolt on the louvered dressing-room door and stepped out to meet his public.

"Take me out the to ballpark," Daniel whistled as he and Deb made their way to their seats at Three Rivers Stadium.

"For my money the Terrace Box seats are the best in the house," Deb explained as she marched into the second tier of the stadium as if she were walking out. "But I got a deal on these tickets, so today we're sitting with Andrew Carnegie behind home plate. You can't catch a foul ball from here, and personally I like to sit behind first base. It's a better view of the game and you can see the JumboTron easier. But I thought it'd be interesting to sit down here behind the batter for a change and see things from a new perspective."

She went on chattering nervously as she led them down the steep, oddly spaced stairs through the rows of red folding seats to their pair just behind and to the right of home plate. She figured if she just kept moving and kept talking, the game would soon be done and she could just go home, and it would be all over and she'd never, never as God as her witness, never do anything similar again. What had she been thinking when she'd asked this guy, way out of her league, to a baseball game? she thought to herself as she explained, "Joel Johnston is having a pretty good season, but nobody's having a great season."

She glanced over as she took her seat and found that he was looking right at her. She gestured to his seat as she explained, "We have to win these next two games against Philly or it's over and we're out of it. If we do, then we're off to Montreal. So, these are really valuable seats when you think about it."

"You know I'm from Pittsburgh," he said when she took a breath.

"Originally?" she said, a little light-headed from the walk and the extended monologue.

"I mean I've heard about the Pirates all season." He smiled.

"So, you're a fan?" she said, grasping at straws and trying to maintain the reins of the conversation.

"Not really." He shrugged.

"Then why'd you come?" she'd asked before she'd thought about it and then flushed so hard she felt faint. "I mean, well, I hope that you are, that is, what I meant to say . . ."

"Would you like something to drink?" he asked easily. "A dog maybe?"

"Yeah," she sighed, catching her breath and his mood. "That would be nice."

"Hot dogs are my guilty pleasure," he said with a grin as he turned to scan the stands for vendors.

"Well, these're nothing compared to The Big O," she said, then began stammering incoherently, trying to get out the name of The Original Hot Dog Shop, an area institution near the Pitt Med School also known to locals simply as The Big O.

"And their fries," he said, unaware she was having a nervous breakdown. "The best ever. I don't see dogs," he said, turning back. "But there's the damnedest cotton candy vendor I've ever seen."

She turned to see the nine-foot-something pillar of pink coming up a nearby aisle hawking the confection. The vendor was tall, six foot at least. But what gave him the real height advantage over pretty much everyone in the NBA was the three-foot spire of pink, spun-sugar updo on his head. No one was buying cotton candy, but no one was distracted by anything happening on the field while the sugar-frosted French twist was scraping the sky nearby.

"Emmett," Deb said without thinking.

"You know him?" Dan asked, far more interested than he had been with the season's box scores in the car on the way over.

"Yeah. I think so. It's a friend of my son's. Emmett?" Deb called.

The vendor's head snapped in their direction, clearly startled, as the whole fuchsia obelisk made the turn with him, signaling passing planes and, unfortunately, some late-season yellow jackets.

Emmett was horrified. He'd taken the god-awful job for want of anything else. After the fire at Kaufmann's and their threat to recover damages, his name was kind of mud in local retail. The vendor's gig seemed like a lark, and who for God's sake would Emmett know at a baseball game? Deb's shouts were the proof he'd needed that it could possibly be worse. It had already been a nightmare. Up and down the cement stairs, his calves and glutes had never been so firm. But despite the prospect of being able to leave off the StairMaster at the gym, the work was grueling, the hours were long, and the conditions were hideous. Worst of all, his pay was based on sales and the competition was fierce. People could have Häagen-Dazs or Pizza Hut, so old news like cotton candy was a tough sell. It had literally been uphill until he'd hit on the idea of the wig.

He'd had a lot of leftover product at the end of his first day on the job. He'd been playing around with it in front of the mirror in the employee lounge when the idea had hit him. Day two was off to a great start, the gawk factor was upping sales already and the game hadn't even started.

"Emmett?" Deb called again. "Is that you?"

Dazed and confused, he'd been trying to think of a plan when the first yellow jacket hit.

All Deb or the rest of the crowd in the infield section observed of the massive pink pole was a bloodcurdling scream and then extremely animated choreography as Emmett attempted to battle and flee the swarm of stinging yellow jackets. The crowd began cheering and even emulating some of his more distinctive moves and Tarzanesque yodels as he ran up and down the aisle trying to elude the tiny monsters that had developed a taste for the combination of sweat and liquefied sugar that had begun to run down Emmett's face in pink streams. And the more he ran, the more he sweat.

It being a play-off game, cameras abounded, and one vigilant cameraman, unoccupied as the game had yet to begin, picked up Emmett's wild dance of the cotton candy macabre and piped it onto the stadium's JumboTrons.

Finally, heedless of the free publicity, and stung several times, Emmett could stand it no more and gave up his brief but intense television career as he ripped the wig from his head, threw the crate of candy floss to a group of adoring fans, and ran screaming from the stadium.

Years later, when the city voted to blow up Three Rivers Stadium to replace it with more modern facilities, Emmett sat enigmatically on the hood of his car in a parking lot at his nearby alma mater, Allegheny Community College, and toasted the stadium's implosion.

Despite the trauma to Emmett's pride, the incident had broken and melted the ice between Deb and Dan. They laughed, they cheered, they led the neighboring crowd in their own version of Emmett's Cotton Candy Watusi. Caught up in the moment and how adorable Deb always was, he kissed her. Owing to Emmett's proximity and popularity, and though they were unaware of it, their first kiss was broadcast on the JumboTrons to 23,000 screaming Pirates fans.

"Congratulations," Melanie said, handing Ted a bottle of Rolling Rock and clinking hers against it. "A toast, to my best bud, there's nothing you set your mind to that you can't do."

"Thanks," Ted said, clinking his bottle against hers.

They both drank.

"Now all I've got to do is all the research and the writing," Ted said with a rueful little laugh.

"Well, yeah." Mel nodded. "But the tough part is getting the thesis committee on board, right?"

"Sure, after that, it practically writes itself."

"Oh my God," Lindsay said, spotting them and grabbing Brian's arm as they hit the door of Woody's for an after-shopping drink. "Do they do anything besides sit here and drink?"

"Glass houses," Brian cautioned as Michael pushed passed them.

"What's going on?" Michael asked.

"It's Lindsay's new girlfriend."

"I didn't know you were seeing anybody," Michael said, brightening from his harrowing afternoon.

"I'm not," Lindsay insisted.

"Not yet," Brian said, taking her arm. "Actually, my dear Mikey, Melanie's seen quite a bit of Lindsay. In fact, the last time we came here, Lindsay's drink was on her."

"Go to hell, Brian," Lindsay said, digging in her heels as Brian began to drag her nearer to where Ted and Melanie were seated.

"So, how'd you meet?" Michael said, taking Lindsay's other arm and helping, glad that it was someone else's turn in the barrel after starring in the fashion show at Rose's. He hadn't bought anything himself, though his modeling had sold a couple of things and he had put a couple more on hold.

"Lindsay was doing her Venus-on-the-half-shell imper-sonation at the fountain in front of the art department at Pitt," Brian said.

"Oh, she's the one," Michael said, recalling the story. "Lindsay, I've seen the painting and your hair's just a little short for the full Botticelli. I'm thinking it must have been quite a show."

"Brian Kinney, so help me," Lindsay said through gritted teeth. "If you don't let me go, I'm going to rack you so hard that you'll be able to give Mariah Carey a run for her high notes."

"Don't be so difficult," Brian said as he and Michael lifted Lindsay off the floor between them and began propelling her toward Melanie's table, her feet flailing wildly in midair. "We talked about this. You need to try to be nice to the other les-bians. Particularly the ones who are showing an interest in you."

"And an appreciation for seeing you naked," Michael pointed out as he strained to keep Lindsay airborne.

"And here we are," Brian said as he and Michael set Lind-say on one of the barstools around Mel and Ted's table. "Mind if we join you," Brian said, struggling to keep Lindsay in her seat.

"Melanie, Ned," Brian said by way of introduction. "You

remember Lindsay. And this is our friend Michael. Ned," Brian said, putting an arm over Ted's shoulder.

"It's Ted," Ted said with quiet irritation.

"Of course it is." Brian dragged Ted off his stool. "Why don't you come with Michael and me to go get drinks so Lindsay has something to throw?"

Brian did not wait for an answer and dragged Ted over to the waiter's station, Michael in tow, leaving Lindsay and Melanie in excruciating silence at the table.

"Okay," Brian said, his arm over both Michael's and Ted's shoulders. "You two kill some time at the bar. There's a guy over there by the pool table who's been dying to meet me since we got here," Brian concluded, dropping them off. "Lindsay will want a white wine." He put some money in Michael's hand and took his leave.

"Jesus," Ted said. "Is he always like that?"

"Pretty much," Michael said with a shrug. "Although sometimes he can be kind of pushy and controlling."

Ted laughed.

"Hi, Ned," Michael said, extending his hand. "I'm Michael."

"Hi, I'm Ted." Ted took Michael's hand.

"Sorry. I thought . . . Yeah, that's Brian. A real charmer."

"He is a bit. In an obnoxious, aggressive, won't-take-no-for-an-answer kind of a way. If you like that sort of thing."

"I don't think they're saying anything to one another," Michael said, looking covertly at Lindsay and Melanie, who were sitting facing in opposite directions at the table where they'd left them.

"Should we go over?" Ted asked, concerned.

"Oh, yeah, 'cause what I want to do is get closer before the lesbians get violent," Michael snorted. "I haven't had nearly enough to drink. Let's not go back empty-handed."

"You're funny," Ted said, taking a better look at him as Michael leaned over the edge of the bar to try to get some service. "So, I take it you and Brian are not together?"

"Since grade school, but just best friends. Hey, Ray, can we get some drinks over here."

"That's great," Ted said, not meaning it in the least and disappointed that he still did not have the information he wanted. "So, where is your boyfriend tonight?" He winced as he said it, but the more Michael hung over the edge of that bar, swinging his legs, the more Ted needed to know.

"Single," Michael answered, oblivious as usual, assuming that Ted's interest was in Brian and mildly irritated for it. "You?"

"Very single," Ted said, as pleased with Michael's question as his answer.

"Really?" Michael said, genuinely surprised. "You don't seem like the type."

"Me?" Ted said, taking his drink. "It's not exactly like I'm one of the hotties that everyone's throwing themselves at."

"Believe me, they are the terminally single," Michael snorted.

"So what type do I seem like?" Ted asked, not at all sure he wanted to hear the answer.

"I don't know." Michael shrugged. "Smart, successful, or well on the way. Stable, dependable, trustworthy."

"I sound like a Boy Scout."

"Those are actually good qualities you know. Marriage material."

"Thanks." Ted was charmed. Was this guy flirting?

"We should probably take the drinks over."

"Right," Ted agreed, taking Mel's Rolling Rock by the neck and following Michael over.

"I'm sorry if I embarrassed you at the fountain the other

day," Melanie ventured, making sure that no drinks were in arm's reach of Lindsay before saying anything.

"And I'm sorry about the drink," Lindsay said, turning to give Melanie at least a sideways glance. "It was a little soap operatic."

"I kind of deserved it," Melanie said with a little shrug.

"Yeah, you did," Lindsay agreed with a smirk. "Even so . . ." She left it at that.

"You did, you do, look really . . . you know," Melanie said, afraid to say too much and get things started again.

"Thanks."

"So, do you mind if I ask you," Melanie said after a little lull in the conversation, "why you were, you know, by the fountain that day?"

"Oh," Lindsay said, laughing a little.

She was beautiful when she laughed, Melanie thought.

"It was a fire drill."

"Oh," Melanie said, knitting her brow.

"I work there," Lindsay said, seeing the bewildered look.

"At the fountain?" Melanie asked, still not getting it, especially since Lindsay was not explaining it.

"In the art department," Lindsay said, hoping not to spell it out any more than necessary. "As a model."

"Oh, of course," Melanie said, the light dawning. "A life model, right?"

"It was my first day on the job, so to speak." Lindsay took a little pretzel out of the bar mix in the bowl on the table, thought better of it, and tossed it back.

"And there was a fire drill," Melanie filled in.

"I was nervous about . . . doing the job," Lindsay said, trying not to lie about the feelings she was experiencing on the job, but not to reveal them either.

"And this loudmouthed dyke came along and started heckling you." Melanie knocked herself in the forehead with the heel of her hand. "Now I really am sorry."

"Because you weren't before?" Lindsay said, flirting just a little.

"Because now I know how you must have felt before I showed up," Mel said, trying so hard not to lose the ground she'd gained that she missed the flirting. "I just thought you were some stupid straight sorority girl doing some pledge haze."

"Well, I might have been. And the people in that class don't need to know all my personal business," Lindsay said with a tense little smile. "I don't think anyone noticed though, so no hard feelings?"

"No, I feel like I got off easy for being such a heel," Melanie said, a little put off by the tone but not wanting any more trouble. "You really don't have any reason to be nervous about . . . your job." She sidled up to the compliment. "You've got nothing to hide."

"Thanks," Lindsay said, out of things to say.

"And here you are, ladies," Ted said as he and Michael returned with the drinks, since the storm warning appeared to have passed.

"So, where is Brian?" Lindsay asked, looking around.

"After some guy," Michael said flatly.

"Our loss," Ted said with a nasty little laugh that irritated Michael.

"You know, you really don't know him," Michael said as easily as he could.

"And he doesn't seem to know me," Ted said, still smarting.

"Because he called you Ned?" Michael asked.

"Yeah," Ted said with a terse nod of his head.

Michael knew, from years of experience, better than to try to defend Brian's behavior. Even so, Brian was his best friend and he was not simply going to stand by. "Well, you should get to know him before you decide."

"So should he," Ted said, not pleased to be having this conversation with the best-looking guy in the room.

"Well, good," Michael said, going cold. "Then you'll give him the chance."

"I'm off to the ladies'," Lindsay said, rising to go.

Michael looked fleetingly around the room for Brian, unsure of what to do in the event of Lindsay's escape.

"I'll be back, Michael," Lindsay said, observing his moment of uncertainty. "Unless you want to come along. We can share makeup tips in the lounge."

"Very funny," Michael growled, stacking arms.

"Oh, come on," she nettled. "You had such a good time with Rose."

She pinched his cheek and disappeared.

"What was that all about?" Melanie asked, interested since it involved Lindsay.

"We were getting costumes for a party," Michael said, trying to gloss it off.

"The Red Dress Ball," Brian said, taking the barstool next to Michael and putting an arm around him affectionately.

Ted was visibly disappointed by Brian's return.

"What happened to your pool game?" Michael asked, steering wildly at the conversation to avoid a retelling of his fashion show incident.

"He's ditching his date," Brian said offhandedly.

"Charming," Melanie said, rolling her eyes and taking up the fresh beer Ted and Michael had brought her.

"Melanie doesn't approve," Brian said, catching the waiter's eye and pointing at his nearly empty glass.

"What's the Red Dress Ball?" Ted asked, not having the least interest in talking about Brian's love life and wanting to know more about Michael.

"It's a fund-raiser for PFLAG," Brian explained, finishing his drink. "Michael's mom is hosting it. The idea is that everyone in attendance must wear a red dress, so we went shopping for red dresses this afternoon and Michael was quite the hit."

"I bet he was," Ted said proudly, even though he knew nothing about Michael whatsoever.

"You should come," Brian said, looking squarely at Melanie. "It's for a good cause."

"Did, uh, Lindsay find a red dress to wear to the party this afternoon?" Melanie asked casually.

"You mean is Lindsay coming to the party?" Brian asked with a little edge to his voice. "Why don't you just ask me?"

"Never mind," Melanie answered, disgusted.

"Look, Mzzzz Marcus Butthead," Brian said, throwing an arm over Melanie's shoulder and leaning in so that they were nose to nose. "I can help you with Lindsay or I can hurt you with Lindsay, but if you want to be a part Lindsay's life, you get to be a part of mine."

Melanie grabbed Brian's wrist and, using the swivel stool to her advantage, spun Brian around and twisted his arm behind his back. "I don't need any help from you where Lindsay is concerned," she snarled into his ear. "Got it?"

"Yeah, I do," Lindsay said. "Now, could you let go of my friend?"

Melanie sighed as she released her grip on Brian's wrist and resisted the urge to put her face on the table again.

"Brian, I'll see you later," Lindsay said, bussing him on the cheek.

"Want to split a cab?" Michael asked her.

Lindsay nodded in response and dashed back her wine.

"Are you leaving, Michael?" Ted asked.

"Yeah, long day," Michael said coldly. "We just stopped in for a drink on the way home. And, well, this was it."

"Great to meet you," Ted said, extending his hand.

"Yeah," Lindsay said, taking it. "Always a treat."

She and Michael turned and left without another word.

Brian's drink arrived. He paid and thanked the waiter, lit a cigarette, and made himself comfortable. Ted stared after Michael, and Melanie said nothing. The silence at the table grew painful, though Brian's smile only broadened. "That went great," Brian said cheerfully at last. "You really don't seem to need any help from me," he went on, chucking Melanie playfully on the chin with a pulled punch.

She sighed deeply and put her face back on the table.

"She'll be there," Brian said, rising to leave. "And so will I."

"We'll see you there," Ted said gamely as if supporting Melanie.

"Good for you, Ed," Brian said, punching him painfully in the upper arm.

"Ned," Ted corrected, and then realized his error as Brian walked away. "I mean Ted."

chapter seven

"Brian," Evan shouted across the office.

Brian sighed as he rose to cross from his office into Evan's. It was ten thirty and the lights of the city tantalized him as he caught a glimpse of the spectacular view of the nighttime skyline. He'd not left the office before midnight for the past week and still with the screaming. He and Evan had come to an understanding when Brian moved into his new office, but aside from the proximity of the screaming, little else had changed.

They were preparing for a huge event in Texas celebrating the merger of their Pittsburgh-based client One Bank as they bought their way into the Texas market by acquiring the largest bank in the state. The multicity event was going to be simulcast between several different venues in Houston, Dallas, Austin, San Antonio, and smaller cities throughout the state with all of the bank's thousands of employees in attendance at each location, symbolically linking the combined operation and allowing the new leadership to address all the employees at once.

In short, it was a logistical nightmare and Evan was directing the entire operation.

He had spent five hours on a conference call that afternoon with all the relevant clients, suppliers, venues, and broadcast services, carefully going over each detail of the massive event from satellite uplinks to pom-poms. He would be leaving the next day for Houston, and then on to Austin, San Antonio, and finally Dallas, where he would be directing the operation. It had been a grueling couple of weeks as they moved into the countdown, and Brian was looking forward to getting Evan on the plane the next day. So, while he wasn't thrilled about the hour or the screaming, the end was in sight, and Brian could be cheerful in the knowledge that he would be back on the town and getting laid the next night and, more joyously, Evan would be away for several days laying waste to the lives of the residents of Texas.

"Brian," Evan screamed, turning to see that Brian was standing there in front of his desk. "Right, where the hell have you been?"

Brian pointed toward his office door a few yards away.

"A couple of things," Evan said without acknowledging. "I want you to mark the pyrotechnic cues separately in the final prompt script, so pick another color and retab all the copies."

"Great," Brian groaned.

Evan gave him an odd look.

"Idea," Brian added none too convincingly. "Great idea."

"I figured that's what you meant," Evan said, not cracking a smile. "Secondly, I need a drink. I know," he said, waving Brian off. "I'm not asking you to fix me a drink. I'm asking if

you want to join me. I think we're done, other than the retab-
bing, and frankly we could get a chimp to do that."

"But the chimp went home at five," Brian said caustically.
"And I'm still here."

"Anyway, the point is, I'm going to make myself a martini. Would you care for one?"

"Sure," Brian said, too surprised to affect an attitude.
Evan had never so much as offered for Brian to take a lunch
break, so offering to fix him a drink was almost an acknowledgment that Brian was human.

"Great," Evan mimicked, rising and crossing to the bar
that was built into the wall of his office. "The only other
thing you need to do tonight is call the travel agent. I want to
change my reservations a bit."

Brian fought not to say anything as he picked up a pad to
write down the zillionth version of Evan's proposed travel
itinerary. They had been through this before. Evan kept
changing things around and the travel agent was on the
verge.

"Tell them I want to double everything," Evan said,
swishing vermouth around in the shaker, then tossing it out.
"I want you to come along, so two of everything, got it?"

Brian wasn't sure how to react. He was actually quite
pleased about the prospect of getting out into the field, working the event, working with the client, and participating in
more than just the concept and the theory, in the realization.
On the other hand, he was horny as hell, hadn't been out with
his friends, and Deb's Red Dress thing was the end of the
week. What's more, he knew that if he went, he'd be with
Evan all day every day until they returned.

"You've been invaluable putting this together, and I
think you'd be a real asset down there." Evan shrugged, pour-

ing the frozen Absolut over the ice in the shaker. "And you've earned it."

"Thanks," Brian said, overwhelmed by what was by Evan's standards the gushing show of sentiment. "Was that praise?"

"Don't get all misty on me," Evan said, pouring. "Just drink your fucking martini."

First class, Brian thought as he stretched out on the roomy, blue leather seat.

"Something to drink?" the handsome young steward asked.

"Absolut on the rocks with olives," Evan said without looking up from the report he was reading.

"Certainly, Ev—Mr. Steele," the attendant said, as though making a joke of referring to Evan so formally. Evan for his part only looked over his reading glasses irritably in reply.

"And for you?" the attendant said to Brian.

"The same is fine," Brian said, intrigued by the exchange between his boss and the young man.

"You know him?" Brian asked.

"Possibly," Evan sighed. "I fly to Texas a lot for this client."

"And so you're on a first-name basis?" Brian said without thinking.

"Something you want to know?" Evan asked, looking all the way up from his reading and clearly not happy about it.

"No," Brian lied. "Just making conversation."

"With me?" Evan snorted. "Try to avoid that." He put the glasses back on and sank back into the reading.

Brian had a little laugh seemingly at his own expense, but in fact at the unexpected moment of dawning realization.

Evan was so complete, so about the work, so smart and competent and engaged and so, well, Evan, that Brian had never really thought of him as a flesh-and-blood man before. It wasn't that Brian had never paused to consider Evan's sexual preference, it was that he'd never considered Evan sexually at all, which was quite remarkable given Brian's own nature. Evan was in fact an attractive, successful man probably in his midthirties, with impeccable style and tastes, which Brian both admired and more and more was adopting as his own.

But Evan, a bone smoker?

Brian laughed to himself again.

The image and idea were entirely too human to be attributed to Evan.

The drinks arrived and Brian observed the attendant again as he made a point to brush up against Evan, who was sitting on the aisle. Evan ignored it or, more likely, never even noticed.

"Here you are, sir," the attendant said to Brian, handing him his drink and giving him a knowing look as if to say, that's my seat you're sitting in. It made Brian uncomfortable. "We'll be taking off shortly. Let me know if there's anything else you need."

"Quiet would be lovely," Evan said, not looking up.

Brian smiled as the attendant huffed off.

"Mr. Steele," the concierge called warmly from across the lobby of the Four Seasons Houston as he rushed to greet them. "Good to see you, sir." He gestured meaningfully to the bellman, who seemed to understand.

Brian was already enjoying the first-class life that he was experiencing vicariously with Evan. The limo that had picked them up, the private club at the airport, the first-class cabin on the plane, the limo and humpy driver waiting in Houston to fetch their bags and deliver them here, and now the concierge at the Four Seasons booking across the lobby to greet them had Brian giddy with luxury.

"Are you really so impossible that everyone remembers you wherever you go?" Brian asked Evan quietly before the concierge reached them.

Evan laughed out loud. "That's probably the mistaken impression. But I thought you'd be bright enough to see that I'm not so much difficult as I am specific."

"Is that what we're calling it?" Brian said, laughing as well.

"Good evening, sir," the concierge said in some Eastern accent that Brian could not identify. "I saw that you would be staying with us, but I did not realize you were traveling with someone."

"This is Brian Kinney," Evan said. "A work associate."

"Oh, I see," the concierge acknowledged.

Again Brian had the same odd feeling of something unspoken that he'd had with the attendant on the plane.

"Well, then, let me arrange for a two-bedroom suite," the nattily dressed man suggested with a little bow. "If that would be satisfactory?"

"Certainly, but not necessary," Evan said as though mildly irritated.

It felt to Brian as though they were speaking in code, exchanging information like parents spelling in the presence of a preschool child.

"No trouble at all," the concierge said.

"We'll have a drink at the bar," Evan said. "You'll have someone come for us once things are ready. I've got some calls to make."

He didn't really even ask. Brian wondered at the imperious way that Evan conducted himself. Brian followed along to the booth that was instantly readied for them in the lobby bar, a telephone on the table as quickly as the drinks, which came without being ordered.

No one asked Brian; it was just assumed that he would have what Evan was having. It was a life that Brian found immensely appealing. So much so that he forgot to be offended at the slight.

George Brown Convention Center looked rather like a cruise ship that had run aground in downtown Houston. The gleaming white structure was fitted with massive porthole windows and exposed red vent pipes, an homage to the fact that Houston, sprawling and beachless, was after all a port city.

The limo the concierge had arranged took them the three blocks to the structure's flag-draped main entrance on Avenida de las Americas, where Evan was met and received like visiting royalty. As the event's account director and various senior facility staff directed them on a brief tour of the center, it seemed to Brian that they were presenting the place for Evan's approval, not simply as a matter of fact. Aside from the event director, they did not know Evan's name, had never met or worked with him before, and still it was the same as everywhere they had been.

Brian, who only knew Evan as the resident despot at the I/M office back in Pittsburgh, had always assumed that the respect and awe with which he was treated there were simply byproducts of a combination of fear and reverence for undeniable talent. But that wasn't it at George Brown Convention Center. Evan simply expected to be treated the way that he was treated and so he was. He commanded respect in the most literal way.

As their tour of Texas continued, Brian saw that Evan was as likely to receive princely treatment from the street vendor on the River Walk in San Antonio as he was from the night manager at the Hilton Midland, where he was spending a small fortune and buying out the entire hotel for two days around the event. They may not have said nice things about Evan after he was gone, but face-to-face, they gave him the reverence of a king.

When their whirlwind tour of Texas landed them in Dallas, where the main event was to be staged at what was preposterously called the World Trade Center, Brian had fallen into a comfortable three paces behind as Evan shaped all that he encountered before them, from lunch waiters to CEOs, sculpting all to his will as Brian watched over his shoulder. It was an odd and unaccustomed feeling for Brian. He felt safe, secure, protected as if he were shielded from the world somehow, observing it without his usual need to tame it.

As their car took them from their lavish suite at the Anatole down I-35 to the venue, the driver, describing the sights in Dallas, mentioned the ice rink at the Plaza of the Americas. Brian had been as gifted at hockey as he had been at soccer, in many ways he liked it more, but he hadn't gotten any scholarship offers for hockey so he'd hung up the skates but not his love of the ice. The trip had been informative, enlightening, and first-class all the way, but there had been no time for anything but work, and a turn on the ice sounded like a week in Tahiti to Brian, who, for all intents and purposes, had not left work at all since they'd left Pittsburgh, and he looked longingly at the rink as the car sped past.

"Earth to Brian," Evan said, throwing a paper cup.

"Sorry," Brian said, shaking it off.

"Where were you?"

"On the ice." Brian grinned an apology for his day-dreaming.

"You a skater?" Evan asked, startling Brian with an unaccustomed show of interest in anything other than the world according to Evan.

"Used to be," Brian said with one long last look out the window as they hurtled down the straight, flat freeway toward the Market Place, a sort of convention mall where Dallas kept their broad, squat version of the World Trade Center.

"Rosebud." Evan grinned.

"Yeah," Brian said, smiling.

"Well, Citizen Kinney," Evan said sternly. "Those remarks for the local guy aren't going to write themselves. I need your draft by the satellite uplink check so I can change everything before we give them to the prompter guy."

They rode the remainder of the trip in relative silence. Evan read reports and memos, messages and faxes he'd collected at their hotel, as Brian alternately took notes on what else Evan needed from him and worked on the speech.

They arrived at the WTC West to find that, much to Evan's surprise, everything was not only in readiness but ahead of schedule. So much so that they were left with several hours before the actual event.

"Great," Evan sighed after they walked the stage, checked the sound and video, previewed the satellite uplink during their scheduled test window with all the other locations, and even tried out their chairs in the master control truck from which vantage Evan was to direct the show. Evan stretched as he arose from his expensive, black leather, ergonomically correct director's chair. "I've got some things that need to be taken care of before the show begins. I'll be back here an hour before we go live; the rest is just catering, and if we can't handle that, set the place on fire and call the local news."

"I'll lay in some Sterno," the technical director joked.

"Come along, Brian," Evan said, raising a mirthful eyebrow but not laughing. "We've got an appointment."

"We do?" Brian said, slightly alarmed, checking his notes as he followed, almost tripping on the metal steps outside the mobile master control trailer set up in the service alley behind the diminutive World Trade Center.

The limo driver looked startled when he saw Evan return and quickly ditched his cigarette, checked himself in the limo's side mirror, and inhaled two quick blasts of Binaca. He hustled for the door and just beat Evan. The effect was that the door was opened as Evan approached, never having to break stride. Brian stepped in behind him and was just about to ask when Evan said to the driver, "Plaza of the Americas."

Brian couldn't help but smile. It was so completely out of character. It was unproductive, it would not earn them any money, and most of all, it was not technically Evan's idea, despite his making it seem as if it were.

"Why?" Brian asked as he eyed the ludicrous orb atop the Reunion Tower that held sway over the city's skyline.

"It'll be a lark." Evan shrugged. "I've never skated before. I like to try new things. Who knows, I might like it. Best of all, if I break my leg, I get to blame you."

"That kind of takes some of the lark out of it for me."

"I'm doing this so I can have a good time." Evan looked out the window. "You much of a skater?"

"I played some hockey when I was younger," Brian said, leaving out the trophies and youth league championships.

"Younger," Evan repeated, then laughed.

It was the middle of the day in the middle of the week

and the ice was completely abandoned. They had the rink completely to themselves.

"Try getting them a little smaller than your shoe size," Brian advised as they approached the skate rental counter. "You want them to be especially snug. Skating is really about your ankles."

Evan nodded. "So, only fourteens?"

"In women's, yes."

After careful consideration, they selected a couple of pairs and made their way over to a wooden bench in a small enclosure on the ice but just off the rink. Brian attempted to explain, then simply knelt to lace Evan into his skates and quickly put on his own.

"Okay, getting your footing on the ice is completely different from getting your footing in real life," Brian explained. "It's why people fall down. Standing on the ice is an act of will. You have to think the correct muscles and will them to keep you standing. Off the ice it's only about balance; it's the resistance that holds you upright. On the ice, there's still gravity and balance, but there's no friction, nothing to hold you in place, nothing to resist. You have to fight the natural attraction."

"Sounds just like real life," Evan snorted.

"Your ankles will have the tendency to go sideways and your weight will push your legs apart. It's actually the same tendency to fall that will move you forward. It'll make more sense when you try it, but the main thing is to stiffen your ankles and tense your thighs, hold your legs together and you'll stay up. Ready?"

"Sure." Evan planted both feet firmly on the ice, pausing for a moment to feel the correct muscles and will them to follow instruction, then stood. Brian rose to stand at his side and kept his hands raised slightly just in case, but not so it would appear that he was helping or even expecting a fall.

After a moment of awkward jitters, Evan found his center of gravity and then stood firm.

Brian was impressed, but figured that the indignity of a tumble would come as they made their way out to the rink and began to skate. No tumble came. Evan did not master skating and he could never propel himself backward, but he got the hang of it and they actually had a pretty good hour on the ice. Once Evan got going on his own, Brian was free to recapture the long-forgotten freedom of flying that the ice offers when you surrender control.

Despite his remarkable performance, Evan was not in Brian's league, and Brian was actually skating circles around him, which Evan pointed out laughingly. The only sound had been their shouts to one another and the scraping of the metal blades on the ice. And as both men took to their respective workouts, the conversation died and it became just about the ice.

A young woman who was to teach lessons in the space a bit later that afternoon arrived to test some music on the sound system, and suddenly the meditative quiet of the rink echoed with Tchaikovsky's "Dance of the Sugar Plum Fairy." Brian could not resist the moment and swooped in on an unsuspecting Evan, his approach covered by the music. Grasping Evan one-armed, firmly around the waist, he swept the novice into a thundering, Tchaikovsky-driven circuit of turns, maneuvers, and spins that would have paled an experienced roller-coaster enthusiast. Evan tensed initially as Brian dragged him along for the high-velocity ride, threatening both of them with a spill. "Just let go," Brian said easily, his face near Evan's ear.

It was an improbable sight. Two men in Armani business suits in blazing Indian-summer heat ice-skating to the delicate ballet music. Evan kept struggling for the lead, hindering their dance and hobbling their stability. Finally, unable to overcome the drag, Brian skated them out to the center of the rink and stopped. He turned to face Evan, forcefully took both of his hands, and concluded their impromptu waltz with a cyclonic spin facing one another. Both hands clasped, they spun in place, faster and faster until the world behind them became a blur and the only thing either man could see was the other's face.

"That was great," Evan panted as they unlaced their skates and prepared to return to dry land.

"Yeah," Brian said a bit wistfully. "I'm a little disappointed."

"Well, we're not exactly Tai and Randy, but it's my first time out," Evan joked.

"Oh, it's not that," Brian said. "I didn't get to see you fall."

"And you never will." Evan smirked as they made their way to the rental desk.

The event was a triumph.

After their adventure skating, Brian and Evan had gotten a light lunch at the Adolphus and then headed back to the WTC. The crowds were gathered at all the locations as Evan took up his place in their mobile master control center.

Brian was mostly just a spectator once things got under way. The staff and facilities were in place, and with a surprisingly gentle hand, Evan coaxed the best performance from each. There were costumed characters, live music, dancers, indoor and outdoor pyrotechnics, giant-screen airings of the upcoming ad campaign that Evan had developed to introduce the new bank to the state, interspersed with interviews and speeches from bank officials and employees simulcast by satellite throughout the state.

Brian's seat, just next to Evan's, was the second best of the night to see the splashy hype that was unfolding before them. Brian watched Evan throughout it all. Late cues, misfires, muffed lines, Evan rolled calmly through it all, always knowing exactly where they were or how they needed to catch themselves back up, never lost, never at a loss, always in charge.

Despite the spectacle unfolding on camera, Evan was the more amazing sight for Brian.

"And that makes us the one bank for the future," the CEO wrapped up his speech and the evening to music, a balloon drop, fireworks, and thunderous applause in locations all across Texas. The director called shots from the different locations throughout the state with an occasional suggestion from Evan until they ran out of satellite time and the screens all went to local signal of the bank's new logo.

"And that's a wrap," Evan said into his headset. "Try not to injure any guests as you strike this shit so we can all go home." Evan pulled off the headset and turned to Brian.

"How about a martini?" Brian asked.

"What's the catch? My legs are already killing me from the skating so I'm in no mood to bargain for it."

"I thought I'd have one. Thought you might be ready for one as well."

"I've got to hoof it out there to schmooze the head cheez-its," Evan said, pointing at the stage in the main room on a nearby monitor. "Why don't you see that the load out gets started and then catch up with me?"

Brian felt a bit stung not to be included in the moment with the client, but he was after all just Evan's assistant.

"Sure thing," Brian said with a little nod, fingering the lighter and cigarettes in his pocket as he edged toward the door.

They went their separate ways and the evening drew to a close. Brian saw to everything being loaded up, moved out, and to the final paperwork and details of the moment, while Evan was lauded and toasted by the bank's top officers on the stage as long as it was standing and then, as even that was torn down, in the hospitality suite the WTC provided as a sort of greenroom for event VIPs.

"All done," Brian said from the door of the room as he caught Evan's eye.

"Good job," Evan said, motioning him in. "Everyone, this is my assistant director, Brian Kinney. Brian, are you ready for that martini you mentioned earlier?"

"No thanks. We've got an early flight tomorrow and I'd like to get back to the hotel."

"Brian, good to meet you," the CEO of the new bank said, clasping Brian's hand warmly. "We've talked so often on the phone; it's good to meet you in person."

A martini was thrust into Brian's hand, and with the CEO's blessing every other executive in the room made his introduction. It took forty-five minutes of determined effort, but at last Brian and Evan were on their way back to the car.

"Did the research on the frozen-food people ever turn up for my meeting tomorrow?" Evan said as they walked through the now empty concourse.

"At the hotel," Brian said tersely but politely.

"God damn it, I asked that those be sent here."

"So I could carry them around all day?" Brian snapped. "Or so you could read them in the car on the way back to the hotel?"

"Bark, bark, bark," Evan said with a dismissive laugh.

"Fuck you," Brian said, getting in the front with the driver.

Evan seemed not to notice as he stepped through the door the driver was holding for him.

"The hotel, sir?" the driver asked as no one was speaking when he got into the car.

"Yes, quickly," Evan said with yet another sigh.

The ride was devoid of any sense of victory. No one spoke after Evan agreed with the driver's suggested destination. When they arrived at the hotel, Brian popped open his door before the staff there could open it for him, moved swiftly though the nearest entrance and across the lobby to the elevators. He stepped onto a car that was just headed up and saw through the closing doors the arched brows of a very much irritated Evan Steele, glaring at him across the room.

Once back in their suite, Brian began filling the enormous tub in his bathroom. He tore off his tie and was unbuttoning his shirt as the suite's front doors banged open and Evan came bellowing into Brian's room.

"What in the pluperfect hell are you up to?" Evan shouted as he followed the sound of running water and charged into Brian's bathroom.

"I'm taking a bath," Brian said, adding bubbles to the steaming water. "Do you mind?"

"You know what I'm talking about," Evan said, not giving an inch.

"Okay then," Brian said as he undid the buttons on his cuffs.

"I can't believe you are acting this way," Evan snarled, leaning against the glass wall of the steam shower opposite the Jacuzzi, clearly not daunted by Brian's personal-space ploy and not leaving. "What is it? Your time of the month?"

"I guess I just overestimated you," Brian said calmly, turning off the taps and switching on the jets.

"Overestimated me?" Evan said, his volume rising. "Where do you get off—"

"You fooled me into believing you had human qualities." Brian sat on the edge of the tub.

"You presumptuous little shit," Evan rumbled, ready to erupt. "How dare you talk to me like an equal!"

"There's the inhuman son of a bitch I know," Brian said calmly as he began to remove his shoes. "What would it have cost you to include me in your little after-party? Were you really that afraid that someone else would get some of the credit?"

"I did invite you to the party." Evan was shouting.

"After I'd cleaned up the World Trade Center West." Brian tossed a shoe aside and raised his foot to take off the other. "Were you afraid that people would think we were together?"

Evan caught Brian off-balance as both men fell backward into the sudsy water. They struggled ineffectually in the soapy morass, a mess of wet clothing and bruised dignity before Evan broke up and began laughing. Brian was not far behind as he stopped struggling and settled into Evan's arms.

Brian slid forward and the laughter stopped abruptly when their erections met through the soaked gray and charcoal Armani wool. Their eyes locked for an instant of revelation and then their mouths were fused as they tore mercilessly at the soaked fabric keeping them apart.

Evan ripped open the front of Brian's trousers and, grasping them by the waistband, pulled them up and off along with the Calvins underneath. Brian's legs came to rest on Evan's shoulders as he hung onto Evan's neck. Evan drove insistently forward, struggling to free himself of his own soaked trousers as Brian's hands slid down his back urging him on, never once breaking the kiss. Once free of the hobbling wet trousers, Evan rose and carried Brian, still bent double, to the marble counter by the sink to retrieve the condoms and the lube, and unable to wait for the greater comfort of the bed or even the bath mat, they consummated the mood.

The sex was about power and submission and control and surrender without need of affected dialogue or mail order costuming. Despite their arguments, Brian had found in Evan a superior intelligence and nature he could trust, and he gave himself more completely then he ever had before.

"I'm starving," Brian said at last, back in the Jacuzzi by way of the vast chenille bath mat and the bidet, where they had just finished round four. "You're pretty persistent for an old guy."

"Still not full? Let's order something," Evan said, picking up the phone, which had fortunately been mounted to the wall nearby or, given the state of the rest of the room, it would surely have been in the tub with them. "What do you feel like?"

Brian grinned as he thrust his hand under the water demonstratively.

"After dinner." Evan flinched. "Concierge, please. . . . Hello, Jacques? . . . Yes, this is Mr. Steele. I need to order dinner, but I'm going to need discretion as the main course. My companion and I will be dining in the Jacuzzi."

Brian wasn't sure if he could wait until after dinner.

chapter eight

"What am I going to do?" Michael said aloud in the empty apartment, staring at himself in the mirror. The Red Dress Ball was that night and Michael was wearing his bathrobe and even that wasn't red. Despite the apparent success of his initial shopping excursion to Second Hand Rose, Michael had not settled on a red dress. Where the hell was Brian?

The phone interrupted his thoughts.

"Hello," Michael said hopefully.

"Hey, baby, want to suck Daddy's big dick?"

"Brian?" Michael asked, not at all sure.

"I said I wanted you to call me Daddy."

"Brian." Michael grinned, certain.

"God damn it," the man shouted before hanging up.

Michael winced at the banging of the receiver. "I guess not," he said to the dead receiver as he hung up.

"Hey, sweetie," Emmett called, breezing in the front door laden with groceries and even a bundle of flowers.

"Groceries," Michael cooed. "My favorite. You remembered." He took a couple of bags off Em's hands and bussed him on the cheek.

"Sorry it's been such a long wait," Emmett giggled. "And look." He reached into one of the bags, more or less dumping the load on the drainboard half of the old-fashioned kitchen sink.

"Cap'n Crunch," Michael shouted as Emmett held the enormous box aloft triumphantly.

"The supereconomy size," Emmett corrected. "There's weeks of oral lacerations just waiting for you in every box."

"There used to be cool prizes too," Michael said, examining the box for special offers.

"That may be in there as well," Emmett said, only half listening as he went about putting away the groceries in the tiny alcove of the Pullman-wannabe kitchen.

The phone rang.

"Daddy?" Michael answered mischievously.

"No, it's your mom," Deb said. "I have the deeper voice. Who the hell were you expecting?"

"Oh, hi, Mom." Michael slouched into the orange-striped chair by the bookcase and draped his legs over the arm.

"Hey, honey," she said, clearly in a rush and not waiting for a reply. "Listen, I need a favor. Can you and Emmett and the rest of your little posse come a little early tonight? We're shorthanded. These queens are great at decorating ideas but a little slower on construction."

"I don't know," Michael said. "Brian's not even home from Dallas yet. I'll ask Emmett and I'll call Lindsay and see what I can do."

"Okay, sweetie, thanks," Deb said, making kissy noises. "Come about an hour early. Even if it's just you, it'll be a huge help. And don't worry about your outfit. There's enough beauty technicians around to make Barbara Bush beautiful."

"Okay, Mom, great," Michael said through gritted teeth to the dial tone. "Oh my God, I'm going to have to move to another city," he shouted, burying his face in the white satin pillow Emmett had added to the chair to "liven" it up, though Michael wasn't sure why an orange-striped chair needed livening.

"The weather in L.A.'s nice," Emmett suggested, emerging from the kitchen. "But the people . . ." He held his hand out and wiggled it back and forth in a the-jury's-still-out kind of gesture.

"Emmett," Michael said so seriously that Emmett actually stopped talking. "I don't have anything to wear to the party tonight."

Emmett clutched the spot where his pearls would be one day if he ever owned any and sucked in air for a remarkable length of gasp. "What do you mean! It's your very own mother's drag party. What will she say? What were you thinking?"

"I know," Michael sighed forlornly. "I really don't know what I was thinking other than I really don't want to go to this party or any party in girl drag. So, I just kept putting it off and Brian kept being out of town and now . . . God, Em, what am I going to do?"

"Well, fortunately you room with the valedictorian of the fashion merchandising class of 1990," Emmett said proudly.

"You were not," Michael spluttered as the enormity of the lie dawned on him. "You were on academic probation until the last possible minute, and even then you practically had to blow the dean of men to get your diploma."

"What do you mean practically?" Emmett demanded

indignantly, then, thinking better of it, changed the subject. "Don't try to change the subject." The best offense was a good defense. "Despite being passed over for the academic honors I should have received, I know exactly what to do." He eyed the coatrack by his own bed, the idea dawning even as he spoke. "When will Brian be home?"

"I don't know." Michael shrugged. "I thought I'd have heard from him by now. He's called most every day and then nothing."

"We really need a third little maid for this to work," Emmett called back from his room where he was pulling kimonos off the coatrack. "Who can we call?"

"Oh, that reminds me," Michael said. "I've gotta call Lindsay. Mom wants us all there an hour early to help fluff."

"Lindsay will be perfect," Emmett said, clapping his hands. "It's surprising, it's ironic, it's totally unexpected, and it's just crazy enough to work. It will be the first time since the days of Gilbert and Sullivan that any of the three little maids were actually women."

"What are you talking about?" Michael asked, dialing Lindsay's number.

"The reason I should be given an honorary validick and the answer to your prayers," Emmett crowed, holding up three red silk kimonos.

"What the hell is a validick?"

Michael was so pleased with the Three Little Maids solution that he had been willing to grant Emmett his "validick." They were not only in red dresses but Emmett and Lindsay had pooled their makeup resources and knowledge and all three were wearing the clown-white masks of Kabuki geishas. Lindsay had been only too happy to go along as simply wearing a red dress to a party had not been much of a thrill for her since third grade; the costumes had seemed like much more of an adventure.

"Oh my God, you three look amazing," Deb had screamed when she figured out who they were.

The three gave the salute they had practiced, balancing their chins on an index finger, holding out their kimonos at the side with the opposing hand, and slipping one foot behind the other in a quick little curtsy, which only made Deb laugh harder. "Vic, you have to see this," she shouted to the red-sequin-spangled Farrah in the work boots at the top of the ladder stringing up enough red paper lanterns to light up the Great Wall.

"What?" Vic called back from under the wing-swept blond locks.

"Guess who it is," Deb said, pointing at the Pacific Rim knockoffs.

The three did their curtsy/salute.

"Why it's Yum-Yum, Peep-Bo, and Pitti-Sing!" Vic exclaimed, hooking the heels of his boots on the outside rails of the ladder and sliding to the ground in a most revealing and unladylike manner.

"Who?" Emmett said, creasing the thick white Pan-Stick on his forehead alarmingly.

"Vic," Deb shouted. "Do I have to remind you you're supposed to be in a wheelchair?"

"The three little maids," Vic said, bounding over to them and ignoring Deb's mothering.

"Is that their names?" Lindsay asked. "I'm Peep-Bo," she said, raising her hand and jumping up and down, even more pleased with her costume now that her character had a name.

"Vic, are you listening to me?" Deb insisted.

"A woman?" Vic intoned as he got close enough to realize who the three were. "Very daring, Emmett." He knew full well whose idea it had been and didn't bother asking.

"I thought the time had come," Emmett said, fanning himself coquettishly, confirming Vic's surmise. "And call me Yum-Yum."

"So, what does that leave me?" Michael said, trying to remember the name choices.

"It leaves you the rose garlands to drape the gazebo with," Deb said, thrusting a handful of the floral swags at him and shoving him toward it. "And if you two could help Pitti-Pat and then string the last of the lanterns and put away that ladder."

Em and Lindsay curtsy/saluted and then scurried after Michael in a cloud of geisha giggles they'd been practicing in the car on the way over.

"No, no, Buttercup," Vic corrected. "It's Pitti-Sing."

"Hey, watch it, Farrah," Deb snarked. "Who are you calling Buttercup? And you can have a seat now that the reinforcements have arrived."

" 'Have you scissors and watches and knives?' " Vic asked, singing the Gilbert and Sullivan lyrics with a plaintive little shrug.

"Yeah," Deb said, waving a fist threateningly in his direction. "And a mean right hook, not to mention a big ass, so you can keep the cracks about Buttercup. Now, sit your skinny ass down."

"Mrs. Cripps has the same problem with the nickname in *Pinafore*," Vic relented, taking the garland off his wheelchair and having a seat.

"Who the hell is . . ." Deb gave it up. "You know what? I've got to get out of this conversation 'cause I really do have scissors and knives and I can't be responsible for what happens."

"Hi, Deb," Daniel called, spotting her from across the room.

"Daniel," she chirped, her mood shifting so dramatically that Vic and Emmett exchanged a quick look all the way across the hall. "What are you doing here so early? And aren't you just a vision in that gown."

"Yeah, I'm a vision all right," Daniel chortled as he spun to model the diaphanous red dress he'd worn for the occasion before crossing to where she stood beaming at him. "I'm a vision like Cassandra's. I came early to see if you need any help and to set up the ticket sales, though we're mostly sold-out."

"And where's Cassandra?" Deb asked, looking behind him as he took her hand and gave her a little one-armed hug.

"Mired hopelessly in Greek mythology," Daniel said, making it a two-armed hug as her naïveté was just too cute to resist. "But trust me, it's for the best she's not here this evening."

"Well," Deb said over his shoulder, "that's too bad. I'm sorry she couldn't make it." She wasn't really sorry this Cassandra wasn't going to be there, whoever she was. She and Daniel had managed to share quite a bit of pie during the planning stages of the party. And while they hadn't been to any more ball games, they had seen a lot more of one another than anyone else knew.

"Hello," Vic said, bumping them apart with his wheelchair, hand extended to Daniel. "I'm Vic, Deb's brother, although tonight I guess we're all sisters."

"Very profound," Daniel said, taking Vic's hand and shaking it heartily. "Good to meet you, Vic. Deb thinks the world of you. She talks about you all the time."

"So, you two spend a lot of time together, do you?" Vic said, on the scent.

"These things take a lot of planning," Daniel said with an expansive gesture to include the room where the ball was taking shape around them.

"And way too many meetings," Deb said, rolling her eyes as she went along with the unfolding cover story. She knew what Vic was up to and she was not ready to deal with his opinion, his advice, or his big mouth.

"So it's been, what? Every other Tuesday at the committee chairs' meeting," Daniel said, counting on his fingers.

"And every second Sunday at PFLAG," Deb said, pointing at a couple of his fingers.

"The two emergency planning sessions when the local lodge figured out who we were and what we were planning tonight at their lodge," Daniel added, upping the count.

"That was a close call," Deb said, hanging on Daniel's arm.

"Good thing their grand pooh-bah had already picked out his gown for tonight or we'd be dancing in the streets." Daniel laughed.

"Yeah, his dress wasn't the only thing that was red at that meeting," Deb said, laughing along. "Hi, I'm your grand pooh-bah and the queen of the May."

"So, you see, we're practically inseparable," Daniel said, laughing with her and giving her a little squeeze.

"You're one of the other PFLAG parents?" Vic asked, not taken in by their good-natured misdirection.

"I am," Daniel said.

Vic nodded. "And your wife?"

"Lives in Ohio with her husband," Daniel said.

That was really all Vic needed to hear, and his face lit up as he shook Daniel's hand again warmly. "Good to meet you, Daniel," Vic said. "I can only think that little Buttercup here didn't mention you because you were both so busy planning tonight's big event."

"Buttercup, huh?" Daniel intoned. "I like that. Family nickname?"

"Daniel," Deb said, pointing to the ladder to distract him as she hit Vic in the back of the head, "could you help me finish hanging these paper lanterns? The kids were going to but they've got the garlands and you're here now."

"By the way, Deb," Vic said to her, rubbing his head dramatically. "Before I forget, I'm staying at Godiva's tonight. I figured that you'd be here late and that way you won't have to give me a ride home and I don't have to stay."

"Oh," she said, distracted by the unexpected change of plans. "Well, I don't mind taking you home whenever you're ready. Or I could give Michael the car."

"Please," Vic said, waving it off. "It'll be like old times. We can sit up all night, do each other's wigs, make s'mores, and compare medications."

"Don't joke about that," Deb said, laughing. "Okay. You have a good time then." She tried not to run as she turned to catch up with Daniel and tell him the news. It wasn't that they had the house to themselves—or rather, it wasn't just that they had the house to themselves. Daniel actually lived alone. What they had was a night when they could go missing and no one would wonder where they were.

"Now, all I've gotta do is tell Godiva," Vic said under his breath, wheeling his chair around in the opposite direction and making for the pay phones.

Brian had still not showed up or called by the time Melanie and Ted arrived. That the two were there was a ploy so patently Brian Kinney that Michael began to worry when

Brian was not there to bear witness to his own craft, though that was often a part of the Kinney method as well.

"What the hell are they doing here," Lindsey snarled into Michael's ear when she spotted them.

"I'm not saying," Michael said, laughing as he recognized his old friend's handiwork. "But his initials are Brian Kinney."

"That son of a bitch," Lindsay said with convincing delivery, but she had never taken her eyes off Melanie, who looked way excellent in two bands of shiny red something, the upper band so short that it left her midriff bare, and the second to the floor but slit almost up to the first.

"Relax, Peep-Bo," Michael said, looking back at her and catching her reaction. "She'll never recognize you in samurai drag. Unless of course you drool it off."

"Oh, yeah," Lindsay said, still not looking at him and missing the dig as well. "They do look a little lost."

It was true. Both Ted and Melanie were looking around the room for familiar faces, and without Brian there and Michael and Lindsay in full makeup, no one was in view. Ted looked particularly lost as he had followed the direction that he wear a red dress, but only just. There was no wig, no makeup, no shaving, not even girl shoes, just hairy-chested, -armed, and -legged Ted in a red gingham housedress. Michael had to laugh at the goofy realness of it in a room filled with such convincing forgeries; here truly was a man in a dress and no more.

"Let's have some fun," Lindsay said, grabbing a tray of hors d'oeuvres off a nearby table.

"What are you up to?" Michael asked.

"Here," she said, handing him the hors d'oeuvres and getting another tray for herself. "Just play along."

"You have been spending too much time with Brian again," Michael cautioned, following almost against his will but too intrigued to drop out. "Where is he, by the way?"

Lindsay's answer, if she gave one, was lost in the noise of a party already way over the top. Not only was the room filled with hundreds of men and women in red, Deb and her committee had made sure absolutely everything at the party was red. Red flowers, red linens, red lanterns, red lighting, red drapes, red furniture, and what wasn't red was gold. One of Deb's committee members owned one of the tawnier shops in the Mellon Park antique district, and the result was enough ormolu to fill Belle Watling's red-light residence for a remake of *Gone With the Wind.*

"You likey yum-yums, boysan?" Lindsay said in a high, squeaky voice, giving an already uncomfortable Melanie a quick feel.

"No yum-yums," Melanie said. "And I'm not a boysan."

Lindsay put her hand over her face and issued a truly obnoxious giggle. "I not yum-yum, I Peep-Bo," Lindsay corrected, launching her very own Gilbert and Sullivan's *Who's on First?* "You must be boysan," she insisted, reaching for one of Melanie's well-displayed breasts. "These not real."

"Look, fella," Melanie said, grabbing Lindsay's hand. "They're real, okay?"

"I can't stand it," Ted sighed. "We come to the gayest event of the Pittsburgh season and you get hit on by a guy. What am I chopped liver?"

"You likey chop liver?" Michael said, thrusting the tray of canapés into Ted's face. "Want a rittle goose?" Michael said, providing that as well.

"Hey," Ted said, jumping. "Thank you, that's better."

"You're welcome, Ted," Michael said in his regular voice.

"How do you know my . . . ?" Ted trailed off, pointing at himself.

"It's Michael. We met at Woody's the other night?"

"Oh, right," Ted said, even more pleased about the goose. "We came looking for Lindsay. Your friend Brian said she'd be here, so here we are."

"I knew it," Lindsay shouted.

"That would be her." Michael managed to catch her hors d'oeuvre tray and set both on a nearby Louis Quatorze table.

"So, you decided to enlist Brian's help after all?" Lindsay said, grabbing two champagnes off a passing tray and downing one of them. "Are you stalking me?"

"Not so much stalking," Melanie said. "Legally it would really be more lying in wait, the difference is subtle——"

"Oh my God," Lindsay said. "Is your plan to ambush me and talk me to death?"

"No, I thought I'd just continue to humiliate myself pretty much every time I see you until you take pity and dance with me or get a restraining order, whichever comes first," Melanie said in a way that Lindsay had to admit was pretty adorable.

"So, a dance and you'll leave me alone?" Lindsay asked.

"Well, I'm kind of hoping that you won't want me to leave you alone after our dance."

"I don't know about you, Ted," Michael said, holding his fan in front of his face and batting his eyes absurdly, "but it's getting to be pretty embarrassing to be standing here."

"Yep," Ted agreed, more than a little pleased to have Michael suggest that they do something together. "Let's go anywhere else."

"Anywhere it is," Michael said, making for the bar as Ted followed.

"Look, it just doesn't seem to be working out," Lindsay explained. "I mean, can we build a future based on one or the other of us being humiliated every time we're in the same place?"

"I'd kinda hoped we'd get past that eventually," Melanie said.

"I have to admit, that dress is pretty amazing on you," Lindsay said, trading in the two empties for two new glasses of champagne.

"Thank you," Melanie said, unconsciously adjusting the upper band. "Ted helped me pick it out. I really only have business suits and jeans."

"Not a debutante, eh?" Lindsay offered one of her champagne flutes. "What were the odds?"

"Yeah, okay, I'm not really of the lipstick variety, save for work."

"You clean up pretty good," Lindsay teased. "What do you do?"

"I'm studying law." Melanie took a sip and adjusted the uncomfortable dress, which always seemed to be sliding down. "I clerk at a judge's office, both for credit and a few shekels."

"What'll you have?" Michael asked, beating Ted to the bar slightly and, as was his habit, hanging over the side and leaning across to get the bartender's attention. He really only did it because it helped level the playing field where his height was concerned, but Ted could watch him swing on the edge of the bar all evening. "To drink?" Michael prompted.

"Oh, right," Ted sputtered. "Of course. Amstel Light would be great."

"You got it," Michael said, hiking himself up farther and leaning over the bar.

Ted looked heavenward and mouthed the words *Thank you.*

"Michael, there you are," Emmett said, rushing to catch Michael at the head of the line at the bar. "Get me a gimlet, will you? My gin level has dropped to a dangerous low." He had to laugh at his own joke. Ted did too. "Well, hello, guy in a dress," Emmett said, unable to think of a single other word to describe Ted.

"Hi, I'm Ted," he said, taking the hand Emmett had extended, fingers down, to be kissed and shaking it awkwardly.

"Well, you certainly are," Emmett said. "And this evening I'm Yum-Yum, though my friends call me Emmett."

"Great costumes," Ted said. "You're friends with Michael and Lindsay?"

"Who?" Emmett said. "Oh, you mean because we're in the same . . . No, complete coincidence. I was really embarrassed at first. You know how it is. You spend days shopping for just the right dress, and then you get to the party and two other people are dressed and made up identically. Don't you just hate that?"

Ted was at a party and actually laughing and having fun. He couldn't quite believe it. He couldn't remember it ever happening before.

"Here you are," Michael said, passing out the drinks to Emmett and Ted. "Ted, this is my friend Emmett."

"Michael, please," Ted said with a stern look. "He prefers to be called Yum-Yum."

"I bet he does," Michael said. "So, you two have met? I should have guessed that. Em is a bit hard to ignore."

*   *   *

"I don't see what harm one dance can do, counselor," Lindsay said, pensive, arms folded in a stance suggesting negotiations rather than an invitation to dance.

"Well, I don't either." Melanie grinned, enjoying the game because they were at least both playing and, better still, Lindsay's friend Brian was nowhere around.

"Maybe I should get separate counsel?" Lindsay suggested, dragging it out long enough to finish her champagne and enjoying the sport of it. It had been a while since Rebecca, and she had to admit it was nice to have someone paying attention, even if there was no way it could ever get serious.

"I suppose, but there is the time factor," Melanie suggested helpfully. "Maybe if we agreed that it's a no-fault dance and that nothing that happens tonight counts after tonight, we can just enjoy the dance."

"It's agreed then," Lindsay said, finishing her champagne. "One no-fault dance, deliverable on demand and with no further obligation for further dances, never to be discussed again after this evening by either party except by mutual consent."

"Agreed," Melanie said, shaking Lindsay's hand officially.

"Ladies and gentlemen," Deb shouted into the microphone, heedless that her voice was being amplified. The feedback did as much to get everyone's attention as the shouting.

"Tonight we're celebrating red," she said as the focus of the room shifted in her direction. "Red is the color of passion and of love. We're celebrating the love of our family and our wonderful gay family members, and we're celebrating the passion that makes life worth living. Okay, it's time for party games, so here's the deal. We have this wonderful band, Morton Saltz and the Shakers; let's give 'em a hand."

Everyone applauded.

"They're doing this for free tonight just like everyone else, so every penny goes back into outreach and other great PFLAG programs." There was more applause.

"Anyway, we've got this band and we figure we need a dance contest worthy of such an event. So we asked ourselves what was the perfect dance for celebrating love and passion, and we decided it had to be the tango. Now I don't know about you, but I've got no idea how to do the tango, and so that I don't look bad, we've devised the Instant Tango contest. Here's how it works. This is Vinnie, Sandy, Raul, Yolanda, Maria, and Whitey from Tighty Whitey's Ballroom Dance Academy. They'll teach us how to tango, and then we'll have a dance contest to determine the winner. So, grab your partners and join the dance of love."

Lindsay's heart sank as Melanie grinned and extended her hand.

"How did you do that?" Lindsay demanded, giving Melanie her hand to be led to the floor.

"Maybe we really are the chosen people," Melanie said, shrugging as they joined the crowd.

"So, Michael," Ted began, half speaking, half clearing his throat as he tried to get up his nerve to ask Michael to dance. But that was all he managed.

Brian clicked his heals together as he bowed and kissed Michael's hand. It surprised Michael, who had been staring out at the dance floor as the couples were getting further directions before they began. Brian looked amazing if for no other reason than he was not wearing red, though that was not the reason. He had on the perfect, vintage tuxedo he'd found at Second Hand Rose that afternoon, it seemed so long ago. He would have looked spectacular anywhere, but in a room filled completely with red, he looked exceptional. His only nod to the event was a gleaming red Barbie evening gown pinned to his lapel as a rather remarkable boutonniere. He had, in fact, worn a red dress.

"You would find the loophole," Michael said, giving a little curtsy.

"Tokyo Rose, I presume," Brian said, being uncharacteristically silly. "May I have the honor of this dance?"

"Charmed, I'm sure," Michael said flatly.

"Hold this, will you, Ed?" Brian said, handing Ted Michael's drink. And with that Brian swept him up into his arms and onto the dance floor.

"I thought they weren't together," Ted said out loud, his fallen crest showing a bit.

"They're not," Emmett sighed, passing Ted the bowl of red hots. "But they're never with anyone else."

Ted looked at him blankly.

"I'm sorry, sweetie," Emmett said, popping a couple of red hots and inadvertently washing them down with his gimlet before he realized. "You're new on the Mikey and Brian show. I remember what that's like. Here's how it works. Brian is always with someone else, and Michael never is, so that whenever Brian needs him, which is constantly, Michael is available."

"So, they're not together?" Ted asked, puzzled by Emmett's explanation.

"Oh, yeah, for years," Emmett corrected.

"So they are together?" Ted tried to clarify.

"No, darling." Emmett shook his head.

"It can't be both," Ted said, turning up his palms.

"Ah, but it can Katie Scarlett," Emmett said with a brogue that could only have been from southern Ireland.

"How can that be?"

"It's like Sam and Diane," Emmett explained. "Remember when *Cheers* first came on? When it was actually a good show?"

"Oh." Ted nodded, understanding at last.

"Where have you been?" Michael asked as they began to follow the steps that Whitey and company were demonstrating for them on the stage in front of the band. "I take it you're leading?"

"I was in Dallas," Brian said as if that answered the question.

"Until two minutes ago?" Michael asked as Brian walked him backward in broad steps across the dance floor.

"Yep." Brian turned them and stepped Michael backward the other way.

"Brian," Michael said with a plaintive note in his voice.

"I had to work." Brian spun him under one arm. "Big trip to do a meeting for a bank merger. Lots of details. I got them wrapped up when I got back this morning. It took all day. Then I came here. It's not very interesting. And of course I'm leading, you big bottom. You're the one in the dress." And he dipped an unprepared Michael so low that the black lacquered wig touched the ground and nearby couples applauded.

"*Whee,*" Lindsay shrieked as Melanie pulled her up out of the dip. "I can't wait till we get to that part again. You're very graceful, Melanie."

Melanie smiled. It was the first time Lindsay had ever said her name.

"Good lawyers have to be light on their feet," she joked.

"And fast talkers," Lindsay teased.

"Well, yes, of course," Melanie agreed as she pivoted around Lindsay, arm extended, holding her hand. "How else could I have gotten you onto the dance floor?"

Lindsay laid her head back and laughed the musical laugh that Melanie loved as they switched hands and Melanie reversed directions.

"You're very funny," Lindsay said, only partly regaining her composure, just in time to have Melanie spin her across and away, bringing her momentum to a halt with a snap as she reached the extent of the arc possible without letting go of Melanie's hand and then spinning her back in the opposite direction.

"Wheeeee," Lindsay squealed again as she spun the other way.

"They seem to be having fun," Michael said as he snapped to a halt, dizzy and suddenly on Brian's opposite side.

"That's the plan," Brian agreed coolly. "Are you?"

"I knew it," Michael hissed as Brian clutched him to his chest and they began to retrace their earlier steps. "And, yeah, now that you're here."

"Me too," Brian said, pulling Michael a little closer than was being demonstrated by the instructors. "Maybe we could blow this off after Mom has seen us both and go back over to my place, just hang out, blow a joint, something. I'm beat after this trip."

"Sounds perfect. Except for the fact that I'm in drag and wearing a wig and enough makeup to white-out three mimes and Dr. Frankenfurter. How did you know it was me?"

"There's a fire hose," Brian suggested as he once again surprised Michael with what turned out to be another spectacular dip. "And your mom ratted you out, but I'd know you anywhere."

"They do look good together," Ted admitted reluctantly.

"Oh, they're perfect for each other," Emmett chimed in. "In fact I don't know that there is anyone else who will put up with Brian's ill-mannered, inconsiderate, rude, selfish, self-centered, childish, and inexcusable behavior."

"Why does he?"

"Well, honey," Emmett said, taking the lime out of his gimlet and gesturing with it, "everyone puts up with Brian. And they all do it, despite what they might say, because Brian is a brilliant, beautiful, oversexed, charming son of a bitch and they want a slice. What's different about Michael is that he puts up with Brian because he loves him."

"And they're not together?" Ted asked as he watched them flicker across the dance floor.

"Yes."

chapter nine

Aswath of sun fell across Brian's face and he opened his eyes.

It was a beautiful room. Everything about it was understated but the price. Leather, steel, and fine woods interlocked together like parquetry to create a pattern of design simply by the brilliance of the way in which the disparate pieces were assembled. It was as perfect a reflection of the man nestled against Brian's back as any mirror image might have been.

Brian snuggled back against the sleeping Evan, drawing the powerful, well-sculpted arm that was draped over his shoulder more tightly around himself. The nameless and unaccustomed feelings that Brian had in that moment were as unaccountable to him as all of the moments he had spent with Evan since that night in their hotel room in Dallas. He only wanted the feelings to go on. Evan wasn't even awake, even a conscious participant in that moment, and still the feelings came.

Equally as unaccountable to Brian was his own behavior since the shattering sex they had shared on most every flat surface in that suite in the Dallas Anatole. Brian was not a stranger to great sex. But he had never had this reaction before, and somehow it had enhanced what was already truly amazing sex. What Brian found most notable in a long list of his uncharacteristic behavior was that he had lied to Michael and left him at the party the night before without a good-bye or explanation, not unprecedented but unsettling. All it had taken was Evan's voice on the phone. "Brian? Come over" was all Evan had said, and Brian had left the party without so much as a word to the people watching the door, let alone to Michael or Deb.

It had been much the same on their return from Dallas.

When they'd landed at Pittsburgh International, Brian had moved through the concourse to the Landside Terminal to collect his bags in a kind of fugue state. He didn't want to end their time together, and so, when the car that was there for them had taken them across the river to the Gateway Tower where Evan's condo overlooked Point Park, Brian had simply gotten out of the car and followed Evan inside. There had been no invitation, but Evan said nothing to dissuade him.

Brian took it as confirmation when, just inside the condo's door, Evan had turned Brian to face him, touched their lips together, and then, placing his hands on Brian's shoulders, pushed him to his knees. With their luggage still at hand, they had had access to condoms and K-Y enough to finish what they'd started without ever leaving the company of the Hockney and the Warhol that flanked the front entrance.

Evan rolled over.

Brian turned to see if he was awake. He watched the older

man sleeping for a moment and thought about what he should do. What he'd done a hundred times before in that moment was dress and leave without another word ever being spoken; not just on the given morning, but ever. And there was Michael to be called. And the finishing touches to be put on his own apartment. All he wanted to do was stay in bed, wake Evan, and start again.

Brian sat up and put his feet on the floor. It was a rare moment in his young life. For the first time probably since he'd first met Michael Novotny, he did not know what to do next. He was naked and had no idea where his clothes were. He had memories of their struggle to both strip one another and make their way down the long gallery that led to the bedroom, but not so much as the Barbie dress from Brian's lapel was in evidence there. He crossed to open the large teak door on the other side of the room and found a whole world to be discovered beyond. In one direction racks of clothes and shoes and socks and shirts and sweaters filled the spaces perfectly hewn for them, more a showroom than a closet. In the other was what looked more like some black marble shrine than a mere bathroom. And in the middle, a sitting room of sorts as though one might take a seat and contemplate what to wear as models flaunted the expansive wardrobe.

Brian sat on the black toilet and pissed away his morning wood as he looked out through the wall of glass over Three Rivers Stadium, silent and monolithic in the gray morning light across the steady flow of the same broad, immutable Al he could see from his own place. He wandered without flushing into a shower so large that there was a place to sit down and reveled in the smells of Evan's soaps and shampoos even as he washed the more truly Evan smells from his hair and body.

He slipped on one of Evan's perfectly pressed oxford-cloth dress shirts and a deliciously soft pair of gray, woolly socks, made his way back through the bedroom where Evan lay still sleeping, and down the gallery to the stainless-steel and black-and-white-tile kitchen. Even the coffeemaker was black and a bit on the complicated side as it ground beans he had had to find and used a filter he didn't recognize, but eventually it yielded coffee.

Little was in the industrial-size, stainless-steel refrigerator besides the cream that he knew only too well from experience that Evan took in his coffee. Brian warmed a little of the half-and-half in the microwave before adding it to one of the chunky Svend Jensen coffee cups and making his way back toward the bedroom.

"There you are," Evan said, suddenly there showered and immaculately dressed for tennis, meeting him in the gallery that ran the length of the condo and connected all the rooms like a central courtyard. "You forgot to flush," he said, taking the coffee. "Isn't that my shirt?"

"I didn't want to wake you," Brian said, not sure what else to say.

"So you put on my shirt? Look, I've got a hot date with this twenty-year-old tennis pro I've been fucking, so lock up on your way out, okay?" Evan walked down the gallery to the front door without a backward glance toward Brian. "See you at work on Monday."

Evan was gone, only to be replaced by a sensation that Brian was completely unprepared for. Smashing the cup on the floor helped.

It wasn't as if it were the first time it had happened or that Michael was completely unprepared. It was mainly just that

he and Brian hadn't gotten to spend any time together for
such a long time. He knew that Brian was working and trying
to make the most of the new job opportunity he'd gotten.
That and Michael's still vying for the promotion to assistant
manager at the Big Q didn't exactly make Brian's neglect any
easier to bear.

He tried Brian's number again. No answer. Only the stupid machine, and he'd already left a message there. He hung
up.

He checked the fridge for comfort food, but aside from the
Cap'n Crunch everything else seemed to have been chosen for
aesthetic value. Little bundles of fresh herbs and vegetables,
fruit, cheeses, and mineral water. He loved Emmett, but this
was what came of letting a display queen do the grocery
shopping. What's more, he knew Emmett for the white-trash
cook that he was, which meant that the fridge was entirely
filled with trick food. The kind of stuff you want the trick to
find in your fridge the next day, but not anything you'd actually really eat.

The phone rang.

"Finally," he said aloud, closing the refrigerator door and
crossing to pick up the receiver. "Hello."

"It's so hard and so big," the man on the phone sighed.
"Do you think you can take the whole thing?"

It definitely wasn't Brian this time or the guy from last
night for that matter. He hung up the phone without speaking. It began to ring again.

"I've got it," Emmett called from his room, picking up the
other extension.

No comfort food and calling Brian was out so long as
Emmett was on the phone.

He was too despondent to go to the grocery store or the

diner, so he made the decision to do the next best thing—Deb's. He couldn't call to warn them, but he never did. Vic and Deb were always glad to see him, and if they weren't there, Michael had a key and he wouldn't have to put up with her mouth while he ate the cold lasagna and cheesecake out of her fridge.

Michael was just about to use his key in the lock on Deb's kitchen door when she answered his knock. She was disheveled and clutching her untied robe together when she answered.

"Hi, sweetie," she said in a raspy voice.

"Were you still asleep?" Without waiting for an answer, he barged past and made his way to the refrigerator. "The door was locked."

"No, but it was a really late night last night and Vic stayed at Godiva's," Deb said, keeping the robe closed with one hand and fishing around behind for the sash with the other. "What brings you over here at breakfast time on Saturday morning? Did your trick go home early?"

"Mom," Michael chided. "You know I was at your party last night. I just thought I'd come by for a snack."

"What did he do?" Deb said knowingly, pushing Michael out of the way with an elbow as she firmly tied her robe and leaned into the refrigerator with a purpose.

"What did who do?" Michael asked unconvincingly.

"You know who," Deb said, building a plate of cold pasta, chicken, and hors d'oeuvres from the night before.

Michael looked at her as though he didn't understand.

She sighed, paused, and gave him a look that said, *You're just about to get hit in the back of the head with this cannoli.*

"He asked me to come over to his place after the party and then just vanished."

"You don't mean it." Deb smothered a couple of loaded plates in foil and plastic wrap. "Brian Kinney picked up some slut at a drag party and took off with it without saying anything? No?"

"Mom," Michael warned.

"Sorry, honey." She shook a paper bag noisily open. "But you have to admit, if he'd been on time, stuck around, and kept his word, it would be a much bigger shock than this."

It was true. Michael hated to admit it, but it was true. It was just that he missed Brian, what with the weeks of merger preparations and then the unexpected trip.

"I know you're right," Michael sighed. "I guess I just wanted to see him, especially last night. I found this really cool light-up beer sign that'll be great in the new place and I wanted him to see it."

"Here." She thrust the bag into his arms. "There's enough comfort food in here for two. Borrow the car, get the sign, take it over, and surprise him. Otherwise you'll just spend all day sulking and then forgive him the minute he shows up anyway."

"I guess," Michael admitted with a self-deprecating little laugh.

"You know I'm right." She pushed him toward the door and pressed the car keys into his hand.

"Yeah, I know." He sounded like a little boy and grinned when she stroked his hair.

"Mama knows best," she said, kissing him. "Now go on, you two have a good weekend."

"Thanks, Ma," he called as she closed the door.

"That was close."

"You're telling me," Daniel said, emerging from the pantry in one of Vic's old bathrobes. "You were good with him."

"I love him very much," she said simply.

"Then why not tell him?"

"You see that," she said, pointing to the little shrine to Lieutenant John Michael Novotny. Daniel only sighed and kissed the top of her head.

"Brian?" Michael called, coming up the stairs balancing the ancient, mint-condition neon Miller High Life sign and the Deb Novotny shopping-bag lunch. "Are you here?"

He balanced the sign on the rail and tried the door. "Brian?" he called again.

No response. Michael regarded the car parked in the alley and was considering leaving when the door opened.

"Mikey, hi," Brian said as though the most frequent and only visitor who had ever come to the apartment, other than tricks Brian had dragged home himself, was somehow a surprise.

"I wondered," Michael said, handing Brian the bag of food and hoisting the sign. "I saw the car. Look what I found."

"Yeah, what is that?" Brian said a little distastefully. He opened the bag and sniffed as he followed Michael inside.

"Isn't this the coolest?" Michael propped the sign on the former jewelry display case that was now the kitchen counter and plugged the sign into one of the many extension cords that crisscrossed the apartment to provide electricity. "It bubbles when it warms up."

"It's a bit much," Brian said, putting the food on the counter and picking up the vodka on the rocks he'd left there when he'd answered the door.

"Isn't it?" Michael said enthusiastically, heedless of Brian's none too warm reception.

"I mean, I don't like it much," Brian said, enunciating the words as though that was the problem.

"Oh," Michael said, stung and unsure of what to say next. They had found the old jewelry counter, the 7-Eleven glass-doored beer cooler, and the glass-topped, top-loading Good Humor ice-cream display freezer together and been thrilled with the kitsch value of each new find.

"I mean, it's a little dorm-room, isn't it?" Brian said, cocking his head as though examining a poorly executed expressionist painting.

"You're welcome," Michael said flatly. "I kind of thought it went with everything here." He switched on the light in the jewelry case filled with mismatched dishes and junk food as a little demonstration.

"All these things have a function," Brian said dismissively, walking away from both the sign and Michael.

"It's a clock," Michael snapped.

"It's a beer sign."

"You're both right," Michael said, trying for humor. "It's a dessert topping and a floor wax."

"Put it in your own apartment," Brian said, not turning back or taking the bait. "It's too juvenile for me."

Michael said nothing. Brian found and lit a cigarette and looked out across the same river he had first seen that morning out the window at Evan's. The view was the same and completely different despite the fact that the two places were not far apart and overlooked almost exactly the same stretch of land.

Finally, Michael's silence was too weighty and Brian turned to find an empty room.

"Michael?" he said, retracing his steps. The sign had begun to bubble. He looked through the curtain that passed for a bathroom door. "Michael?" He walked over and reopened the door and looked down the steps. Deb's car was gone.

"Shit," he said, sitting on the top step.

*   *   *

"Daddy, I've been a really bad boy," Emmett said convincingly into the phone as he lay on his bed leafing through the Banana Republic catalog.

"Hello," Ted said in reply from his end. "Is Michael Novotny there?"

"Oh." Emmett sat up and closed his robe as though Ted could see him and he'd been caught. "I, sorry, thought you were, someone else," he stammered.

"It's Ted." He wasn't at all sure that he shouldn't just hang up and pretend that the whole thing had never happened. "Ted Schmidt? Melanie's friend? From the party last night and Woody's the other day? Red gingham dress?"

"Oh, Ted. Of course, I never forget a dress. This is Emmett, Michael's roo—houseguest. We met last night."

"Yum-Yum," Ted said, remembering.

"Ah-so." Emmett laughed. "Michael's not here right now. Can I take a message?"

"Oh, sure. I just wanted to ask him something. Nothing important, just—"

"Wait. I think he's just come in. Hang on. Michael," he screamed, deafening Ted on the other end of the line. "Phone."

"That didn't take long," Michael muttered to himself, stalking over to the phone and snatching the receiver from the cradle.

"Crawl up my ass and eat a ham sandwich," Michael said.

"Doesn't anybody just say hello over there?" Ted asked, as perplexed by Michael's phone manner as he had been by Emmett's.

"Oh my God. Who is this?"

"Ted Schmidt. Melanie's friend. Red gingham dress . . ."

"And Emmett," Emmett said. "I fortunately had not hung up yet. And what I want to know is, who you thought it was?"

"Brian," Michael sighed, slouching into the orange-striped chair and dangling his legs over the arm as was his habit when he talked on the phone.

"The tuxedo with the red Barbie dress?" Ted asked by way of clarification.

"The same," Michael groaned.

"The one who blew you off last night," Emmett added not so much for clarity.

"That's him," Michael said with a tense little lilt.

"He blew you off last night?" Ted asked.

"Oh, that's old news," Michael said with an exasperated little noise. "You know that Miller High Life clock I found at the used-restaurant-supply place last week when I went with Mom to get a new sneeze-guard pie-dome thingie?"

"Sounds cool," Ted acknowledged. Even though he had no idea what they were talking about exactly, he knew kitsch. "Did it bubble?"

"Yes," Michael said triumphantly.

"And it was in perfect condition," Emmett added.

"And it was, is, perfect for Brian's new place," Michael said, topping it.

"Which, if you don't know, Ted, Michael has worked like a slave to help renovate, ever since Brian moved in," Emmett added for color.

"So, I took it over there this morning, with food, and he takes one look at the clock and says, 'It's a little juvenile for me.'" Michael finished with a none too flattering but creditable impersonation of Brian Kinney.

Michael was gratified to hear Ted and Emmett gasp into the line in unison and harmony.

"Michael, Michael, Michael," Emmett said. He'd been in this place before and knew that it was a lose/lose position. If you said anything mean about Brian, even if Michael agreed with you in the moment, he'd blame you for it when he and Brian inevitably made up. But more likely was, if you said anything against Brian, Michael would rise to his defense and in attacking you find a new enemy and be instantly over whatever Brian had done to provoke the comment in the first place. Undiluted sympathy was the only safe course here. "That's awful, honey," Emmett cooed.

"That son of a bitch," Ted said, unaware of the rules of the game.

"I don't know," Michael said, hurt enough not to take Ted's head off, but not far from it given the indecisive nature of Michael's reply.

Emmett saw that he had to act quickly and talk to Ted later when Michael wasn't on the phone. "So, Ted," he said, cutting in and changing the subject, "what was it you called to ask Michael?"

"What?" Ted said, taken off guard and not at all sure how to proceed given the way the conversation was going and who all had ended up on the call. "Oh, yeah, right. Well, Michael, I've wound up with an extra ticket to the Pittsburgh Opera's *La Bohème* and thought maybe you'd like to go?"

"Well . . ." Michael drew out the word as he turned the idea over in his head. "I don't really know anything about opera but, yeah, sure, what the hell. It'll get dickhead off my mind and get me out of the house. What time?"

"Well, it's at eight," Ted said, the conversation completely out of control. "Maybe we could meet up early and have a little dinner or a drink beforehand?"

"Oh, I think that sounds great," Emmett said. "Just what

the doctor ordered. You can wear that new jacket I made you buy, Michael. I told you you'd get use out of it."

"This is the first time I've ever been to the opera," Michael said. "I think it's too early to start amortizing the purchase."

"So, I'll come by about six?" Ted said, trying to get in on the conversation. This was not at all how he'd planned to ask Michael out on a date, but the important thing was he could tell Melanie he had asked someone out the next time she gave him shit about not asking anybody out on dates.

"Perfect," Emmett said. "It's 1422 Edmond Street. I'll have him ready. You'll see."

"It is a good jacket," Michael admitted. "Just things I needed more."

"Like beer clocks for Brian's apartment?" Emmett teased.

"Bitch," Michael giggled, and hung up the phone.

Emmett hung up in reply.

"Six it is," Ted said to the dial tone.

Lindsay was parked on the canned-goods aisle of the Giant Eagle with her basket of ramen and tuna, trying to guess what was in the unlabeled cans.

"A bargain but always a gamble," a familiar voice said.

It took Lindsay a moment to realize that she was being addressed at all as she listened intently to the silver can she was turning over in her hand to try to determine if it was dog food or tomato paste.

"Oh," she said at last, turning abruptly as she realized she'd been caught. "Melanie, I've never seen you here before. You live nearby?"

"Yep. Once a month, just like clockwork, whether I need to or not," Melanie said in a good-natured tone. "I was out of beer."

"Un-huh, so you just stopped by for a month's supply of beer today." Lindsay folded her arms and gave Melanie a smug look.

"No, not really," Melanie said unexpectedly. "I was across the street checking the air pressure in my tire and I saw you come in here."

"You're following me?" Lindsay asked, some of the smug wiped off her face by shock.

"Well, not exactly, but sort of. I was there by accident. So technically we ran into each other by accident."

"Ask a lawyer." Lindsay was smirking.

"I really enjoyed the party last night," Melanie hedged. She really enjoyed getting to be with Lindsay, and the party was okay too.

"It was great." Lindsay nodded.

"Congrats again on the trophy for the three of you."

"Yeah, it was only honorable mention, but we gave it to Emmett since we were really his creation," Lindsay said with an affable little laugh at her own expense.

"We should do it again," Melanie blurted out.

"I'm never doing that makeup again," Lindsay said, rolling her eyes. "That clown white is still oozing out of my pores, and I spent almost an hour—"

"I mean you and I should go dancing or something together again. Not that you should remount the Gilbert and Sullivan . . ."

"I know what you mean, Melanie," Lindsay sighed.

They regarded one another for a moment.

"I thought we had a deal?"

"We do, we did," Melanie said resignedly. "I just can't keep it."

"Melanie—"

"Listen, I know we got off to a bad start, but once you get to know me you'll see—"

"Get to know you?" Lindsay said with a little laugh. "I may not be one of the Dykes on Bikes, but I think I have a pretty good idea who you are."

"You do?" Melanie said, taken aback.

"Your motorcycle and your radical feminist politics are just not my cup of tea."

"Who are you talking about?" Melanie said, a bit offended by the description. "I ride a motorcycle mostly because it's cheaper than a car."

"Look, I'm not saying that there's anything wrong with your choices, I'm just not sure they're for me."

"What choices exactly are we talking about?" Melanie asked, folding her arms.

"You know." Then looking around to make sure no one was around to hear, Lindsay whispered, "Being a lesbian."

"You think that's a choice?" Melanie whispered back before she thought about it. "Why are you whispering?"

"I just don't know that it's what I want. It's too hard."

"Lindsay, honey," Melanie said, more than a little concerned. "It's not like you're ordering Chinese. Either you are or you're not."

"Well, I wasn't before," Lindsay said, gesturing decisively with the unmarked can.

"Before what?" Melanie asked, puzzled.

"Look, the point is, I just want more out of life." Lindsay put the can in her basket, then thought better of it and fished it back out. "I want to get married and settle down and have a house and kids and someone who'll always be there."

"What makes you think you can't have that?"

"The federal government for one," Lindsay said, tossing the can aside. "Look, I can have all that, just not with another woman. I've tried."

"Not with me," Melanie said, trying not to cry.

"No, not with you. Look, Mel, you're a babe and I really appreciate the attention, and if I were in the market to get mixed up with another woman, I'm sure that you'd be just the kind of woman to get mixed up with. But that's just it. I'd be all mixed up. I'd get caught up with the funny and the smart and the sexy and that dress you wore to the party. But I just can't go through that again. Or at least I'm not sure. And this way no one gets hurt."

"Too late," Melanie said, abandoning her cart and stalking out of the store.

"It just seemed odd that she was dying of TB and singing so much," Michael said as he and Ted made their way down Liberty Avenue from Benedum Center to Woody's for a little after-Puccini drink. "And that whole huge song about my name is Mimi. I mean, okay already."

"It's not a very realistic medium," Ted agreed with a little grin. Ted loved the opera, and while he'd found that night's production less than stellar, he thought Michael was the cutest thing in pants, talking about it as though they'd been to see a documentary or an indy film.

"I'll say," Michael agreed with a nervous laugh.

"You know the thing I love best about the opera?" Ted asked to fill the silence.

"The fact that it's the gayest thing ever?" Michael giggled. "Have you ever seen so many homos in one place outside of Babylon?"

"Well, there's that," Ted said, laughing heartily.

"Seriously." Michael took Ted's arm and gave it a tug. "What do you love best about opera?"

"It's a mistake." Ted grinned.

"What?" Michael wrinkled his nose in a way that made Ted shiver slightly.

"It's true." Ted turned and started to walk down the street again to cover. "Opera literally means the 'great work' as in big or vast, but it's all a mistake."

"How is that possible?" Michael laughed.

"Well, during the Renaissance there was a big interest in things classical, meaning Roman or Greek," Ted explained, tucking his hands in his pockets against the chill of the November night. "But, thanks to a little thing called the Dark Ages, there was not a lot of information. So, in an effort to re-create Greek and Roman tragedy and based on the information they had at the time, they created opera. But it turns out they were wrong. It was nothing like this. And so they created a whole new art form by accident."

"I see," Michael said, intrigued by this unexpected poetic side to Ted's nature. "And why do you love that exactly?"

"Because opera is wonderful," Ted said expansively. "It really is the great work. It's huge. It's vast. Giant sets, lavish costumes, enormous halls that can barely contain the music, and voices so large as to be in scale with such expansive productions. It's a huge amount of work to mount. The singers train for years for careers that are usually briefer than pro athletes' and for which they are not paid even half. It's not bigger than life, it's just big enough to describe life. And it's a mistake. Just like life. Did you ever notice how all the best stuff in life happens by accident?" Ted said, pausing just outside the door to Woody's to catch Michael's eye.

"Yeah," Michael said with a smile and a little nod, caught up in Ted's enthusiasm. "Yeah, you're right. Like birth, family, careers, success, winning the lottery, inventing opera."

"Or falling in love. It's the accidents, the happy ones and the bad ones, that make life divine."

"Can I buy you a drink so we can toast to that?" Michael said, holding the door.

"You bet your ass," Ted said with a borrowed Three Little Maids curtsy that made Michael laugh.

"Oh, look, it's your friend what's her name," Michael said, following Ted in.

"Who?" Ted said, looking in the direction Michael was pointing. "Oh, Melanie. Great," he said, not wanting to have to explain to Melanie he was on a date with Michael, at least not in front of Michael, who Ted was not entirely sure knew either.

They walked over to the spot at the bar where she sat.

"Mel, hey," Ted said, putting a hand on her shoulder.

"Oh, Ted, hi," Melanie said, looking up only long enough to see them.

"You remember Michael," Ted said by way of introduction, and bracing to be unmasked with a few surgical questions from her keen legal mind.

"Michael, hi," Melanie said, shooting him a quick, forced smile.

The lack of prying put Ted off so completely that he actually stopped thinking about himself long enough to react to Melanie's strange manner.

"What's going on?" he asked suspiciously.

"Nothing." Melanie shrugged.

"Really?" Ted took the stool beside her. "You trying to score?" He looked around for possible prey, but the only other woman at the bar was actually a man, and he was pretty sure that Melanie wasn't drunk enough to make that mistake. "Which one is it?" he asked just to be sure.

"No," she sighed. "I'm not on the hunt. I just got shot down and I'm here licking my wounds."

"What'll you have, Ted?" Michael asked, doing that thing he did, leaning over the bar. "My treat."

Oh, the treat's all mine, Ted thought, grabbing an eyeful of Michael's perky little butt. "A light beer'd be great, thanks," he answered, so concerned by Melanie's mood that he was actually able to look away as Michael leaned in over the bar and signaled to the bartender. "Who shot down the hottest lesbian in Allegheny County?"

"Actually that's apparently why I got shot down," Melanie said with a drunken laugh.

"What is?" Ted asked, wondering if he could get her to switch to coffee by just ordering her some and putting it in front of her without asking.

"Because I'm such a fucking babe," Melanie said, toasting herself.

"Michael, could you get a cup of coffee too?" Ted asked, deciding to chance it.

Michael nodded.

"Well, you are, honey," Ted said. "But why is that a problem?"

"Because Miss Lindsay is trying to avoid temptation," Melanie explained, hoarse as if from shouting, but probably more from alcohol dehydration.

"Here's the coffee," Michael said, sliding the cup over toward them. "Cream or sugar?"

"Just cream," Ted said for her without thinking.

"Some cream," Michael called after the bartender. "What's this about Lindsay?" he asked, turning back.

"She's not a lesbian anymore," Melanie said, tapping Michael on the chest with her index finger.

"Since when?" Michael said, thinking that Mel was just being self-indulgent.

"Since she told me so at the Giant Eagle earlier this evening."

"What were you doing at the grocery store with Lindsay?" Ted asked, screwing up his face.

"Stalking her."

"And she thought that was a turnoff?" Ted asked, still trying to get the story out of her.

"No," Melanie said with the laugh again. "She thinks I'm a turn-on but she wants to get married."

"Don't lesbians usually wait until the second date?" Michael asked, adding cream to the coffee and stirring it, the spoon ringing against the sides of the cup.

"I don't know." Melanie shrugged. "She doesn't want to go out with me because of my radical feminist politics."

"That sounds like Lindsay." Michael nodded.

"Well, there are plenty of other fish in the sea. No offense," Ted added, thinking better of his choice of words. "You'll find someone else."

"Or you could show Lindsay she's wrong," Michael said with a little toss of his head. "She's just a little gun-shy, you know?"

"What do you mean?" Melanie said, taking a sip of the coffee before she realized she hadn't ordered it.

Ted smiled, pleased.

"When I first met her, she was dating a guy who I ended up dating," Michael said with sigh. "Then she fell for Brian before she realized. And when she figured out that part of the reason she had so much trouble with boys was that she was into girls, she fell for this angry radical lesbian feminist basketball center named Rebecca Tucci, who dumped her when she graduated because she didn't want a 'parody of heterosexual marriage,' as she put it. Lindsay hasn't gotten involved with anyone since."

"How long ago was this?" Melanie asked, her self-pity forgotten.

"Since she graduated college," Michael said. "I think she's just afraid and doesn't trust her own instincts."

"Jeez," Melanie said, taking another sip. "Maybe she's too much trouble."

"Oh, yeah." Michael grinned. "She is. But she's worth it."

"What we need is a way to show Lindsay that you're as solid as the Rock of Gibraltar," Ted said, catching Michael's drift. "We could have a little dinner party over at my place."

"Good," Michael agreed, nodding. "You clean up great. We can lose the leather jacket and the motorcycle. You bring up some long-term goals over canapés—do you have any?"

"Duh." Melanie shrugged. "What's with everybody? I'm a nice Jewish girl in law school. When did I get to be Jessica James?"

"Excellent," Michael said with an expansive gesture. "A quick makeover and we can reveal the real you."

"Perfect," Ted said. He was pleased to help Melanie, but he was even happier to be planning more time with Michael.

chapter ten

Things between Brian and Evan had been just as before when they returned to work. Aside from Evan's passing mention of the broken coffee mug, he had made no reference to what had passed between them during the trip or on their return.

For his own part Brain said nothing. He was troubled more by the feelings he was having about the situation with Evan than he was by the situation itself. He had not been out. He had not heard from Michael since his last visit with the clock. He had focused on work and on getting the apartment into shape. Or at least that was his cover story. What he was really doing, what really troubled him, was that he was waiting for Evan.

And Evan did nothing.

The apartment was looking great and Brian was more favored at the office for the quality of his work, and still there was no word, no call, no sign from Evan.

Brian was working late at the office refining his ideas for a presentation on personal electronics based on his earlier concepts that had landed them the account. No one was around, except for Evan, whom he heard talking on the phone and banging around in his office next door. They had not spoken at all that day save for officially at the afternoon staff meeting. Brian had managed to lose himself in the work for the moment.

"Brian?" Evan asked from the door of Brian's office. "What's your favorite restaurant in town? Something romantic, that'll score me points and put me on the sleepover express?"

"Well, J. Frank's is fun," Brian said with a flirtatious grin. "But the best is probably the Limelight. It works for me anyway."

"Yeah?" Evan grinned back. "Great, could you make me a reservation for two for Friday? Or get whosits to do it," he said, hiking a thumb in the direction of his current assistant's desk.

Brian watched Evan's back recede as he walked away. Brian was stunned. He felt a lot of conflicting emotions, but the one that was clearest to him was anger.

"Excuse me?" he said, rising and following Evan as far as the door.

"Oh, don't get all het up," he said, waving Brain off. "I said get the assistant to do it. I just wanted your advice."

"Is that all?" Brian asked, his voice rising enough that Evan turned back.

"Yes," Evan said, speaking clearly. "That's it. There's this kid I'm trying to get in the sack. I've got a date on Friday and I appreciate your help—" He ducked to avoid the electric pencil sharpener that narrowly missed his head and smashed on the parquet nearby. He looked up in time to see Brian's door slam hard enough to knock a framed certificate off the wall, which also smashed on the floor.

"You could have hit me with that," Evan shouted, storming toward the door and finding it locked. "Open this door," he demanded, pounding.

Brain snatched the door open. "The only reason that it didn't hit you was that you moved," Brian said, opening the door briefly, then closing and locking it once again.

"Brian," Evan said, pounding on the door. "God damn it. That pencil sharpener is company property. So help me it's coming out of your salary."

Brian's office door sprung open and Brian handed Evan his checkbook and a pen. Evan heard the lock click in the stunned silence that followed.

Brian sat on the edge of his desk facing the locked door, his breath short, his chest pounding. The only time he could remember being as angry was the last time he'd spent time with his father. And yet this was completely different. What was the matter with him? What did he care? Evan could fuck whomever he wanted to. And so can I, Brian thought as he grabbed his things, resolved to get to Babylon and prove just how little he needed Evan.

"You seem upset," Evan said, scaring the hell out of Brian. He'd walked around and come in the hall door to Brian's office.

Brian only jumped.

"You have two doors on your office," Evan added. "You might want to stay out of the military strategy arena; it doesn't seem to be your long suit."

Brian tried to push past, but Evan blocked his way. They didn't struggle, but there was a definite physical challenge.

"What's up with you?"

"Not a thing," Brian said. "Just leaving for the evening."

"Well, I encourage people to clean off their desks when they leave each day, but that is not what I had in mind."

"Fuck you."

"As I recall, that's not the way it works with you and me," Evan said, shoving Brian back toward the desk. "As I recall, this is the way it works." He pushed Brian against the desk. Brian fell backward hard on the desktop from the force. Evan pushed his body against Brian's, knocking things out of the way as he lay Brian down on the desk. In the same forceful and abrupt movements he ripped open Brian's slacks and pushed the trousers and underwear down Brian's legs to his ankles. "Here's how I remember it," Evan said, opening his slacks and rolling on the condom he'd put into his pocket with the lube packet when he'd made to circumvent Brian's locked-door defense. "Fuck you," he grunted as he shoved himself inside.

Brian shouted but pushed back into Evan, greedy for more.

There was considerably more breakage by the time they were done, and Brian's desk had never been so cleared off. Evan pulled out and rolled off the used condom, tossing it in the trash as he zipped up. Brian lay gasping on the desk.

"Brian," Evan said, unlocking the door to his office and opening it, "if you want to fuck, we can fuck. All you have to do is ask. But that's all we do. I'm not your boyfriend and we're not going steady; this is what this is and it's all it is. I like this, but no drama, no tantrums, or we're quits. Got it?"

He didn't wait for an answer before slamming Brian's door.

Michael had been keeping an eye on the public restroom at the Big Q, wondering if the incident had been a onetime thing or if he'd really been so clueless about the comings and goings right under his nose. He worked there and he wasn't really into even the idea of tea room sex, so he didn't keep a constant vigil, but the proximity of sex was still unavoidable as he replayed the incident in his mind.

Occasionally he'd used the public restroom instead of the employee facilities just to look for any signs or activities, but he'd seen nothing since the one time, and since the appeal was largely voyeuristic, he'd not given it much thought. His boss had recruited him to rehang new curtains for the displays on the wall by the entrance to the public bathrooms. He and a college kid, Kirby, who'd been hired as extra help for the upcoming holidays, were assigned to curtain duty.

As they started out the day, Michael was keenly aware of the restroom's proximity, but as the day wore on and little to arouse suspicions let alone anything else transpired, Michael slowly forgot the nearby possibility and got lost in the curtain wall. Michael's friends found it amusing that Michael, despite not being out at work or to any of his coworkers, was always the one chosen to redo displays, put out the holiday decorations, and generally pull "fag duty," as Emmett called it. Meaning anything from hairdressing to decorating to furniture placement at which a sizable number of gay men were presupposed genetically to excel.

So, Michael was deep in "fag duty" when Kirby excused himself for a moment. In fact, Michael was so engrossed in draping the chintz valance on the new fluted fruitwood dowel hardware that he completely lost track of how long Kirby had been gone.

"Michael," Kirby hissed.

"What is it, Kirby?" Michael said in a normal voice, despite Kirby's more theatrical tone, as he descended the ladder. "And where the hell have you been?"

"There and back," Kirby said huskily but sotto voce still.

"And that mean's what exactly?" Michael asked, planting both feet back on the ground.

"You want to take a real break?"

"What are you talking about?" Michael said, suspecting that Kirby must have gone and gotten stoned. "Did you?" he asked elliptically holding up the universal sign of thumb and forefinger pressed together held to pursed lips and inhaling sharply.

"Nah, but that would have made it even better," Kirby said, rubbing his crotch perhaps unconsciously.

And Michael understood. But he couldn't let on that he understood.

"So you want to have some fun?" Kirby asked.

Michael's face flushed, his head swam, and he was totally unsure of how to handle the situation. Kirby was plenty hot and Michael would gladly have and had already imagined all manner of fun with Kirby. But he had also met Kirby's girl-friend and listened to his ongoing rating of every female of the species who passed within a hundred yards of his "peter meter." So Michael was at sea.

"What kind of fun?" Michael was whispering now.

"You can get a blow job in there."

"In the men's room?" Michael said, acting his part well.

"Yeah. There's someone in there now."

"And you just walked in and asked for it?" Michael asked, genuinely curious as to how it worked.

"Nah, it happened by accident first time."

"You've done this before?" Michael was truly incredulous.

"Shit, yeah. Don't get me wrong, I'd rather have a girl any day. But if some fag's giving out BJs, I'm not passing it up. You just close your eyes and it's Heather Locklear . . ." Kirby trailed off into silent laughter.

"Still, aren't you afraid someone will find out?"

"That I like getting my dick sucked?" Kirby was laughing again. "I figure the more people who know the better. Go get one for yourself. I'll cover out here. If someone opens the door, the ceiling tiles rattle and you stop till they leave. He's in the last stall."

"I better not," Michael said, gathering up some loose fabric to cover his reaction to pretty much everything Kirby had said and moving down to the next display. "Come on now, we've got displays to finish."

"Your loss, dude." Kirby shrugged it off. "But if you change your mind, it's a pretty regular thing between noon and four Tuesday through Thursday and again on Saturday morning before the store gets crowded."

"So you've done this a lot?" Michael asked as casually as possible.

"Every chance I get," Kirby said, packing up the old curtains that Michael had taken down during Kirby's extended absence and catching up on his end of the job.

"But you're not gay."

"No, but nobody gives head like a gay boy." Kirby gave Michael a look.

Michael could not believe what he was hearing. "So this isn't your first time letting a guy?"

"Every chance I get means every chance I get." Kirby laughed.

"So how long?"

"Is what?" Kirby laughed.

Michael blushed but laughed along to hide it as he struggled to stay focused on the task at hand.

"It started around eighth grade, I reckon," Kirby said, offhand. "There was this kid at school in my PE class. It's, you know, kind of above average and he was always looking at it. So I asked him one day on the bus after school if he'd like to do more than look. He got off at my stop. And so did I." Kirby chuckled nastily.

Michael was amazed at Kirby's complete ease with the topic.

"We were in school for a long time and so I got used to it," Kirby said. "The girls started relaxing in the next year or so, but it was always a good standby."

"And in there?" Michael said, prodding the story along.

"I had just started a couple of weeks back." Kirby took a case cutter to the next sample box. "I had to take a whiz. I noticed someone was in there. I smelled cigarette smoke. Means someone's been killing time in the bathroom. No reason to do that unless you're waiting, you know? So I stepped into the next stall, sat down, took it out, and patted my foot. The fucker was motioning under the stall before I got my pants pulled down. I knelt down and slid it under and he blew me. Never have to see each other's face. So it might have been Heather for all I know."

"You just pat your foot?"

"Yeah, usually." Kirby laid out the organdy panels as Michael tucked them over the tension rods. "Sometimes there's holes in the stalls and you just stick your dick through, or a finger to let them know, or they do to motion you over. But here you gotta go under the stall 'cause they're metal and so there's no holes."

"You sound like an expert," Michael teased, once again scaling the ladder.

"Like I said"—Kirby handed him the curtains that Michael had strung on the tension rods—"every chance I get."

*   *   *

"Hi, Deb," Daniel called as he came into the diner.

"Daniel," Deb called back casually, grabbing a menu and pausing before coming from behind the lunch counter. "Good to see you. Coffee?"

"Tea."

"Hot or ice?"

"Hot please, Earl Grey if you got it."

"Sure do," she called over her shoulder as she siphoned off some hot water from the coffee machine into the tiny stainless-steel pot and pocketed an Earl Grey tea bag. She knew perfectly well that Daniel did not drink coffee, and she had recently purchased Earl Grey for the house. She teased him about being a lesbian because of it. But they had gotten expert at hiding their affair as a friendship between two PFLAG parents, which wasn't hard because they were that too.

"Here you go." She set the teapot before him with a cup. She pulled the bag from her pocket and untucked the menu from under her arm to hand it to him.

"Thanks," he said, then in a lower voice, pointing as though he were asking a question about the menu, asked, "Can you meet me later?"

"For a while, but it'll have to be late," she replied quietly and nodded as she pulled out her guest-check pad. "One of the other girls quit so I'm working a double shift. I'm not off until ten. And I can't be out too late 'cause Vic's home and there's a Susan Hayward marathon on so he'll be up and see what time I come in."

"I'll take what I can get. I've got a room at Swingers." Daniel nodded as though he'd made up his mind about the entrée, knowing full well that Deb would bring him whatever she wanted for him to have anyway. "See you after work?"

"Coming right up," she said, taking the menu and retucking it as she wrote down his order, deciding that he'd like the turkey meat loaf with salad, since he'd not been getting as much exercise now that the weather was getting cold.

"Emmett," Michael screamed from the front door.

"Oh, Daddy, yeah, that's so good," Emmett said hurriedly into the phone in his room. "Come on me. Shoot it for me. Now, Daddy, now."

Emmett could tell from the gasps on the other end of the line that he'd earned his by-the-minute rate once again.

"Emmett, are you here?" Michael hollered. "I need to talk to you."

"You want me to be home from school the same time tomorrow?" Emmett asked, trying to wrap it up.

"Not tomorrow," Daddy said. "I've got to work late, but the day after."

"Emmett, are you in there?" Michael pounded on the door to Emmett's room.

"I'll try not to be late," Emmett said. "I'd hate to be punished again. Bye, Daddy."

"You be a good boy." Daddy hung up.

"Emmett," Michael said. "I hear you talking."

"Coming," Emmett said, straightening his bed as he arose from a grueling afternoon's work. He opened the door and gave Michael an air kiss. "Sorry, angel, I was on the phone."

"Funny you should mention that." Michael held up the phone bill. "Our phone bill this month is twelve hundred dollars." He waved it at Emmett, who was heading to the kitchen.

"And that's high?" Emmett poured himself a Tab and got a doughnut out of the box on the counter.

"It's usually somewhere between twenty-four and thirty dollars. So, yes, it's a little high."

"I'll take care of it." Emmett took the bill out of Michael's hand. "Will cash be okay?"

"Emmett, what's going on?"

"Nothing special. Is there a problem?"

"Why is the phone bill twelve hundred dollars?"

"It's work-related," Emmett evaded, perusing the coffee table for fresh magazines.

"What work? And for that matter, where the hell did you get twelve hundred dollars in cash?" Michael's pitch was on the rise. "Emmett, are you dealing drugs?"

"No," Emmett sighed sadly. "I hear it's great money, but I thought I'd end up using more than I sold, and you know what pariahs the cokeheads are at the bar. Never shut up, can't keep it up, the attention span of a gnat. And who needs crystal dick? Fun but so unattractive."

"Emmett," Michael said sternly. "Focus. What's going on?"

"Oh, it's just phone sex, Michael," Emmett said, passing it off.

"You're running a phone sex parlor out of my house?"

"You make it sound so sordid." Emmett winced, screwing up his nose.

"It is a bit. What happened to the job at the law firm?"

"I called one of the partners a cocksucker." Emmett sank onto the sofa.

"And was he?"

"No."

"They hate that." Michael nodded. "And the department store?"

"I burned it down." Emmett rolled his eyes back. "Not the whole thing."

"There's the blessing," Michael said, beginning to despair. "And the vendor thing?"

"There was an incident." Emmett sighed. "And the season's over anyway."

"They play football in the fall and winter months."

"In Pittsburgh?" Emmett scoffed at him. "I don't think so. It's a little cold for outdoor sports here this time of year, don't you think?"

"Yeah, I do, but that's not really . . ." Michael trailed off with a sigh. "It all makes sense now. The obscene phone calls that are not Brian. No one's ever able to get through. You always in your room on the phone."

"The twelve-hundred-dollar phone bill," Emmett suggested helpfully.

"Yes, the twelve-hundred-dollar phone bill. It must pay well."

"Not really." Emmett shrugged. "I'll get reimbursed for the phone bill, and I only get an hourly wage based on the charges."

"Still, it must be hot, talking dirty on the phone all day," Michael said, imagining.

"You'd think. It was at first. I had a boner for like eight hours straight. Now, I read fashion magazines while I do it, it's so dull."

"But the work's easy and fun," Michael said, trying to lighten the mood.

"Boring and gross, but I don't know what else to do," Emmett wailed, throwing himself back dramatically across the sofa, the back of his hand across his forehead.

Outside, there was a persistent high-pitched beeping.

"So you hate it, you're not making any money, and I never get to use the phone again?"

"I could get a separate phone line."

"Emmett, surely you can find something that you like better."

"I thought that I could work on my fashion designs in my spare time."

"And have you?"

"No. I don't make enough to have any spare time."

"Michael, Miiiii-challllllllll," someone was calling outside in concert with the beeping.

"Someone's calling you," Emmett said.

Michael looked suspiciously at the phone, which began to ring. Startled, he picked it up.

"Hi, cocksucker," the voice said on the other end of the line.

"Hang on a second." Michael passed the receiver to Emmett. "It's for you."

"Miiiiiii-chaelllll," the voice called again from outside, and Michael crossed to the window to see.

"Hello," Emmett said, and listened for a bit, making theatrical noises of shock and dismay. "How did you find out? Who told you? What do want? I'll do anything to keep this a secret."

Michael looked out the window and Ted was waving up at him as he struggled to keep the motorcycle he was straddling upright. Michael opened the window. "I'll be right down," he called.

"Tonight," Michael said, pointing at Emmett, who saluted, and then dragging the finger across his throat. "I want the money when I get home."

Emmett nodded broadly. "What do you mean, everyone already knows? But how is that possible?"

"Blind people know you're a cocksucker, Emmett," the man on the phone said.

"How do you know my name?" Emmett asked, genuinely shocked for the first time in the conversation and none too pleased about it.

"Don't play games, Emmett, put Mikey back on the phone," Brian said.

"Oh, Brian," Emmett giggled. "Michael just left."

"What the fuck? Didn't he answer the phone?"

"Yeah, but I don't think he thought it was you. I've been getting a lot of obscene phone calls lately so he just assumed it was for me."

"I didn't think it was possible for you to get any weirder." Brian hung up.

"Always a pleasure, Brian." Emmett scowled at the dead receiver.

"So what do you think?" Ted said, following Michael into the diner like an attention-starved beagle.

"The motorcycle?" Michael shivered from his inaugural and final ride. "I hope you got a good deal on it," he said, fishing for something positive to say as he discreetly checked his teeth for bugs.

"Yeah," Ted said, moving toward one of the booths that was already occupied. "But don't take my word for it. Ask the dealer. Tell him, Mel."

"Tell him what?" Melanie asked, looking up from her coffee and her copy of *Gilbert's Law Summary* on torts. "Hey, guys."

"Michael was just asking if I got a good deal on the bike," Ted said, sliding in beside her. "And since it's your bike, I thought you were uniquely qualified to field that one."

"It's on consignment," Melanie said. "I'm driving Ted's Saturn and he's trying out Matilda."

"Trying it on to see how it fits," Ted explained.

"To see if Lindsay's buying it," Melanie added ruefully.

"Hey, boys," Deb called. "You want something to drink?"

"Ma," Michael said, glad to escape the discussion of the hideous motorcycle that had nearly frozen his ass off in the few life-threatening blocks from his apartment on Edmond to the diner on Liberty. "What are you still doing here?"

"Gloria quit." Deb shrugged. "She eloped with Prince Charming."

"That hustler who bar-backs at Meat Hook?" Michael asked disbelievingly.

"The same." Deb smirked. "So, she'll be back after he's run through all her money and gone back to boys. Meanwhile, lucky me, I get double shifts until we find someone."

"Well, it is extra money for the holidays," Michael consoled, slipping onto a nearby barstool. "Maybe I can get that pony this year?"

"Only if you keep it at the apartment," Deb said, unable to resist the impulse to stroke his cheek at that moment.

"I don't know," Michael said, taking the hand against his face. "I'm not sure if we could get Emmett and a pony into the extra room. Wait, that's it."

"It is?" Deb asked, not sure what he meant.

"Em needs a new job."

"I thought he was a big designer in L.A. or something," Deb said, abandoning her side work and leaning on the bar between them. "Although, now you mention it, I saw him selling cotton candy at Three Rivers the other day, but he ran off before I could talk. He was wearing a pink candy-floss wig so I thought it could have been somebody else."

"It was him. Long story." Michael waved it off. "And you didn't hear it from me. But he's home to stay and he's staying with me. And I need his half of the phone bill. And you need another waitress."

"He'd be perfect," Deb said, beaming. "Get him to call. I'll do what I can."

"Oh, yeah, right." Michael smirked. "Like they'd hire anybody here you didn't want to work with."

"Yeah," she said with a hoarse little cackle. "Like they'd dare."

"I'd better go sit down. We're having a strategy meeting."

"Uh-oh. Should I call the *federales?*"

"No, we've postponed world domination until we've got Lindsay fixed up with Melanie over there," Michael said in a sinister tone, twirling an imaginary mustache.

"Matchmaking." Deb shook her head and clicked her tongue. "Honey, take my advice, stick with world domination, there'll be less trouble."

"It'll be okay," Michael said, backing toward the booth. "We've got a plan."

"I'll bring over some coffee. You hungry? A sandwich?"

"Not really. Maybe some fries?" Michael said. "Thanks. Ted, you want coffee?"

"Yeah, great," Ted said, looking up from his conversation with Melanie.

"Two," Michael said. "Thanks, Ma."

They fell into a deep conference over exactly how best to showcase Melanie as they devoured the fries that Deb brought.

"Well, the problem is that she doesn't really know the real Melanie, right?" Michael said, trying to get them back on track after a long discussion of Melanie's long-term goals.

"No," Melanie said. "It's that she thinks she does know the real me, but she has me confused with somebody else."

"So, who are you, Mel?" Michael asked.

"Who knows? I'm a work in progress. So's she. Am I a small local law practice, a Victorian in Squirrel Hill, and two point five kids? Maybe, if I found the right partner."

"She'll love that," Michael said as they agreed on a final draft.

"So would I," Melanie said, falling more in love with the portrait they had been painting as she wondered if Lindsay might be the right partner. She'd only asked for a date, but as she took out her dreams and polished them up, she couldn't help but see Lindsay as part of them.

Brian spotted Michael through the window of the diner where he sat talking to Ted and Melanie.

"Hello, boys," Brian said, sliding into the booth with them, an arm possessively around Michael.

"There's a lady present," Ted sniped.

"Is Emmett powdering his nose?" Brain said, looking in the direction of the toilets. "Nice bike, Mel, is that yours?" he asked, pointing through the window.

"Actually it's mine now," Ted said irritably. "I'm buying it."

"Teddy boy," Brian mocked. "Did you buy her testicles as well?"

"What do you want, Brain?" Michael asked, pulling away from the familiar embrace.

"You," Brian said, grabbing Michael again with both hands. "I'm going to look at a painting that I'm considering for the new place. A Lukacs actually. I think it'll be a good investment."

"I think you can pick out a painting without any help from me," Michael growled.

"Oh, so do I. What I need is the wall space. What do you want me to do with your beer clock?"

"Shove it up your ass." Michael pushed Brain out of the booth and almost onto the floor as he got up.

"Mikey," Brian said, pursuing him a couple of steps. "Don't be like that."

"Don't call me Mikey," Michael snapped, wheeling on him and stepping him off. "My name is Michael."

"I know that," Brian said quietly. "It's not disrespect, Michael. That's not why I call you that and you should know that by now."

"You take too much for granted, Brian," Michael said coldly, then turned and stalked out of the diner, slamming the door.

"What's eating him?" Brain asked just before he was suddenly struck in the back of the head.

"What did you do?" Deb demanded.

"Nothing, I didn't do anything," Brian said, suddenly a defensive adolescent when faced with Deb's unspoken power in their long-standing relationship.

"So, Michael just went stomping out of here with not so much as good-bye for no reason when he was fine and laughing not a minute before you got here?" Deb grabbed Brian by the ear. "Could you two excuse us a minute?"

"Certainly," Melanie said, smiling politely as she enjoyed watching Brian's fate.

Deb dragged Brian by the ear to the back.

"That was fun," Ted said as they continued to watch covertly.

"It's the most I've enjoyed being around that guy since I met him. Do you think she'll kill him?" Melanie asked hopefully.

"She doesn't seem like the type to let him off that easy," Ted said. "Okay, so we're all set for tomorrow, right? You've got the new outfit we picked out. Your hair appointment at Chez Cheveux is right after your contract law class at three."

"Are you sure she doesn't suspect anything?"

"I don't know. I doubt it. We haven't actually asked her to come yet so she doesn't really have any reason to suspect anything."

She looked up and saw Deb lecturing Brain while feeding him pie over the counter at the back of the diner.

"Oh, God," Melanie moaned. "We're going to have to ask him, aren't we? Am I ever going to be a part of Lindsay's life without his constant presence?"

"I don't know," Ted said. "But he's going to be at dinner tomorrow or Lindsay won't be."

"What is he doing here?" Michael demanded as he saw Brian and Lindsay walking through the door of Ted's apartment, which Emmett was holding open.

"What is she doing here?" Lindsay hissed, grabbing Brian's arm and trying to pull him back out the front door.

"He's how I got Lindsay to come," Ted said quietly to Michael, who was by contrast making no secret of his displeasure at seeing Brian.

"Hi, Ed." Brian waved across to them. "What happened to your face? It doesn't always look like that, does it?"

"Believe me," Ted said, still speaking under his breath to Michael, "I'm not any happier about it than you are. But this is for Mel, remember?"

Ted made his way over to greet Lindsay and Brian.

"Can I get your coats?" Ted asked.

"Thanks, Ed," Lindsay said.

"It's Ted," Ted said as nicely as he found it possible, but wanting to kill Brian more each time they met.

"Oh, sorry," Lindsay said, letting the old camel coat she'd had since sophomore year slide down her arms. "I know that. Of course it is, Brian just said . . ."

"Yes, it seems to be a real challenge for Brian," Ted said with a laugh that was as insincere as it was mirthless.

"Right you are, Theodore," Brian said, tossing his coat into Ted's arms.

Ted made a hissing noise as he drew in a sharp breath.

"Are you okay?" Emmett asked, still holding the front door for Brian and Lindsay since Lindsay had not come in far enough to close it.

"I'm fine," Ted said, clearly not the least bit fine. He had scratches and bruises all over those parts of his body that were visible, the makings of a black eye shaping up on his badly marked-up face, and an Ace bandage wrapped around his wrist.

"You don't look fine," Emmett said, taking the coats from Ted and having a closer look at his face.

"Don't worry about it, Tedward," Brian said, clapping Ted painfully on the back. "You don't look any worse than you usually do."

"Thanks," Ted said, wincing from the pain of the hearty pounding Brian had given his back. "Just a little motorcycle accident."

"You have a motorcycle?" Emmett said, surprised and secretly impressed.

"It's actually Melanie's," Ted said. "She's getting rid of it."

"Oh?" Lindsay said, taking the bait.

"Yep, she's behind the wheel of a Saturn, these days," Ted said. "We've all got to settle down sooner or later."

"Fuck that," Brian said. "Michael," he said formally to

make sure it was clear he was not calling him Mikey. He made his way over to sweep Michael up in his arms and give him a big, messy wet collection of kisses. "Let's get out of here. Come away with me." He put Michael in a fireman's carry and headed for the door.

"Put me down, would you?" Michael demanded, still too irritated to be charmed by Brian's obvious effusiveness.

Lindsay stepped aside to avoid Michael's flailing feet, and Emmett took the opportunity to close the front door. Brian set Michael down next to the door and held him against it, hands pressed to it on either side of Michael's head as he tried to plant another kiss. Michael turned his head to avoid Brian's advances and got Brian's tongue in his ear instead.

"Get off me, Brian," Michael growled as he slid down the door and slipped out from under Brian's arm. He darted across the room.

"You can't stay mad at me forever," Brian said, following.

"Oh, yeah?" Michael called over his shoulder as he fled. "Just watch me."

"This isn't going to work," Lindsay said quietly to Melanie, who was trying to look as conservative as possible in the smart little suit Ted and Michael had picked out.

"What isn't?" Melanie asked, puzzled.

"This whole *I Love Lucy*, madcap, let's-trick-Lindsay-into-falling-for-Melanie scheme." Lindsay sighed.

"Is that what you think?" Melanie asked, hurt and humiliated by the accuracy of the observation and frustrated by her own feelings of desperation.

"The suit, the Saturn—your hair looks great by the way. Did you buy a house?"

"No, but I've settled on a neighborhood."

"I need a drink." Lindsay stalked off.

"Me too," Melanie said disgustedly as she followed.

Ted and Emmett were left standing by the door, Emmett clutching most everyone's coats, Ted rubbing his sore arm.

"Well, that went well," Ted said expressionlessly.

"A motorcycle accident?" Emmett chided.

"Don't remind me." Ted rolled his eyes.

"Skipping over the whole 'What the hell were you doing on a motorcycle in the first place?' question for the time being, what happened?"

"Here." Ted pointed toward his bedroom door. "Let me show you where you can put those."

"And then what happened?" Emmett asked, following him.

"I got these great Barcelona chairs at this little high-end junk shop," Brian was explaining to a bored and cornered Michael in the kitchen. "The chrome's a little flaky, but they really set the tone."

"Cold and uncomfortable?" Michael asked, topping his drink off for the third time since Brian's arrival.

"That wasn't exactly what I was going for, no," Brian said, trying to keep his sense of humor.

"So, just pretentious?"

"This is all really sweet," Lindsay said, sipping her wine on the sofa with Melanie. "I can't believe how much trouble you all went to."

"I think maybe you're worth it," Melanie said.

"And that's maybe the most romantic thing anyone's ever said to me." Lindsay took her hand. "But the assumption here is all wrong. You don't need to change. There's nothing wrong with you. This is about me. This is about who I am and what I want or don't want."

"I just wanted to show you who I really am, Lindsay."

"By driving Ted's Saturn?" Lindsay asked gently.

"No, by letting you see that I'm not a motorcycle any more than I am a Saturn. In the store the other day you made it sound like being a lesbian ruled out getting married, settling down, having some kids, and having a life. I wanted to show you that those things are not mutually exclusive, at least not in my case. I haven't really spent so much time thinking about that kind of thing lately. Not because I don't want it, but I've been too busy living my life, working, going to school. But what you said the other day reminded me that that kind of life is why I'm doing all this work in the first place. It's what I've been dreaming of all my life."

"But it's just a dream," Lindsay said with a sad smile.

"Every great thing in life starts out as a dream. Why not this?"

"Because every dream doesn't come true."

Melanie was quiet for a long time.

"You're right," Melanie said, nodding. "I gotta go."

"I understand," Lindsay said with the same sad smile.

"Ted, I'm leaving," Melanie called as she made her way to the door. "And I'm taking the motorcycle back."

"Was that Melanie?" Ted said, emerging from the bedroom. "Leaving? Where did she go?"

"Back to real life," Lindsay said, setting her glass on the table. "Coats in here?"

Ted nodded, stunned.

"Ready for yours, Brian?" she asked.

"Yeah, I'm ready," he called after her.

"Who's life are you going back to?" Michael asked him.

"Look, Michael." Brian tossed back the last of his drink in a shot. "I'm sorry you can't be happy for me. Is it that you're jealous of what my life is becoming? Of who I'm going to be? If you don't want to be a part of my new life, then maybe you don't want to be a part of my life."

"Sorry, Brian," Michael said sadly. "I always thought you were already good enough." He pushed past them and out of the apartment.

"Ready?" Lindsay said, handing Brian his coat.

"You bet." Brian slid into his leather jacket. "Thanks for a memorable evening, Ned."

"Sorry you went to so much trouble." Lindsay bussed Ted on the cheek. "I do appreciate it. Melanie's very lucky to have a friend like you."

She closed the door behind them.

"That was shorter than I had thought it would be," Emmett observed.

The oven timer went off.

"You feel like eating dinner three times?" Ted asked.

"I can try," Emmett said, following him into the kitchen. "So, now this motorcycle accident, what exactly happened?"

"The official story is that I spun out driving up the Ohio on Highway 65," Ted said, taking the rosemary chicken out of the oven.

"That smells great." Emmett began to toss the Caesar salad. "And the real story?"

"It fell on me while I was trying to start it and then spun around in circles a few times until the engine died," Ted said. "You want white meat or dark?"

chapter eleven

Lindsay was watching the Norelco gurgle out enough coffee to cheat a cup out of the pot before it finished brewing. This cold Saturday morning, she did not have anywhere to be. She'd had a nice hot shower, wonderful in that way that hot showers can be only on cold mornings. A teacher at one of the elementary schools where she taught art classes had given her a copy of *Having Our Say*, and it waited for her virginal and wholly unread on the nightstand. She was heading back to bed with her coffee to spend the morning reading.

It all sounded a bit like the Saturday morning of an old-maid schoolteacher, she was thinking to herself. Still it was better than the pain of same-sex femme fatale. She smiled a bit as she thought of how Rebecca used to make the coffee hobo style or, as Lindsay preferred to call it, burnt. It was their regular weekend argument, each trying to beat the other into the kitchen to make the coffee.

There was a steady knocking on the door.

Lindsay tried to imagine who it might be and settled on

Brian—though his usual knock was more percussive and the time was not typical, which she chalked up to his and Michael's fighting—as no one much else came to visit her. That thought was sharp and unexpected and made her more acutely aware of her loneliness.

She opened the tiny metal hatch mounted at eye level in her front door.

"Brian?" she said, peering through.

"Hi, Lindsay," Melanie said.

"Melanie, hi." Lindsay was puzzled but pleased to see her. She felt much better about the finality of their last talk at the Ted disaster dinner. She'd gotten to say what she needed to say without hurting Melanie, and perhaps more important, Melanie had heard what she'd said. "Hang on." Lindsay took off the chain and undid the various locks her mom had installed on the door to protect the precious daughter she hadn't called since Easter. "Come in," she said, opening the door. "Would you like some coffee? It's just fresh."

"Okay." Melanie stomped off her boots on the mat before stepping in.

"Great." Lindsay was conscious that she was wearing a nightshirt under her robe and that all her makeup was still in the bathroom and none of it was on her. "Right this way," she said, touching her face nervously.

"So, you got big plans today?" Melanie put the two motor- cycle helmets she carried on the kitchen table.

"I've got a date with two women," Lindsay said coyly.

Melanie gave a low whistle and nodded. "That's hot."

"Yeah, only they're both over a hundred years old," Lind- say said, scrunching her nose as she poured the coffee.

She looked cute when she did it, Melanie thought, and smiled. "Like 'em older?"

"Not usually." Lindsay shrugged. "But these two came highly recommended."

"Working girls?" Melanie asked, puzzled.

"Maybe, I'm not sure yet. Cream or sugar?"

"Both." Melanie's heart sank a bit. She should have called first. "Not sure? How can you not be sure?"

"Well, I know that my friend paid twenty-two dollars for them. So, there's that. But I don't know what, if anything, either of them do."

"I see," Melanie said pensively, taking her mug from Lindsay and sitting at the table. "You going over to their place?"

"No, they're back in the bedroom," Lindsay said playfully. "Want to see?"

"I'm not sure," Melanie said, knitting her brow. "I don't think so."

"Wait, I'll bring them out." Lindsay laughed as she dashed out of the room.

Melanie reached up to smooth her hair and straighten her clothes a bit, not knowing exactly how to handle the moment and wondering how quickly she could drink her coffee and get the hell out. The book hit the table beside her.

"*Having Our Say: The Delany Sisters' First Hundred Years,*" Lindsay said. "You heard of them?"

"Oh." Melanie laughed, deeply relieved. "I, yeah. I haven't read it yet but it looks great." Then she laughed again, the tension broken.

"Got you, didn't I?" Lindsay asked, laughing too, taking the seat beside Melanie.

"Yeah, you did. I was totally ready to run out of the room. I thought these two ancient, naked women were coming in and I was considering ditching."

They laughed for a bit.

Lindsay grinned as she gave a little eyebrow wave at her own deviousness. She propped her feet up on the rung of the chair below her as the cold in the floor was beginning to seep through the bottom of her slippers. "So why the two helmets?" she asked, tapping the one nearest her with her fingernail.

"Like two condoms. In case the first one breaks."

"Sounds painful. But very practical."

"I want to ask you to do something with me."

"Okay," Lindsay said, curious.

"I've spent a lot of time on your turf trying to show you who I am," Melanie said, running her index finger around the rim of her coffee mug. "I'd kind of like the chance to just be me with you for the day. No obligation, no expectation, just a day in the life of the real Melanie Marcus."

"I've never ridden a motorcycle," Lindsay admitted, not entirely ruling it out.

"Would you like to? I thought it might be a nice day to have a drive up the A1, maybe have lunch at this little place I know, Two Moons, out by the river. I don't know exactly. Just go."

"Is this a date?" Lindsay scowled.

"Absolutely not." Melanie raised both hands in unconditional surrender. "This is just possibly the last sunny day in Pittsburgh until next March. Thought you might like to see it. Maybe bring your sketch pad. Or your book for that matter. What do you think?"

"I think the Delany sisters have waited a hundred years for me. They can wait one more day," Lindsay said, knocking her mug against Melanie's.

"Okay, honey," Deb said, concluding her half-hour-long orientation speech in honor of Emmett's first day. "I guess that's everything I can think of. The main thing to remember is to set your own pace. You let the customers or the kitchen start setting your pace and it's your ass on toast."

"Got it," Emmett said with a little salute, still not able to take his eyes off the babe sitting at the counter who looked just like Emmett's favorite Baldwin, Stephen, and completely oblivious, as a result, to a word Deb had said to him. "My own pace," he repeated, completing the illusion that men create when they are cruising and don't want their companion to know by parroting the last few words said to them.

"Okay, great," Deb said. "Today, why don't you take the counter orders and I'll cover the booths. Usually you'll have both together, but on weekends and special occasions there'll be two of us."

"Usually two," Emmett said, grinning as he'd succeeded in establishing eye contact with Baldwin.

"That's right. So, grab some coffee and go ahead and clean the toaster before the lunch crowd starts building in."

"Toaster. Right."

Deb poured them both a cup of coffee and sat down at the bar to marry the old ketchups she'd collected from the booths while she'd been talking to Emmett about his duties.

Emmett set about to clean the toaster. He had just managed to fill the bus sink with warm, soapy water and was pulling the large industrial toaster over to plunge it into the bubbles, a choice that would not only have killed him instantly as the nonimmersible unit was still plugged in, but would not in fact have cleaned it.

"Could I get some more coffee?" Baldwin asked Emmett in a voice that was actually better than the original's, in that it was speaking directly to Emmett.

"Sure," Emmett said, setting the toaster carelessly aside on the edge of the sink and going to get the coffeepot from the warmer, bending over gracefully to pick it up even though the warmer was at eye level. "More cream?" he asked, leaning his face as close as possible to Baldwin's face as he poured.

"Please," said Mr. B.

"Coming right up," Emmett said with a Loretta Young twirl as he returned the coffee to the warmer and continued his late-breakfast ballet to include another low bow headfirst into the fridge just below the counter to get another pitcher of cream. He struck his head on the inside of the refrigerator and recovered nicely, realizing that Stephen was watching his every move. Their eyes locked as Em returned with the cream. "Here you go." Emmett put the little steel pitcher down and leaned both elbows on the counter to stare balefully into those dreamy Baldwin eyes, which had not left his.

Thus engaged, neither noticed when Darnel, the fry cook, rang the bell, either the first or the second time.

"Pick up," he yelled again.

"Yo, Tinkerbell," Deb said, throwing a dishcloth and hitting Em in the side of the head. "They're playing your song."

"Yeah?" Emmett said, looking up and listening intently to the tune on the jukebox. "No, this isn't my song." He shook his head. "I do love me some Taylor Dayne, but I'm really still stuck on 'I Will Always Love You.' And I'll tell you a little secret, Whitney's version is good, but Dolly——"

"Shut up, shut up, shut up," Darnel wailed. "Just pick up the food, would you?"

"Oh, right, sure. That bell is for me. I gotta remember that," he sang, pointing his index finger at his temple and pulling the imaginary trigger.

Deb laughed and turned back to her ketchup bottles.

Emmett leaned across to the pickup window, still amused by his little faux pas and bumped the toaster, just enough to start its slow decent over the edge of the sink, such that it didn't actually hit the water until Emmett was standing on the rubber skid mats that lined the space behind the lunch counter, saving his own life for the second time that day.

The explosion was quite remarkable, accompanied as it was by the horror-movie lighting effects as the diner flickered, lit up, and then blew out accompanied by Taylor's rendition of "Love Will Lead You Back" faster and then slower and then faster as the jukebox blew along with everything else in the kitchen, the diner, and at the hairdresser's next door.

It was an unusually quiet morning at the Big Q. It was one of the last sunny Saturdays in Pittsburgh for a very long time. Michael had not wanted to go to work and had even considered calling in sick. There had been no word from Brian since Ted's party. Friday had been a wash, and the prospects for the rest of the weekend were not looking good.

Such was the dark cloud over Michael's world that sunny morning until, admiring his work with the new drapery displays and sipping his battery-acid-strong coffee from the Big Q snack bar, it came to him.

"Tuesday through Thursday afternoons and Saturday mornings before the store gets crowded," Michael remembered Kirby's voice explaining the official store hours for blow job customer service. Michael was only just intrigued by the idea of people having sex at the store where he worked, but the idea of getting to see straight-college-boy hottie Kirby having boy sex was irresistible and the setting almost irrelevant. And Michael knew that Kirby was scheduled to work that very slow Saturday morning.

Michael had stationed himself on the wicker aisle sorting the baskets where he'd have a view of the entrance to the

public restrooms. So far, though, the baskets looked great but
the boys' room had been as slow as the rest of the store. He
was just about to give up when he spotted Kirby moving in
the right direction. Michael's boner snaked down his leg at
just the prospect. His mouth was dry and his breath short as
he watched Kirby turn the corner and move down the aisle
straight toward the men's room.

Michael stopped breathing as he waited and watched
Kirby open the men's room door and disappear.

As the blood left his brain for points south, nothing else
mattered. Not the importance of his job, the potential for
public humiliation or even arrest, and certainly not the
prospect of Kirby finding out. In fact, Kirby was the least of
Michael's worries as he knew that Kirby's job ended the last
day of December no matter what.

In addition to discretion, reason had also moved south as
Michael made his way to the restroom after what seemed like
a discreet interval. Michael had not paused to consider that
though he had seen Kirby headed into the restroom from his
rattan vantage, he had not seen anyone else.

Michael opened the door as quietly as possible and
stepped inside. His heart was pounding so hard that he could
barely hear. He held the door handle for a moment as he considered running right back out. He stood frozen looking at
himself in the mirrored wall above the sinks opposite him
and wondering what to do next.

There was a sharp cough from the back of the restroom in
the stalls.

The sound jarred Michael enough that he let go of the
handle and, figuring he'd better do something as standing
there silently would be more suspicious and perhaps frighten
them away, took a breath and held it as he walked back to the

stalls. Under the second-to-the-last stall, he recognized the trousers Kirby had been wearing when he'd seem him only moments before. An electric shock ran through him as he realized that no one was in first position. He and Kirby were alone in the BJ bathroom at the appointed time.

Unable to think clearly, Michael opened the third stall on the other side of Kirby, where he'd planned to try to catch the show, stepped inside, and locked the door. Trapped, he could not think of anything to do, and the longer he waited the harder it became to think. He sat down so as not to create any more suspicion. Maybe someone would come in soon and Michael would get his little show. He'd wait five minutes, and then, if no one else had come in, he'd flush and leave. Even if Kirby saw him at this point, he was just in a men's room he'd been in a hundred times before.

He sat silently for a moment.

Kirby patted his foot.

It hit Michael as if he were seated in the electric chair instead of fully clothed on a toilet in the men's room at work.

He was alone with Kirby. Kirby didn't know it was him. Kirby wanted a blow job. There was no blood left in Michael's brain. There was nothing outside, no work, no fight with Brian, no consequences, only the throbbing electricity of that moment.

Kirby patted his foot again.

Summoning every ounce of strength and will he possessed, Michael stepped into the blinding fear that he was experiencing and patted his foot.

"You want it?" Kirby's voice whispered.

"Yeah" was Michael's hoarse reply.

In an instant, Kirby's hard cock was sticking straight up from his lap as he knelt and slid his lower body neatly under the partition that separated them. Michael could only stare at first. Kirby, always one to brag, had not been exaggerating. Aside from his looks, it was the only other thing about Kirby that was above average.

"Go for it," Kirby urged after a moment during which Michael remained unmoving, transfixed by the cobra that rose up before him.

For an instant more Michael decided, and then there was nothing but the two of them, Michael and the hard column of flesh and the heat that was passing from one to the other. It was abandon, it was wrong, it was dirty, it was hot, it was just the clean, unclouded act of sex, between two anonymous strangers. That Kirby didn't know it was Michael and that Michael knew it was Kirby only excited Michael more.

As though in response to one of those little impulses that pass through the adult male brain every nine seconds or whatever it was, he had simply dropped to his knees and gone down on the object of his random passing fancy and been allowed.

"I'm gonna," Kirby warned.

And then it happened. Michael didn't pull away but took all he could get as he finished Kirby off and then let him slip from his mouth.

Both men were breathless in the aftermath.

It took Michael a minute to get to his feet, and even then he only took a seat.

Michael could hear Kirby getting himself together as he tried to clean himself up enough to get dressed and return to the sales floor.

"Jesus, dude," Kirby said in hushed tones as he tucked himself away and zipped up. "That was incredible."

It wasn't everything, Michael thought, but it was ten minutes when he'd stopped thinking about his life.

*   *   *

"This place is amazing," Lindsay said as they rounded the bend on the trial in Riverside Park and came face-to-face with the Allegheny River, from which the park had partially gotten its name. "The Al, close enough to touch. I've lived here all my life, seen this river thousands of times, and I don't know that I've ever been this close or even stopped to realize that it was under the bridge."

"Aren't you glad I made you wait for this?" Melanie said, pulling the small brown bag with the burgers, still warm from the vendor, from inside her bulky leather jacket. There had been a struggle, but Melanie had grabbed the sack and run ahead saying that they had to wait for the perfect moment. She had made a show of stuffing the bag inside her jacket, daring Lindsay to reach inside.

"You're right, this is the perfect moment," Lindsay said, taking a seat on a rock protruding from the bank, her legs swinging over the water. She was having a great time. Melanie was so much more fun once they took sex off the table. When it was just them, just friends, just out enjoying the afternoon, it really was the perfect moment. "This is the best burger I ever tasted," Lindsay moaned as she took her first bite.

"Yeah, it's a total hole in the wall, but it's my favorite burger place, in Pittsburgh anyway." Melanie folded back the paper expertly as much to hold the large, unwieldy burger together as to keep her hands clean. "My league plays softball on the diamond here sometimes."

"You play softball?" Lindsay grinned at the notion.

"The Swinging Dykes."

Lindsay choked on her burger and Mel pounded her on the back.

"Good one," Lindsay managed, recovering. She enjoyed being one of the boys, but she'd really missed being one of the girls who was one of the boys, and she was only realizing how much as their day unfolded.

The bike ride had been exhilarating. Mel had sped them expertly up the 130 along the south bank of the Allegheny. The cold, clear day, the powerful, steady river, and the power of the bike between her legs as they flew down the asphalt had blown all the dust out of her brain and made her feel in perspective and truly alive in her own skin for the first time in longer than she could remember.

"Is that how you found this park?" Lindsay asked, breaking the easy silence that had settled as they sat over the river eating their lunch. "Playing softball?"

"Yeah." Melanie smiled at the summer memories. "This insane old friend of mine, Leda, and I used to bring girls out here after the games to score. These trails go all back up along the river here. I kind of found this spot by accident one night. It was the end of the season and you could feel fall in the air. The moon was just up and full, and we came around that corner and there were two moons. It took a minute to realize that it was just a reflection in the river. So for a minute there really were two moons. Sometimes you see something and you're sure it's there, and it's real so long as you believe it. And then it's not anymore, and even though it never really was, there will always be a time in your life when it was real, when there really were two moons. Anyway this kind of became my place. When I want to get away, be in the world that I want to believe is real, instead of the one I know is."

"Two moons." Lindsay nodded. "Very poetic, counselor."

"Nah, I was probably just horny and too many beers," Melanie said with a self-effacing little gesture. "But for a minute it was as real as you beside me right now."

*   *   *

Lunch was well over by the time they got the power back on at the diner.

In addition to having to serve sandwiches prepared and consumed by candlelight, they had been forced to call the owner, who'd called an electrician. Both had wanted to know how the toaster got into the sink.

"Well, how else was I supposed to clean it?" Emmett had asserted huffily.

Deb had made threatening gestures to the owner over Emmett's shoulder, waving off the savage assault and firing that he would surely have received had Deb not silently risen to his defense. The owner took one look around the silent and abandoned restaurant, partially eaten food set at most places, made an exasperated noise, and stormed out.

It had been a singular Saturday lunch at the Liberty.

Due to the complete absence of electricity and hence labor-saving devices of all kinds, Em and Deb had been forced not only to take the orders for the cold plates and sandwiches from those customers who did not flee immediately upon receiving the news about no hot food on a clear and sunny but decidedly cold day. They had also had to help make the sandwiches.

They'd gotten off to a bumpy start, mostly because Darnel was more interested in killing Emmett than he was in making any sandwiches. Once they'd overcome the potential for homicide, Deb had whipped them into a little well-oiled sandwich-making machine. They limited the selection to the easier items, and as the crowd began to grow, the news about the power seemed less daunting to newcomers and they built it into a nice little lunch rush.

Emmett had been put in charge of egg salad, pimento cheese, and chicken salad as they were all premade spread-ables and much easier to make. Deb had taken all peanut butter varieties for the same reason, along with most salads, which were not only cold but always part of her regular responsibilities; that way she had time to be the cash register since the regular one was out of commission due to the outage. This division of labor freed Darnel up to complain bitterly and take on the more complicated sandwich orders.

Things were moving right along and the place was packed and noisy despite the lost jukebox. The sound of a case-knife handle hitting the pie dome that Emmett held aloft rose above the din, but did not still it.

"Hello," Emmett said, pounding more furiously on the ringing glass dome with the stainless-steel knife handle. "Could I have your attention?"

What did finally get their attention and effectively silence the room was the moment the pie dome shattered. Emmett screamed as he had not since earlier when he'd blacked the place out and tossed the lunch he was serving onto the Baldwin he had been trying to pick up.

Everyone stared blankly.

"Yeah, hi," Emmett said, clutching his imaginary pearls and regaining his composure. "This is especially for those of you who ordered egg salad, pimento cheese, or chicken salad, but, everybody, heads up," Emmett said with a sheepish smile. "Those are the sandwiches I'm in charge of and I lost my birthstone ring. So, if you run across it, I'd like to get it back. Thanks and chew carefully."

That had been pretty much the end of lunch. Some of the regulars insisted on paying anyway, but no one ate any more that afternoon, and plates loaded with unpaid-for food had been left sitting on every flat serving surface in the place. And there was no cleanup as there was no dishwasher or hot water.

Darnel just left and Deb locked the door and turned the

Closed sign around to face outward as there was really nothing else to do except wait for the boss and the electrician. The Liberty Diner, an anchor on the avenue and staple in the community, was, for the first and only time that anyone could remember, closed during regular and even irregular business hours. It had taken Emmett less than one day.

"Oh, here it is," Emmett called, holding up his ring. "I took it off when I went to wash the toaster."

The dance floor at Girl Bar was really just a tiny raised spot near the back where they couldn't fit a pool table. Lindsay eyed it warily as Melanie sank yet another stripe. It was the third game of a three-game challenge. Best two out of three, and the loser had to either dance with Melanie or take Lindsay to J. Frank's for steak and lobster, depending.

It had been a great day, and neither had wanted it to end so Girl Bar had seemed like a reasonable compromise. Not as date-like as Kahlo's, with its draped booths and porches and garden, but not as over-the-top and anonymous as Babylon. They'd had a round of beers, and then Melanie had suggested the wager.

Lindsay was actually a pretty good player, having sharpened her skills playing with Brian and the boys on slow nights at Woody's. Brian usually won, but she could beat Michael most of the time and always Emmett. But Melanie was a shark and was taking her time as she cleared the table for the game that would give her the two out of three to win.

"Did you just let me win the second game?" Lindsay asked, leaning on her pool cue to get some use out of it.

"Pretty much, yeah." Melanie leaned over the table and sawed the cue between her two fingers in preparation to putting the 10 in the corner pocket. "I didn't want you to know that you never had a chance." She sank the ball, then rose to get a sip of her beer as she examined the table. She gave Lindsay a grin.

"You could have just asked me to dance," Lindsay said, grinning back.

"Yeah, right," Melanie sputtered with laughter. "Not without an argument or a city ordinance. I figured this way was easier, and the point was to spend more time with you doing the things I do, and I have."

She leaned in and effortlessly tapped in the 15.

"If it's any consolation," Melanie said, rechalking her stick, "I'm still taking you to J. Frank's for surf and turf."

"Oh, don't call it that." Lindsay made a face. "It makes it sound so awful."

"God knows what they'll call it at that place," Melanie said, scoping the table for her next layup.

J. Frank's on Baum was a local theme restaurant. The theme was all things *Wizard of Oz*. That included calling menu items like calamari Calamunchkins and specialty drinks Surrender Daiquiris, so what they'd come up with for surf and turf was worth worrying about.

"What I meant was, you could have just asked me to dance," Lindsay repeated, smiling and not looking away.

"You say that now." Melanie looked up from taking the shot and caught Lindsay's eye, realizing. "I could have, huh?"

"Mmm-hmm."

"It's more fun to beat you." Melanie turned and began hammering the balls into the pockets, clearing the table of her stripes, and the 8 ball delayed only by wind resistance and gravity. "Shall we," she said, tossing the stick onto the table and extending her hand formally to Lindsay.

"I think so." Lindsay smiled knowingly as she placed her hand on top of Melanie's.

As if in answer to their decision, k. d. lang's "Miss Chatelaine" came up on the anonymous loop that played background to the early-evening crowd.

"I love her," they both said, then laughed at themselves like the kids they felt suddenly free to be with one another.

"Just a smile, just a smile, hold me captive just a while," Miss lang sang to them.

No one else was on the dance floor, and the spirited melody took them as they held one another and spun around the little square of polished and beer-stained hardwood, joining in at the chorus.

"Every time your eyes meet mine clouds of qualm burst into sunshine," they sang along, spinning more and more wildly around the empty floor. That they both knew every word and breath in k.d.'s performance only made them laugh harder and sing louder.

It was inevitable. Given the moment, the way they were feeling, and the lyric.

"Just a kiss just a kiss I have lived just for this."

Needless to say, they were no longer singing along, and it wasn't because they didn't know the words.

The high point of Vic's week was vocational therapy. Between the nausea and side effects of the experimental meds and his ongoing collection of opportunistic infections, his idea of fun had been muted. He'd really lucked out on vocational therapy. Considered more a burden or an outright waste of time to many, it was a glimmer of his former self for Vic. There was a culinary track, and after years as a successful chef, Vic felt more himself in the kitchen than anywhere else.

He'd even been able to polish up his dessert skills, never his long suit, in what had turned out to be a really excellent course taught by a cordon-blue-trained dessert and pastry medalist whose career had been sidelined by HIV.

It was a good course made even better by his sharing it with his old friend Godiva, who called it "cake-decorating class," in that husky Southern accent that always made Vic smile. Godiva's HIV had never manifested, but he had few enough T cells to qualify for full AIDS benefits. Another benefit was that Godiva was still driving, still had a car, and often picked Vic up. Just as often, the two made a night of it, hanging out at Woody's or Pistol till late and occasionally crashing at Godiva's.

That particular night, though, Vic's new antiparasitic meds were acting up and he'd wimped out early as soon as class was over. Despite Godiva's offer to put on the full Nurse Nancy drag to attend him, he had opted to go home to Deb's.

The place was strangely dark when Vic got home. It wasn't particularly late as class was out by ten and Deb was off due to the unprecedented closure of the diner. Vic figured the old girl must have taken advantage of the solitude and the time off and made an early night of it, so he was especially quiet as he made his way in from the car.

As he opened the door, he paused. A strange noise, a small strangled sound and other gasping and braying noises, covered his efforts at coming in quietly through the kitchen. The noises seemed to originate in the living room, and Vic was alarmed enough by the racket to arm himself with a dangerous-looking wooden rolling pin.

He peered through the balustrade on the stairs that separated the kitchen from the living room. The noises were definitely coming from the living room, and he was concerned enough for Deb that he forgot his own safety and dashed into the room to the light switch.

Deb screamed and threw a pillow. Daniel pulled the

afghan over his head, figuring that his face was more recognizable than the rest of his body parts. Vic turned the lights back off and ran for the stairs, laughing hysterically.

"Vic Grassi, you keep your mouth shut, or you'll be sleeping with the fishes," Deb bellowed after him, but the only answer she got was the sound of Vic's door slamming and his continued muffled laughter.

"All right, Mr., uh, Kinney," the desk sergeant said, turning the arrest blotter around and reading Brian's name printed next to his signature. "The bail is two hundred fifty. We take cash or postal money order."

"It's hard to believe that indecent exposure is really a crime," Brian chuckled as he dug the money out of his pocket.

"Actually, I think they knocked it down to that so there'd be no real record. Too fucking cold for it, if you ask me," the sergeant said with an irreverent snort of laughter. "You're a good friend to come down here like this."

"It's a good investment." Brian counted out his rent money. "The surprise is that it's not the other way around. Probably only a matter of time."

"Nice young man like you?"

"You might be surprised, Officer. I gotta tell you, I never saw this one coming."

"Well, you tell your friend to get a good lawyer."

Brian was laughing too hard to respond.

"Okay," the officer said, a little put off by Brian's odd response. "You just wait here. We started processing when you first got here. It shouldn't take much longer."

"Great," Brian managed. "Not laughing at you. Private joke."

He stepped out the nearby door and lit a cigarette. The

night air was cold and raw. It was winter for sure. He thought about how warm he'd be back in Evan's bed as soon as this was over. The cigarette tasted funny in the cold air and he stubbed it out halfway and stepped back into the terrazzo-covered waiting area.

"Here we go," the sergeant said, resuming his post.

The blond wood door buzzed and began to open. Brian turned to face it, an irresistibly rude and superior smile spreading across his face in greeting.

"Brian, you can't tell anyone about this," Lindsay said, closing the space between them.

"Don't be silly. I'm going to tell everyone. I may call your mother."

"God damn it, Brian," Lindsay wailed.

"Great," Melanie groaned. "I can't believe there was no one else we could call."

"I've never been happier to be home waiting by the phone." Brian grinned. "I brought you this." He pulled out a bottle of Corn Huskers lotion from his coat pocket.

"What the hell is that for?" Melanie asked as he held the door for them.

"Howling at the moon . . ."

"We were singing a k. d. lang song."

"Nude . . ."

"We only had our shirts off."

"On a rock on the banks of the Allegheny River in Pittsburgh in November?" Brian asserted. "I figure it's gotta be the worst case of windburn since the Amazons."

Melanie paused to face him as she exited the police station. "If you were a man," she said, her eyes burning into his, "I'd give you such a beating."

"I bet you would, missy." Brian laughed. "I bet you would."

chapter twelve

Michael had paid an enormously high price for his ten-minute vacation from care and worry. The interlude with Kirby had Michael gripped with fear that Kirby knew it was him and would out him at work. Fear over having swallowed—something the experts would never say for sure was dangerous or not, though the last time he seemed to remember hearing they thought it wasn't serious. Plus he felt degraded and desperate and pathetic for having done any of it in the first place. All of which was made worse because he was not able to talk to Brian about it. And worse still, every time he saw Kirby at work, he wanted to do it again.

He was sullen and snappish with everyone and unable to explain.

All in all, it had not been worth it at any level. He debated with himself over just telling Kirby and offering to do it again, but under less questionable circumstances. But, though he was ashamed to admit it, even to himself, part of what

made it hot for him and, from what he'd said, Kirby too was
that Kirby didn't know who it was. Kirby could imagine some
bodacious babe and Michael got Kirby.

More than anything, he did not want to stop by the diner
for a "talk" with his mom. But it was a "command performance" according to Deb, and so he was on his way to meet
her. As he made his way across Liberty in the last few feet of
the short journey, he stepped wide to avoid the huge puddle
gathered at the curb. The car came out of nowhere, horn blaring, and Michael jumped back to avoid a brief new career as a
hood ornament and landed, both feet, up to the ankles in the
cold, slushy water. He stood frozen in disgust for an instant
and then hopped up onto the curb just in time for the next car
to hit the puddle at just the right angle to blast Michael with
a wall of the same frigid, murky water he'd only just escaped.

The kind of white anger that simply takes away all reason
carried him flat-footed back through Lake Michael and heedlessly into Liberty Avenue traffic. Tires squealed, horns blew,
and fists were waved out of car windows to herald Michael's
arrival at the diner. He slammed the door, just to complete
the set.

"Hey, sweetie," Deb yelled. "Grab a seat, I'll be right with
you. Is it raining again? You look soaked. Want some coffee?"

"Sure," Michael growled, moving in a straight line to a
booth.

"Michael," Ted said, beaming, clearly pleased to see him,
and bounded toward Michael, puppylike in his enthusiasm,
from where he'd been sitting talking to Emmett at the
counter.

"'Lo," Michael said actually, bumping into Ted, who'd
opened his arms to give Michael a hug. Michael kept moving
and more or less threw himself into a booth.

"So, how's it going?" Ted said like a Jack Russell undaunted by the actual brush-off and Michael's stormy mood.

"Life is a shit sandwich and every day you have to take another bite."

"Bad day, eh?" Ted gave Michael's shoulder an affectionate chuck.

"And life."

"Anything I can do?" Ted asked, still the Jack Russell, happy just to see Michael under any circumstances.

"You know, Ted," Michael said with a sigh, "did you ever feel something for someone and they just totally didn't get it? Not just didn't feel the same way, but didn't even have a clue that you felt anything at all?"

The words pierced Ted's heart like an arrow on target. "Kind of," he said, his mood bruised and hemorrhaging.

"And yet, no matter how badly they treat you or how bad it makes you feel, you still really, really care about them?"

"Yeah," Ted said with a sad and wounded smile.

"I guess it's just best to let go, no matter how bad it hurts." Michael slumped back against the booth. "I mean, it can't be helped that your feelings aren't returned, and it's not kind or loving to punish the person you care about just because they don't feel the same way."

"You're right," Ted said, just this side of tears.

"Thanks, Ted. I appreciate your advice."

"Ted, could you excuse us a minute?" Deb said suddenly there with the coffee.

"Yeah, sure," Ted said listlessly, rising from the table and returning to his spot at the counter and Emmett, who was still standing there reading a magazine, despite the fact that the place was doing a pretty good business.

"What's eating him?" Deb said, looking over her shoulder as she watched Ted shuffle away.

"Who knows?" Michael shoved his coffee mug toward the pot.

"Okay, so you got me into this, you gotta get me out," Deb said, leaning in and speaking with her teeth clenched, not really any quieter than usual but harder to understand. It was what Michael called her spy voice.

"Could I have some coffee?" Michael tapped his cup. "Or do I need to go to another diner?"

"That's just the problem," Deb said, clicking her tongue against her clenched teeth.

"Okay, I give up," Michael said, wet, cold, angry, and well into stage-three caffeine withdrawal. "What have I done now?"

"You've gotta do something about Emmett."

"What?" Michael said, actually looking at her for the first time. "It's not working out?"

"He forgot to lock the door yesterday. He defrosted the freezer with all the food still in it. He flooded the kitchen and put out the pilot lights and then called the gas company and got the place evacuated during the breakfast rush. It's not working at all."

"Accidents happen," Michael scoffed.

"Yeah, but that's all that happens with him. I wanted someone to help around here, and all I've done since he got here is clean up after him."

"Fire him."

"I can't. He's your friend, he's your roommate, he's half your rent."

"Pick up," Darnel called, ringing the bell. Emmett only moved to turn the page in December *Vogue*, which was just out that day.

"I was paying the rent by myself before he got here," Michael said irritably.

"Just encourage him to look for something better suited," Deb said reasonably.

"Pick up," Darnel yelled, ringing the bell again. Emmett still did not look up.

"Oh, God, how bad could it be?" Michael said disgustedly.

"He's blacked the place out, run off customers, insulted the health inspector, caused Darnel to quit three times, caused the flood, broken the toaster, the dishwasher, and the coffeemaker and enough dishes and glassware to set a dinner for all the closeted gay athletes, and he's been here less than a week,"

"Pick fucking up, God damn it," Darnel screamed, throwing the bell at Emmett and hitting one of the customers. "Aw, shit."

"Sorry," Emmett sang, setting aside his magazine. "Be right back," he said to Ted, who was staring catatonic into his empty coffee cup.

"You see," Deb said. "He doesn't seem to get that we serve food here."

"I'll make you a deal, Ma," Michael said. "I'll smother him in his sleep tonight if I can get some coffee."

"There's no need to get nasty." She shrugged, rising. "Just give him a little nudge about how this work isn't good enough for him or something, before someone gets seriously hurt. Let me get you some fresh," she concluded just before pouring coffee into his cup.

His hand shot out to try to grab the pot, but Vic literally waltzed her away, taking her coffeepot hand in his and raising it high above their heads as he slipped his arm around her waist and spun her around the busy diner. "Hello, young lover," Vic sang out.

"Vic, are you crazy?" Deb snapped, struggling to get away. "What's the matter with you?"

"I can't help myself," Vic teased, spinning her under one arm and then grasping her waist firmly for another turn around the diner. "All the world loves a lover."

"Shhh," Deb hissed, putting a hand over his mouth. "Everyone will hear you."

"Isn't it wonderful, Michael?" Vic called out to him. "Your mother is in love!"

"What?" Emmett said, turning back from the people at table eight to whom he was about to deliver food. "Deb? Who?"

"Daniel," Vic sang out.

"You son of a bitch," Deb said, really struggling to get away from Vic while trying not to hurt him. "You let go of me right this minute."

She broke free just as their orbit reached Michael's table, and just as Emmett and the tomato soup, chili, coleslaw, and Cobb salad with extra blue cheese dressing he was supposed to be serving to station eight reached Deb. The result was that Deb, free of Vic, crashed into Emmett and his precarious tray of food, and instead of the coffee he'd asked for, Michael got the food from table eight.

"You are so fired," Michael shrieked, rising from his chair like the dome of Mount Vesuvius on a bad day in Pompeii, coleslaw dripping from his hair, chili and tomato soup staining his clothes as they burned his skin. "You are the worst waiter in the world. Get your things and get out," he bellowed, scooping hot chili beans out of his shirt pocket as he swatted away Emmett's efforts to wipe some of the mess away.

"Michael," Emmett said, taking another swipe at him

with the cloth he'd wondered why Deb had urged him to keep tucked in his belt. "Calm down."

"Get away from me and get out," Michael said in a spasm of flailing and screaming. "You're fired, didn't you hear me?"

"Michael," Emmett said, recoiling slightly. "You can't fire me."

"Oh, yes, I can," Michael snarled, completely out of control. "Darnel, you want him fired?" he shouted toward the kitchen.

"I want him hung," Darnel shouted back. "But I'll settle for firing if it's all I can get."

"How about you, Mom?" Michael demanded, wheeling on her. "Do you want him out of here?"

"Well, I, not really . . ."

"This is it," Michael shouted, waving his finger in her face. "This is your big chance. You can either admit it or work with him every shift for the rest of your life. But you don't get to bitch to me about him again either way."

"You're fired, Emmett," she said without a moment's further hesitation. "It's really for the best for everyone concerned. Someone would have been killed sooner or later."

"How about you all?" Michael said to the restaurant in general. "Who here never wants this man to wait on their table again?"

The hands at table eight waved particularly vigorously.

"It's unanimous," Michael said, untying Emmett's apron and taking the dish towel out of his hand. "Get out before they form a mob and it gets ugly."

"Well," Emmett said indignantly. "I have no intention of staying where I'm not wanted. I'll send for my things," he said to Deb. "Darnel, we need a redo on the order for station eight. I'm out of here."

Ted rose to follow. "Michael, that was just mean," he said as he made his way past to catch up with Emmett.

"Is there anything else, Mom?" Michael said, panting from all the excitement.

Deb only shook her head.

"Then could I please get some coffee?"

"So, Brian, are you going to get to keep the window office or are you going to New York too?" Trish called nastily to Brian from the receptionist's desk as he entered the Inverness/Muir offices.

"Morning, Trish," Brian said expressionlessly as he sorted his messages into his two habitual categories—call later and never call. Still no message from Michael. "What do you think you know today?" he asked, not looking up.

"Never mind," Trish said with a sniffy little laugh. "You already answered my question."

"I'm glad I could help." The messages were all never call, so he tossed them in the bin beside Trish's desk and headed down the hallway to his office without giving her much more thought. But as he made his way down the corridor, the tone of the greetings were a little off-key. Brian was doing a great job, but aside from Evan, a few people in his department, and possibly Angie Howell, the woman in human resources who'd gotten him interviewed for the job, he was just "the new kid in creative" or, Brian's least favorite, "Evan's boy."

So, when people who usually addressed him as "Watch where you're going" and "Ryan, isn't it?" actually made eye contact as though trying to gauge his mood or reaction to something—and in some cases said to him without prompting "Morning, Ryan, how are you?"—he became suspicious and began to try to recall Trish's acerbic greeting. The big clue that something was in fact up and that the little shrike was passing on more than office gossip with the messages, though, was that Angie Howell was waiting for him in his office.

"Brian," Angie said, extending a hand. "I thought we should have a talk."

"Sure, anytime." Brian took off his coat as he joined her in his office. "You need coffee or something?"

"I'm covered, thanks," she said, raising her standard-issue cobalt with gold leaf I/M coffee mug as evidence.

"Do I need some?" he said, wary of a visit from the vice president in charge of hiring and firing, whom he had not even seen since the day he was hired, let alone had her drop by for a visit.

"Grab some if you want," she said easily. "I can wait."

He opened the door and went into Evan's office, still dark save for a lamp on the desk, to make himself something using the espresso machine there. "So am I fired?" he called back to her as he leveled off the coffee grinds and pulled on the wooden handle to twist the tiny filter into place.

Angie made to answer him, but the noise of steam testing the fittings as the espresso machine came to life drowned out the possibility of an answer. She rose and stood at the doorway and watched as he steamed some milk and added it to his espresso in a cup the size of a soup bowl, something she'd seen Evan do dozens of times. What an asshole, she thought to herself of the opulent office's soon-to-be-former occupant.

"Is that a no?" Brian asked, taking the steaming cup and returning to his own, somewhat less spectacularly equipped office.

"I tried to call you, but there was no answer at your place," she said, sidestepping the question again.

"I wasn't home last night," Brian said without further explanation. Probably not the best idea to tell the head of the sexual harassment investigation squad that he'd spent the night examining the ceiling of his boss's bedroom.

"Oh," Angie said a little eyebrow flash and a coconspirator's grin. "Seeing someone?"

"Sort of." Brian sat behind his desk and hid his smug expression with the huge mug of espresso and steamed milk. "So, did you come by to tell me what a great job I'm doing?"

"Brian, I've come to make you an offer," she began in a practiced way.

"Is that why you wanted to know if I'm seeing someone?" Brian asked, raising a brow playfully, relieved, as she had intended, with the way the conversation was beginning.

"As you may or may not know, Evan is leaving for the New York office, to take over as COO for the company," Angie said in a matter-of-fact tone that made the information she knew full well he did not yet have seem less important.

Brian relived the previous twenty-four hours, all but the last two spent with Evan, in seconds as shades of rage, betrayal, and a blazing desire for revenge coursed through his veins. "No, he hasn't mentioned it" was all he said, his face a mask of calm and just the slightest shade of surprise.

"Well, the position came open suddenly," she said, knowing full well that such was not the truth save for the broadest possible interpretation. "In fact, he'll actually be leaving for the New York office later today to finalize the arrangements."

"And this offer you came to make me?" Brian asked, taking another sip of the latte and consciously forcing any thought of Evan from his mind. He focused, as he was always forced to do, on his own survival.

By the end of their little discussion he'd managed to get a

small raise, a titular promotion, to keep his office, the use of the assistant he'd shared with Evan, and to talk Angie into having one of his special lattes.

"Okay, then," Angie said, more than pleased with how well the conversation had gone. "I'll put together the paperwork. Stop by my office around the end of the day and we'll finalize it. And thanks again for the latte. Really nice. Who knew?"

"I'll bring you one this afternoon when I stop by," Brian said, rising and shaking her hand as she rose to take her leave.

"I'm glad we could work this out," she concluded, ever more impressed with him.

For his part Brian didn't hear anything else she said as they parted. All he could think of was the complete betrayal of the man he'd only just left in the bed they'd shared the night before. Of the lie and the deceit in every kiss, every moan, every thrust, every sex act that had passed between them certainly that morning and he couldn't guess for how long before. How long had Evan known? Brian felt the lie as he'd felt the man inside him only hours before.

After Angie left, he'd sat down to the work on his desk, but all of it revolved around his work with Evan so there was really little he could do. Following a few abortive attempts to get started and progressing to the point where he needed to talk to or call Evan, Brian gave it up, grabbed his coat, and headed out.

The looks and the remarks in the hallway made more sense now. The insincere greetings and solicitude all seemed more pronounced and distorted by his new perspective, as though he were traveling down the hall looking through a fish-eye lens. He met each with an impassive half smile and nod with no acknowledgment of the ambivalence that tore at him.

He could smell Evan's cologne, feel the warmth of his body next to his, feel Evan's erection pressing against his back as he held Brian possessively while they slept. What an idiot he had been.

"Leaving already?" Trish asked with an edge that made it clear she knew.

"Leaving?" Brian said, turning to her with a sly smile. "And give up my window office? You're not as well informed as I thought." He smiled at her, turned, and left.

"It's a little early in the day for a drink, don't you think?" Ted said, startling Emmett, who'd just raised the mimosa to his lips. He'd followed Emmett down the street to Woody's, which was open in preparation for the lunch business and for the "hair of the dog" trade.

"I can't see what difference it makes," Emmett said, tossing the drink back. "Got a cigarette on you."

"You don't smoke."

"I can't see what difference it makes," Emmett said dramatically. "Waiter, another mimosa, and don't spare the Mumm's."

"Who are you supposed to be?" Ted asked, taking the stool beside him. "Susan Lucci or Barbara Stanwyck? Coffee," he said in the bartender's direction.

"I'm not just being dramatic," Emmett said, his tears genuine. "They all hated me. They all wanted me out. They raised their hands and voted me out. Do you now how that feels?"

"Look, Em," Ted began, not really sure what to say as a witness to democracy in action at the Liberty Avenue Diner. "It's not the end of the world."

"Do you know how many brothers and sisters I have?"

Emmett asked, taking up his fresh drink. "Of course you don't. I've six brothers and sisters. You know how many of them I've heard from since I left Hazlehurst?"

Ted shook his head as he stirred the coffee.

"Zero, none of them," Emmett said sadly. "I send them cards on their birthdays and at Christmas every year. There's always a return address, my number's always in the card— when I have one. That's how it feels. I ran away when I was really young. I lied about my age to get into Allegheny Community so I could follow my dream and get my degree in fashion merchandising. And when I got my big break, I went out to L.A. and got fired for ordering twice as much sparkle spandex as we were going to need for the line and killing the profits for the whole season, while also not sleeping with the boss. I've never exactly fit in, certainly not in Hazlehurst, or with my family, or even with all those 'straight acting' queers who spend all their time trying to look and act like the people who hate them. But Michael and Deb and Vic and the friends I have here, this is the family I chose. And I thought it was the family that chose me. Now I feel like I'm back in Hazlehurst."

They sat in silence for a bit. Ted didn't really know what to say. Emmett ordered yet another mimosa. Ted drank his coffee. Someone put "Everybody Hurts" on the jukebox and Emmett started crying softly.

Ted put his arm around Emmett's shoulder and Emmett put his head on Ted's. It made them both feel better.

"You know, Em," Ted said, once R.E.M. had run its course, "I keep the books for a couple of the businesses in the neighborhood, and there's this little clothing store, mainly clubwear and T-shirts for the Babylon crowd. They're looking for someone to do sales and display part-time, so if you did both jobs, it would be full-time altogether. I don't know what I can do, but I could put in a good word for you."

"Oh, that sounds so perfect," Emmett said, taking the hand Ted still had resting on his shoulder and giving it a squeeze. "I can't believe that you'd do that for me. You don't really even know me that well."

"You seem pretty great. And I have some experience with that whole not-fitting-in thing."

"Emmett, honey," Deb said, surprising them as her approach was covered by the music and since no one else was really around save for the hard-core drunks, and they weren't there to socialize. "You forgot your magazine," she said, offering it to him.

"Thanks," Emmett said quietly, taking it from her and turning back to face the bar.

"And I didn't get a chance to apologize to you," Deb said.

"Michael, is the one who—"

"No, darling," Deb said, taking the stool next to Emmett. "I owe Michael an apology too. That was my fault. I should have fired you. But I love you and I didn't want to hurt your feelings."

"So you asked Michael to do it?" Emmett said, rotating his stool to face her.

"Well, not exactly. But I did put him in a really bad position. Honey, you are a smart, talented, darling young man, and you make the best coconut cream pie I have ever tasted. But you are a terrible waiter. I can't decorate. You've seen my house. I have the clown figurines to prove it. And what I don't know about fashion is a lot. But I'm a great waitress. It's what I do, 'cause I'm good at it. You should do what you're good at too."

"Thanks," Emmett said. "I appreciate your being honest."

"I should have been sooner and I might have avoided you getting your feelings hurt," she said, patting his shoulder. "Try not to blame Michael. He's in a world of hurt over Brian lately, and I'm not sure that there's not more to it. I know a life working at the Big Q wasn't his dream. He had to put his dreams on hold so I could help his uncle Vic."

"And I did pour chili over his head," Emmett added helpfully.

"There's that," Deb said. "Okay, I've got to get back across the street before someone fires me. I just wanted you to know how much I love you, kid. We all do. You're like one of the family. And what family doesn't have its off days."

"Even if I am the worst waiter in Pittsburgh?" Emmett said with a little grin.

"And Pennsylvania and possibly the whole Northeast," Deb cackled.

"Thanks, Deb. That means a lot more than you know."

The cold five-block walk to Evan's condo on the river from their office had done little to clear Brian's head. He was more confused by his reaction to Evan's departure than he was by Evan's departure. He was just this old guy in his thirties Brian had been screwing around with for a couple of months. No more than that. Evan had made it more than clear that day in his office.

But try as he might, that's not what kept coming into Brian's head as he made his way down Liberty to Commonwealth. That Sunday morning in bed with two papers and coffee, Evan doing Sports and Brian Arts and Leisure and the crossword together with Brian calling out the clues. The stupid argument they'd had about Warhol after the art opening they'd been to and the incredible makeup sex they'd had in the limo on the way home. The easy feelings that came when they were just in the condo together at the same time and not doing anything in particular. It was those feelings he was mourning more than actually losing Evan.

It all kept playing over and over in his head like a film loop as he turned into the wind and down Liberty Avenue.

He'd clear his mind, and then the scene in bed that morning, when Evan knew, had to have known, that Brian was going to find out when he went in to the office. And knowing that, Evan had not only not said anything, he'd still fucked Brian one more time, one last time, knowing that it was over. And then Brian's head was off again to their favorite coffee shop or his mile-high-club initiation with Evan on the flight home from Dallas.

The doorman only waved at Brian as he walked across the Gateway Tower lobby on his way to the elevators. A regular fixture at the luxury high-rise, Brian had been home to his own place in the past month only to work on the apartment, which Evan was helping him furnish and upfit. Evan hadn't paid for it or worked on it. He'd gone with Brian to help him understand value and quality and style as they'd scoured the DIY stores, the salvage yards, the secondhand shops, art galleries, and antique dealers.

Evan's stamp was on everything in Brian's life. He was wearing a suit that Evan had picked out and encouraged Brian to buy. And when Brian looked at his reflection in the gleaming elevator doors, it was Evan he saw.

Brian opened the door with his key, stepped into the central gallery, and closed the door quietly. He had no idea what to say. He left his hand on the door handle debating whether to simply leave and never mention it. He heard the shower running, remembered the two of them in that shower together, and made his way to the master bathroom if for no other reason than to stop thinking about it again.

The bed was still unmade as he passed through the bedroom, odd for Evan, who was a bit on the fastidious side, but not unprecedented. He walked through the dressing room and into the archway that lead into the bath. Evan was leaning, his back against the glass wall of the shower that faced into the room, water cascading down his body as some kid Brian had not seen before knelt on the black tiles, his head bobbing between Evan's thighs.

Brian could tell from the sounds that Evan was making that he was about to climax. He smiled as he heard the familiar wheeze and gasp. It was perfect, complete, done. Calmly he swept the blue glass vase with the wisteria and lilies that was sitting on the marble counter onto the floor, shattering it like blue glass fireworks glittering across the dark marble tiles.

The kid yelped and jumped away from Evan. Evan wheeled to face Brian. There was blood on his erection where the kid's teeth had nicked him, but not hard enough to take the erection away. Evan gasped and then ejaculated against the glass between them.

Brian regarded the scene, arms folded, face impassive.

Evan laughed as he regained his composure. "He's nobody," Evan said with a little gesture in the direction of the shower's other occupant, who still cowered in the corner next to the tub.

"Nobody," the kid said, suddenly self-righteous and drawing himself up indignantly.

"I'm sorry," Evan said grandly. "This is the nameless college dropout who sold me a latte and agreed to come up and suck my dick, for which he will probably receive a Nobel Prize next year."

Brian gave a little snort of laughter.

"Who the hell is he?" the kid demanded, coming out of the shower only far enough to get a towel to cover himself, avoiding the shards of blue glass.

"Get your clothes and get out," Evan said, shoving the kid as he got out of the shower, dodged the broken blue glass daggers, and got a towel for himself out of the Gullah basket from which they sprouted, standing on end, rolled like hot towels at a sushi bar.

The blood stained the white towel.

"Little bastard," Evan sighed, tossing the towel into the trash. "My dick is bleeding. I suppose I'm lucky he didn't bite it off with the scare you threw into him." Evan unfurled another huge white towel.

Brian smiled.

"What is so fucking funny?" Evan said, dabbing at the blood with a bit of tissue.

"I'm leaving," the kid announced haughtily from the door, his hands on his hips. Brian recognized the uniform from their favorite—well, Evan's favorite—coffee shop.

"Use the window, would you," Evan said irritably.

"Fuck you too," the kid said adroitly, turned on his heel, and left.

"That'll be the day," Evan snorted after him.

"When were you going to tell me?" Brian asked quietly.

"I wasn't," Evan said offhand, toweling his hair.

"I was just going to show up and you weren't going to be there anymore?" Brian asked, leaning against the dark mahogany cabinet.

"Did you find out?" Evan said, annoyed.

"Angie told me."

"Am I not here?"

"What?"

"Did I just vanish?"

"No," Brian said tensely, annoyed by what seemed to be Evan's growing anger.

"So obviously that's not what happened," Evan said, throwing the fresh towel in the hamper and grabbing a white terry robe off the hooks by the door. "What did you want? Roses? Perhaps an engagement ring? Come away to New York with me and we'll live happily ever after?"

"No, I didn't." Only the tensing of the muscles in Brian's jaw gave away just how angry he was at that moment. But only Michael would have been able to spot that.

"Then what's the broken vase?" Evan said, stepping him off, but Brian held his ground and their faces were inches apart. "We're fuck buddies. Not more. This was about sex and a few ball games and a dinner or two. I enjoyed it. So did you. And if I hadn't gotten this promotion, it would probably have lasted a little longer, but in the grand scheme of things, aside from the fact that you give better head, you don't mean a hell of a lot more to me than coffee boy."

"Yeah, I get that," Brian said, all the secure feelings of being there, of ever having been there, taken away in an instant as if they'd never existed at all. "You've made it more than clear that I'm just someone to fuck when you're in the mood and you don't have a better offer."

"Then what's the problem?" Evan folded his arms with finality.

"Why not just tell me?" Brian asked, shrugging. "If you don't care, if it's just sex, why not say to me this morning before you shove it in me one last time, 'You know, Brian, it's been fun, but this is the last time'? Hmm?"

Evan turned and walked out of the room and into the

dressing room, picked up a large rectangular package wrapped in brown paper and returned with it. "Here." He thrust it at Brian. "It's that Lukacs you admired. I got it for you as sort of a going-away thing."

"I can't accept it," Brian said, his hands at his sides.

"You can't afford it and it'll be perfect in your new place." Evan shook it insistently at Brian. "Send me a check for it when you can."

Brian took it.

"So that's it?"

"You wanna?" Evan said, shoving his hands in the pockets of the robe and gesturing sideways toward the bed with his head. "Once more for old times' sake now that you know?"

Brian shook his head.

"That's kind of why I didn't say anything this morning. That way the last time we could both enjoy it."

"That's not why I said no," Brian said with a bitter little laugh. "You're really not that good."

Evan laughed. "I'll be flying to New York today to make arrangements," he said, returning to the dressing room to pull out some clothes to wear. "I'll be gone for a week or more. You've got a key, take your time. I know you've got some things here. The place is going on the market today, so you can't stay here anymore, but come and go as you need."

Brian watched as Evan picked out the perfect suit for the day and collected a few well-chosen items to pack for his trip with the same fine eye that guided his every choice and decision. Nothing but the best.

"I guess I better go," Brian said.

"One more thing," Evan said, turning. "And this is the only thing I really did want to say to you other than it's been fun. You succeeded at the office because you're really good at what you do. This was a bonus, for me if not for you," he said, pointing at the bed for meaning. "But your work and your talent are what got you your job. They don't know anything about this there, and they've got plans for you. Don't stay too long. You should be able to learn all they've got to teach you in about two years. Then move on to an operation where you can get a piece of the action. That's where the real money is."

"Thanks," Brian said with an odd smile as he turned and walked out the door. "See you."

"Yeah," Evan said with a little nod, and turned back to his packing.

Brian walked out of the condo as deliberately as he'd walked in. It was over. The loop in his head had stopped. Or rather it had been replaced. He wasn't thinking of Evan at all. In fact the only thing he could think about was the one thing he'd made certain he couldn't have, Michael.

chapter thirteen

Lindsay could not remember being in a better mood. She hated to admit that seeing someone could have such an effect on her, but even though nothing else in her life had changed, everything seemed different with Melanie some-how.

Whatever the future held, the present was a spring day in November that even Brian's wintry tone on the phone that morning when he'd called to ask her to lunch couldn't cloud out.

"Clouds of qualm burst into sunshine," she sang under her breath as she erased the chalkboard, in anticipation of the bell that would free her, until her life-study session later that afternoon.

"Miss Peterson, are you singing?" an adorable little gapped-toothed girl with glasses asked incredulously.

"Yes, Lisa, I am." Lindsay dropped the eraser in the tray on the board and dusted her hands against one another.

"What are you so happy about?" a boy sitting in the desk next to Lisa's asked.

"Nothing special, Bobby." Lindsay shrugged.

"It is for you," Bobby said, rolling his eyes dramatically. "You're never happy."

The words stung a bit. Had she hated this job so much, felt it so beneath her, that she'd punished her elementary art students for it? "I'm so sorry, Bobby," she said, kneeling by his desk but speaking loud enough for the whole class to hear. "I'll try to do better, because you all make me very happy."

"We do?" Lisa said, grinning with what teeth she still had.

"Oh, yeah, you do," Lindsay said, rising and ruffling both Lisa's and Bobby's heads. "Everyone about finished?"

The class made various plaintive noises.

"All right," Lindsay said. "Why don't we work on your self-portraits some more next time."

The suggestion was met with an agreeable racket.

"Put them in the portfolios we made," Lindsay instructed, "and get ready to head out. The fifth-graders will be using the art room next, so let's leave it nice for them."

The children gathered the portfolios Lindsay had helped them make from old boxes and string. The bell rang as they were putting their works away, and with a mad scramble they bottlenecked out the door. The traffic jam was made worse by Brian's presence blocking the exit, and he found himself wading through the waist-high sea of third-graders.

He smiled at Lindsay and she waved to him.

"Is that why you're so happy?" Lisa asked, tugging at the hem of Lindsay's cardigan.

"Is he your boyfriend?" Bobby shouted to Lindsay from the portfolio rack.

"*Ewww, oooo,*" the class made a shame-on-you kind of noise at them as they rushed out the door.

"Hi, sweetheart," Brian said in a stagy voice. "Are you ready to go do girlfriend-and-boyfriend stuff?"

"Not so's you could tell it," Lindsay said, gathering her things off the desk. "I am starving, so if that counts, I'm all yours."

"I thought we wouldn't go to the diner today," Brian said, trying to make it sound casual.

"This must be serious," Lindsay said, looking up from her purse, which she was searching for her keys.

"How about The Big O?"

"That'd be great. I've got a class at Pitt at three so I'd already be there. I'll park at Frick and meet you there."

"Okay," Brian said as he was struck from behind by a fifth-grade projectile. "What the . . ." Brian left it at that, stepping aside to let the little boy in.

"Sorry, mister," the kid said, hardly stopping as he raced across the room to get one of the front desks.

"No problem—" Brian began to say as he was struck with yet another juvenile missile.

"Justin," the young girl wailed. "No fair."

"Excuse me," Brian said, glad once again that gay men didn't have children. "You ready, Lindsay?"

"Too bad, Daphne," Justin said triumphantly. "You snooze you lose."

"Are you two going to be okay in here without a teacher," Lindsay asked, sternly enough that the two youngsters settled down.

"Yes, ma'am," Daphne said politely as Justin nodded.

"Okay, then I'm ready," Lindsay said to Brian as she followed him out of the classroom.

"Two of your more dedicated students?" Brian asked as they made their way down the hall to the exit.

"No, not mine. I'm only here once a week and I only teach the third-graders."

"So we're taking two cars?" Brian asked. "Why did I come over here to meet you?"

"Search me." Lindsay shrugged. "It's a little needy for you. What's up? You want a kidney?"

"The bail money back would be nice," Brian jabbed. "Rent's due the end of the month."

"And you'll have it by then," Lindsay said, giving him a shove.

"Melanie already paid me," he said, shoving her back. "So now you owe her. *Eww, ooo,*" he said, imitating the noise the kids had made earlier.

"I'll see you there," she said, laughing as she got into her car.

"I'll meet you at the Frick parking lot," he said, holding her door. "We can ride together that far."

After a short ride across the Birmingham Bridge and up to Forbes, they were at the lot by the Frick Fine Arts Building where Lindsay had her next modeling session. Lindsay lucked into a good space and Brian pulled up to where she waited by the fountain as he caught up to her.

"Is that the spot?" Brian asked as she got into the car.

"Is what the spot?" Lindsay said, scrambling for the seat belt before he rocketed away from the curb.

"The fountain? Venus rising?" Brian pointed.

"Oh, yeah," Lindsay said with a warm smile as she looked at the place. "It is."

"Your tune has changed on that particular memory," Brian said, squealing away from the curb and plastering them to their seat backs.

"Has it?" Lindsay said airily, not wanting to be dragged down that path. "So what's up with you?"

"Can't I have lunch with an old friend?"

"You turning sentimental?" Lindsay scoffed. "You do want one of my kidneys."

"Your kidneys?" Brian said, patrolling Oakland for a space. "You miss half your life running for the bathroom. No thanks."

"That's my bladder, not my kidneys."

"Yes, Miss Peterson," Brian said in a silly little voice. "There's one." He made a terrifying U-ie into oncoming traffic to bag a space on the opposite side of the street.

"So, are you going to tell me?" Lindsay said as they walked up Oakland. "Or do I have to guess?"

"What would you guess?" Brian asked, stopping and turning to face her. He'd not mentioned Evan to anyone, not really known what to say.

Lindsay paused and searched his face. "I'd say do whatever you have to, to get him back."

Brian was momentarily stunned by the pinpoint accuracy of the remark, and he imagined himself going to New York, finding Evan's hotel, and bribing a bellman so he could be naked in Evan's bed when he came in. "You think?" Brian said, turning and walking slowly up the street.

"Yeah," Lindsay said, matching his glacial pace. "It doesn't seem the same without the two of you together."

"How so?" Brian puzzled.

"I don't know. People ask 'Will Brian and Michael be there?' like it's one word."

"Michael," Brian said, understanding again.

"You've been a bit of a beast lately, but he always forgives you," she said, taking his arm. "And you don't seem to be doing so hot without him."

He stopped again and faced her, examining her expression.

The smile came back to his face like the sun coming from behind the clouds. It was the perfect advice; even though he'd never gotten to talk to her about what he'd thought was the problem, this was the solution.

She smiled as she watched it happen, saw the Brian who kept her coming back for more reappear before her.

"The grand gesture," he said, nodding.

"Yes, the grand gesture. You're going to have to go some, though, after that 'not a part of my new life' speech at Ted's party."

"You heard that, huh?" Brian said, taking her arm again and resuming their progress toward The Original Hot Dog Shop, aka The Big O, at a brisker pace. "I figured you were too busy explaining to Melanie how she should leave you out of her dreams."

"You heard that did you?" she giggled.

"Oh, yeah. That Ed can throw a mean dinner party."

"Vicious."

Michael found himself cleaning the signage on the displays along the aisle facing the public restrooms though he'd cleaned them only the previous week.

The scene with Emmett had only made him feel worse about the whole situation and himself. There had been no word from Brian, and in addition to doing seemingly irreparable damage to his relationship with Emmett, he'd also managed to alienate his mom, his uncle, that new guy Ted, and most of the patrons at the diner with the possible exception of the people at table eight, who'd paid Michael's tab in an unsolicited show of gratitude and solidarity. But he couldn't meet the people at table eight at Woody's and talk to

them about the cute guy at work or the incident in the men's
room or how he was feeling about his job or how he thought
he'd seen that kid Terry who used to pick on him in grade
school in the store. He'd not even been able to get up nerve
enough to tell hot Kirby that he could get a lot more than a
blow job in a more comfortable and better-smelling setting,
like Michael's bedroom.

And so there he was, midafternoon, midweek; he knew
Kirby was working and he'd found something to do that
would allow him to keep an eye out for Kirby making his way
to the facilities. He tried to talk himself out of it, but he
couldn't resist the promise of escape no matter how brief. He
just keep seeing it, feeling it, wanting to escape from himself
and his life for a few minutes of pretending that Kirby cared,
let alone knew.

Michael was so lost in the fantasy that he didn't realize
until Kirby was almost in the men's room door. His heart
leaped. He felt an urge like needing to pee really bad at the
end of a long road trip as his whole body seemed to long to
empty out. He crept closer to the door to wait until it could
seem as if by chance before he entered.

"Michael Novotny," the operator's voice cut into the
canned version of "It's the Most Wonderful Time of the
Year." "Michael Novotny, please call the operator. Happy holidays."

"Damn it," Michael said under his breath. He hesitated a
moment. He did not want to miss his chance, but if he didn't
answer the page, they'd page again and then they'd start to
wonder where he was. As if on cue, the operator paged again
as Michael dolefully made his way to the nearest phone so he
could keep an eye on the restroom just in case.

"Big Q, happy holidays," the operator answered.

"Hello, this is Michael."

"Oh, hey, Michael. How are you, hon?"

"Great," Michael said not very convincingly.

"Good, hon, never see you anymore," she said, not noticing. "Come by the office if you get the chance. Marge brought in a batch of her famous Hello Dollies. They won't last."

"Sure," Michael said without conviction.

"See you then," she said. "I've got Brian on the line for you, hang on."

Brian had called the store for Michael an average of five times a week since Michael had started working there five days a week and so was as recognizable to much of the staff and the operators in particular as Michael himself. The operator had no idea what had passed between them recently and had no reason to suspect, so she'd never hesitated to put Brian straight through even though, technically, personal calls were strictly verboten.

"Michael," Brian's voice came through the phone before Michael had the chance to object.

"Hello, Brian," Michael said coldly. Was he going to have to have this conversation standing in the middle of the domestics department at Big Q? he wondered.

"What are you doing this evening?" Brian asked, wading right in.

Michael could not believe that Brian was just going to act as if nothing had happened. "Nothing special," he answered before he'd thought about it, then instantly regretted it.

"Good. There's some stuff of yours at the house. Could you come by for it tonight after work?"

"Un-fucking-believable," Michael said with disgust. "Is that all you have to say to me?"

"Oh, yeah," Brian said as though he'd been reminded. "Happy holidays. See you around eight?"

"Sure." Michael hung up without saying good-bye. "Fucker," he said under his breath. At least it had been brief, he thought, and he turned and walked toward the public restroom doors without a moment's thought or hesitation.

He was just about to cross the broad curtain-wall aisle off which the public restrooms opened when several uniformed police officers headed him off and rushed to open the door just in time for a cuffed and much embarrassed Kirby to be dragged out, along with the young man who had first accosted Michael on the Corning Ware aisle and led him into the tea room and so much more. Both were handcuffed and handed over, none too gently, to the uniformed officers who'd apparently been signaled by a couple of other very nice-looking men who'd been inside the men's room. Michael had taken note of both of them shopping nearby a few minutes before.

As if from nowhere, Mr. Barbarosa, the store manager, was standing beside Michael, clicking his tongue and shaking his head. "You never know about a person, do you, Michael?" he said, patting Michael on the back in a fatherly kind of way.

"What's going on?" Michael asked, confused and chilled by the moment, such a one-eighty from the hot blood that had been coursing though him only an instant before.

"Don't ask me, Michael," Mr. Barbarosa said protectively. "You don't really want to know and I sure don't want to tell you. You're too nice a boy to hear such things." He gave Michael a pat. "Use the employee lounge for a while. We'll get this taken care of."

Mr. Barbarosa followed the little party as Kirby and Corning Ware boy were led to the front of the store.

Michael began to shake and actually had to sit down on one of the broad bottom shelves nearby between two stacks of welcome mats. If Brian hadn't called. The thought just kept coming.

Vic was practicing his icing rosettes on a sheet of wax paper when the phone rang. He didn't want to break his concentration so he left it for Deb. The phone kept ringing.

"Deb," Vic screamed. "Phone." He made it into two syllables.

"Do I seem to be answering it?" her muffled voice came back.

He heard the flush and chuckled as he set aside the forcing bag and picked up the receiver as he took a seat in the wheelchair he hardly ever sat in.

"Hello, Deb's house of charm."

"Vic?" a man's tentative voice came back.

"Yes," Vic said almost mockingly but not quite.

"This is Daniel, Deb's friend? We met at the Red Dress party?"

"Oh, right. And I then I got to see you naked with my sister a couple of weeks ago here at the house."

"Give me that phone," Deb said, snatching it from Vic. "Hi, honey, sorry. Vic's not himself since he got hit in the head," she said, hitting him in the head. "Couldn't wait till tonight?"

Vic rubbed his head, grinning at Deb as he returned to his rosettes.

"Actually it's about tonight."

"Oh, no, Daniel," she pouted. "Not work again. We've been planning this."

"No, it isn't work. I just don't think it's a good idea."

"What do you mean?" she asked, sitting in Vic's wheel-chair.

"Well, I love the ballet," Daniel said, "Tchaikovsky's a particular favorite. It's just so public. You know? Lots of the parents of the dance company are PFLAG, and they might be there and then there's questions to answer—"

"Daniel," she cut him off. "Are you ashamed to be seen with me?"

"No, of course not. It's just better not to have a lot of questions. I thought you agreed with me."

"Well, now that Michael knows and my brother has seen your wiener . . ." Deb shrugged. "I mean, who's gonna find out?"

"It could be uncomfortable at meetings and with the other members," he said firmly. "Or worse yet, some of my clients could be there and then there'd be awkward questions about where we met. I'm just not ready for everyone to know."

"Oh my God, you're a closet case."

"What?" Daniel asked in two keys.

"You heard me. You're still in the closet."

"Well, that's just ridiculous, Deb."

"I didn't notice it at first 'cause I was hiding out from Michael and my darling brother blabbermouth," she said, wheeling herself near enough to kick Vic.

"Damn it, Deb," Vic said, taking a cut at her as she'd messed up one of his rosettes.

"But you're worse than I am," Deb said. "You don't want perfect strangers to find out. Or anyone. What's the point in that?"

"Deb, don't make a federal case out of this," Daniel sighed. "I just don't think it's the best idea."

"I think you're right, Daniel," she sighed, sinking back

into the chair and rocking herself gently as she rolled it back and forth. "This isn't the best idea. I'll see you around."

"Oh, Deb. We can do something else. Let's go to dinner or Woody's or somewhere down on Liberty."

"You're what my friend Emmett calls a ghetto fag."

"What are you talking about? I'm not even gay."

"No, but it still applies. It's easy to be gay on Liberty Avenue and at the diner and Woody's and PFLAG parties; easy to be proud in the parade. It's a lot tougher in Topeka at the Baptist church. It's really insidious, but it's still in the closet. And it's not going to work for me."

"Deb, you're overreacting."

"Okay, then pick me up wearing your PFLAG button and come with me to Petersen Center for the ballet," she said defiantly, her voice not betraying the tears in her eyes.

"No, Deb, I told you. I'm not comfortable with that," Daniel sighed, a little disgusted with himself. "I guess maybe I am a ghetto fag."

"And there's not even a toothpick left of my closet door. You're a great guy, but that just doesn't work for me. I'll see you at the meeting next Sunday."

"Yeah," he said sadly. "I'll see you there."

She put her face in her hands for a moment and smeared away the tears, leaving black streaks across her face, then startled herself by looking up into Vic's imploring eyes.

"Oh, my little raccoon," he said, reaching for a tissue and dabbing away the mascara trails. "You want to eat all the icing rosettes?"

"Oh, yeah," she said, wheeling herself up to the table. "How would you like to be seen third row center at Petersen Center for the Pittsburgh Ballet Company's thirty-third annual *Nutcracker* ballet with the Pittsburgh's oldest living fag hag."

"Come, come, my pet," Vic said indulgently. "You're hardly the oldest—close though."

She tried to swat him, but he got behind the chair and began spinning her in circles.

"Now, let me see," Vic said as if pondering the invitation as he spun her in circles. "I think the question is, where else would a middle-aged, HIV-positive fag be on a holiday night other than in good seats at Petersen Center watching the *Nutcracker* with his hag?"

"Vic, you're making me sick."

"It's probably the icing," he said, pushing her up to the table again. "What time's the curtain?"

Michael got off the bus on Penn and walked the couple of blocks up to Brian's place on Mulberry Way, grinding his teeth with each step. He was conflicted to the extent that had Brian not called at precisely the moment that he did, Michael would be trying to raise bail on some kind of indecency charge. On the other hand, Brian had no idea the good he was doing by calling when he did, and the reason he'd called in the first place was only to nag Michael about that fucking clock one more time.

On the long bus ride over from Bridge Street near the store, Michael had already made up his mind to stomp the thing to bits, then treat himself to a taxi home.

As he rounded the corner of Twenty-fifth and Mulberry Way, he saw no sign of Brian's Nova in the driveway. His blood began to boil at the thought that he was going to be made to wait to be insulted. So that he was stomping by the time he got to the staircase that lead up the graying whitewashed cinder-block wall with the fading sign Mulberry Electronics writ so large across it that the staircase started at the first *c* and ran to the top of the capital *E.*

He pounded on the door, kicking it once, convinced that there would be no answer and already furious about it.

"Hi," Brian said, opening the door and scaring Michael so badly that he almost fell backward down the stairs and let out a small, girly scream. "If I'd known you were so anxious, I could have just left it open. You okay?"

"I thought you weren't here," Michael said gruffly, trying to butch it up and recover a bit of his dignity.

"I am." Brian shrugged. "I did invite you to come by."

"I just . . . Where's your car?"

"Oh, someone tried to break in. I made a deal with a place around the corner. It's a parts store now, but it used to be an old garage. It's sheltered and locked up."

"Nice," Michael said without feeling.

"They don't have a valet, but it keeps that FM radio in the dash that we waited for, for so long. Would you like to come in?"

"Sure," Michael said, pushing past him.

"You like what I've done since your last visit?"

The floors they had refinished gleamed under exposed top-hat lights affixed to the rafters Brian had put in without aid of a ceiling to conceal them in. The knockoff Barcelona chairs were actually kind of hot; the leather straps were beat-up enough to look like a weathered leather coat, more masculine and less Metropolitan Home Queen.

There was even a hot, retro, Jane Jetson sofa in need of reupholstery, but together with the chairs it meant there was a place to sit other than on the floor or the bed, and a living room of sorts. Brian had created a bedroom for himself with rippled fiberglass roof and awning covering standing on end around his mattress and box springs. He'd even found an old men's room door to replace the curtain that was the former door to the bath closet. The reminder was a little too close for comfort, and despite the effect Michael still shivered. If Brian hadn't called when he did . . .

"It almost looks like a place where people could live," Michael begrudged. "If you squinch your eyes just right, you can't see the holes in the wall, the unfinished plasterboard, and the extension-cord network." Brought up short, he surveyed the room and fell silent once again.

What had caught Michael's eye and stopped his heart was the place of honor on the patch of carefully hand-cleaned brick on the wall that separated the bathroom from the main room, highlighted with a specially focused light in which had been placed the Miller High Life clock Michael had brought on his last visit, bubbling away.

Michael was touched and confused and overwhelmed.

Brian stood back and let Michael take it all in.

When Michael's focus came to rest on the brick wall where the clock hung, Brian asked, "You like that there?"

Michael only nodded.

"That's the painting I was telling you about," Brian said, referring to the Lukacs that Evan had given him, which hung nearer the corner on the same wall. "You want something to drink?"

"Yeah, that would be great," Michael just managed, not quite sure what was going on with Brian.

"Oh, you know what?" Brian said, dashing across the room to the metal ladder affixed to the far wall. "I finally got that metal hatch open, and it's not an attic. This, it turns out, is the attic. It's so you can go up on the roof. Come on, I want to show you something." He darted up the ladder and through the hatch onto the roof.

Michael was reluctant and still a bit off center from the

clock, so he made his way over to the ladder and up to the roof. As he neared the top, Brian took his hand and lifted him up through the hatch and onto the roof.

Michael forgot to breathe for a moment.

The roof he'd never seen before had been transformed into a garden, more pots than plants at that point, but enough to support the zillions of tiny white Christmas lights Brian had strung up everywhere, even over the water-cooling tower and exhaust vents. He'd somehow gotten a couple of bus benches and some used lawn art up there along with a small table and chairs that looked suspiciously like the outdoor café stuff from a nearby bistro. On the table were snacks, two champagne glasses, and a small wrapped package.

"You like it?" Brian asked, a little excited for Brian.

"It makes me wish I was stoned."

"Doesn't it." Brian popped the cork on the champagne, trying to catch the part that sprayed out.

"It's amazing." Michael turned slowly to take in all that Brian had done.

"Here." Brian handed Michael the small package. "This is what I wanted you to come by and get. I need that table space for smoked salmon. Go on, open it," he said, going to retrieve their champagne.

Michael lifted the lid and pushed the cotton aside. The sterling silver Tiffany key chain, the cheapest thing they sold, had a single key. As Michael stared at it and tried to get his mind around the concept, a loud bang and hissing noises caught his attention and fireworks began to go off all around them.

"Happy New Year, Michael," Brian shouted over the noise as he ran from station to station lighting off the fireworks.

"What the fuck?" Michael grinned in spite of himself as

he found he was encircled with fireworks amid a sea of fairy lights. "What are you doing?"

"Here you are," Brian said, rushing to Michael's side and handing him a glass of champagne. "Happy New Year, Michael," he toasted.

"But, Brian, it's not New Year's."

"Just depends on when you start counting. Don't you think we deserve a new year? I know you deserve one, Mikey. I'm not the easiest friend I know, but I'm the best. No matter where I go, who I'm with, or what I do, Mikey, it's always you I love. So I give you a new year just for you, if you want it."

"I accept," Michael said, knowing that this was as close to an apology as he'd ever get out of the person he cared about above everyone else in the world.

Michael drained his glass as did Brian, their eyes locked, Roman candles and spinners and event rockets going off all around them. They smashed their glasses for luck. Brian butted his forehead against Michael's and then, wrapping his arms around him, kissed Michael's lips and rocked him gently as Michael nestled his head under Brian's chin, two scared little boys, warding off the evil spirits of the world around them with fireworks, bravado, and a simple love.

chapter fourteen

9:30-ish.

The hands of the Miller High Life clock were less exact than the crisp red numbers on the digital clock at his place. In fact the Miller clock had no numbers at all, the idea being that any time was Miller time. You could tell because that's what it said on the clock right underneath the Miller logo.

Michael watched the Miller bottle whirl as it counted off the seconds. The sun blazing in through the unshaded windows had crept across the bed and into Michael's eyes, waking him. Brian's breath was warm on Michael's neck as he slept spooned up behind him, his arm wrapped around Michael in that possessive way in which they had slept together since they were boys. More like puppies than lovers, but Michael was glad of the closeness.

The day he could see was amazingly clear, and the sun created the illusion that it was warm.

Michael smiled. It was only a moment, but it was all his.

It had been a great night together for him and Brian. The

apartment had no table other than the purloined bistro two-top on the roof, and it had been too cold to stay up there for long. Brian had laid out a picnic on the kitschy beach towel with the girl in the one-piece and the fifties updo. "Lake Harmony, PA. You are here!"—the model, who looked for the world as if she were screaming, was pointing to the spot on the map of Pennsylvania more in warning than in welcome. It had made the two of them laugh so hard that Brian had bought it.

Though Michael didn't know from where, Brian had picked up a lot of wonderful new bits of information about gourmet dining and put together a pretty great picnic for the two of them.

Full of dinner and wine, Michael had babbled on about what Brian had missed in the interim, though he skipped some of the details, such as his little encounter with Kirby in the men's room. Brian for his part was content just to listen to his favorite voice in the world and fell asleep with his arm around Michael, who nodded off during his own retelling of the situation with Emmett and how he wasn't sure how he was ever going to make it up with him and was afraid to go home until he did.

9:35-ish.

Michael really had to pee but he didn't want to break the spell.

It had been a long time since he and Brian had gotten a night together, and he didn't want it to end. Gently he slid free of Brian's firm grasp and padded across the freezing-cold wooden floor to the relief of the shaggy chenille bath mat that Michael recognized from the Big Q inventory. Without slippers and unsure of the exact location of his socks, he walked the bath mat first to the toilet and sink and then out of the bathroom to the kitchen to make some coffee. Unsure of how to work the surprisingly complicated-looking cappuccino machine, he settled for the more mundane Mr. Coffee.

He leaned on the cold glass jewelry counter as he waited for the coffee to brew. Brian was still asleep and had replaced Michael with Michael's pillow and held on to it in that way he had as though Michael were going to be taken away. Michael wondered why it was so much harder for Brian to show his feeling when he was conscious.

Michael sighed as he looked around. It was far from done, but the place was unrecognizable as the filthy, vermin-infested storage room that they had first seen. If nothing else, cleaning the windows had transformed the room. The sun gleamed off the glossy varnish they had applied to the floor. The memory of being trapped in the corner into which they'd painted themselves that night made Michael laugh softly.

The amazingly noisy Mr. Coffee wheezed out the last gasp of hot water in one extended death gurgle, then was quiet, signaling the arrival of coffee.

Michael walked the bath mat over to the pot and poured two cups, to which he added cream and sugar. He walked the bath mat back over to the bed with the two cups in hand.

"What's the deal with the bath mat?" Brian asked, his first words of the day.

"You're awake," Michael said, climbing back into the relative warmth of the bed and putting his cold feet on Brian, who lurched and yowled. "Imagine how bad that would have been without the bath mat. Coffee?"

"Thanks." Brian took the cup that Michael offered him.

They drank in silence for a bit.

"So where have you been?" Michael asked.

"I slept right next to you." Brian shrugged.

"It's just been a long time," Michael said without much expression.

"Too long. Starting this new job took a lot of time."

"No, it's not that. You've been busy before. It wasn't that you weren't physically there. Finals, soccer season, that semester you took statistics and had to study around-the-clock, you were busy and you weren't around, but you were still there," Michael said, unable to explain better.

Brian gave him a blank look and little shrug.

They regarded one another a moment.

"It's like before it always seemed like you were coming back," Michael said, looking away. "But you don't have to anymore. You're done, you're free, you can go anywhere in the world. And maybe it felt like you weren't."

"Sounds like it had more to do with you than me." Brian took a slurp and sat up.

"Brian," Michael said, trying to look at him, "I just wonder when you're going to move on."

"I meant what I said last night," Brian said quietly.

"And I appreciate it, Brian. I feel the same way. I just feel like my life isn't really turning out and that soon I'll be left behind. I don't think it's how you feel about me. I just don't feel like I can keep up."

"What are you talking about?" Brain said, leaning forward and putting his elbows on his knees.

"My life isn't really turning out."

"Do you really think that?" Brian asked, amused.

"Well, yeah." Michael shrugged. "I'm a clerk at a discount store. The guys are not knocking one another down to get to me. I live in an apartment because it's a good deal, not because it's cool or chic or glamorous, but so I can afford to live on half of what I earn. I don't have a car. I don't have a degree. I don't know what's next except more of the same. And I don't see an end to that."

"Are you kidding with this?" Brian said, actually laughing. "You think you're some kind of failure?"

"No, I think I'm an exceptional failure," Michael said with a big sigh.

"Well, you're not, you're just clueless. Michael, you already have what the rest of us are working to try and get."

"What are you taking about?" Michael scoffed.

"Haven't you noticed that you're the one everyone turns to? You think that's because they all think you're the loser in the group? I know that no one comes to me other than you, and I usually fuck that up. You're not a loser, Michael. You've already won—the rest of us are just trying to catch up. Anyway, I'm never going anywhere without you. Including breakfast, so come on and get dressed." Brian tossed the covers aside and walked across the bed. "We're going to be late. I promised Lindsay that we'd meet her."

"Okay," Michael said, smiling without thinking about it for the first time since he couldn't remember when. "Come back here with that bath mat."

"What the fuck are you people doing here?" Melanie demanded, slamming into the largely theoretical backseat of the Nova, dark glasses and a baseball cap on backward hiding a severe case of bed head. "Is it possible to get away from you or is it some kind of twisted package deal?"

"Just consider us your parole officers," Brian said sternly. "Until you young ladies can be trusted to be on your own together—"

"Brian," Lindsay warned as he got dangerously close to their little secret.

"What am I missing?" Michael said, trying to follow the conversation but still a cup of coffee short of his morning wake-up call.

"Not a thing," Lindsay said.

"All I know is that I only invited Lindsay to join us for breakfast," Brian said. "And it turns out there's a crowd at her house."

"So I'm not invited?" Melanie said, leaning over Brian's shoulder.

"Melanie, you look like you just got up," Brain said. "Is your apartment near Lindsay's?"

Melanie slouched back in her seat, arms folded in response.

"Lindsay, you also look kinda like you just woke up," Brian said, catching her eye in the mirror.

"Shut up, Brian," Lindsay sniped.

"You sound like you just woke up too," Brian said.

They rode in silence for a moment, Brian grinning mischievously.

"Melanie," he began offhandedly. "Are there still roses on the ceiling in Lindsay's bedroom."

"I kept expecting a twelve-year-old girl to come in and tell us to get out of her bed," she said as she and Brian broke up.

"That's not very nice, you two," Lindsay chided.

"Say, Brian," Michael said, coming to a bit. "How do you know what's on the ceiling in Lindsay's bedroom?"

It was Michael and Lindsay's turn to break up.

"Here we are," Brian said, deliberately not answering as they pulled into a parking spot near the diner. "Home at last."

"Lindsay, how does he know?" Melanie asked as they lagged behind the boys on the way into the restaurant.

"Remind me to tell you that story in about a year," Lindsay said, holding the door for her. "And you can tell me the one about your crazy friend Leda."

"Maybe two years," Melanie said, nodding genially.

"Sounds good to me," Lindsay agreed.

"Hi, kids," Deb called cheerily enough to make them all

wince. "I'm guessing I'm the only one who got a good night's sleep last night. Am I right?"

Michael grabbed one of Deb's troll dolls from beside the register and hissed, "Bring us coffee or the troll gets it."

"You heard him, angel face," Brian said, brandishing two index-finger thumb-trigger guns. "You know how Bugsy is without his morning coffee."

"I know that's right," Darnel called from the back, snapping all four corners. "The last time he was in here for breakfast it was the shoot-out at the O.K. Corral, the Saint Valentine's Day Massacre, and Alexis Carrington on the rag all rolled into one."

"Don't remind me," Michael said, putting the doll back and pulling his coat up to cover his face as he slunk into a booth. The others followed.

"Better safe than sorry, I always say," Deb said, pouring them four coffees and then handing Michael the whole pot.

"Very funny," Michael said as they laughed at him. "And you never once in my entire childhood said that to me," he called after her as she flipped him the bird behind her back. "I seriously don't know what I'm going to do about this thing with Emmett," Michael said as they began to examine their menus to make an informed breakfast choice.

"Let's find out," Brian said, leaning across Michael and banging on the plate-glass window beside them. "There he is now, with your buddy Ted." Brian pounded again and waved them over.

"Brian," Michael said, trying to push him away from the glass—too late.

Ted and Emmett smiled and waved back as they squeezed between a couple of parked cars and made their way across the street in their direction.

"Great," Michael said, pouring himself some more coffee.

"Brian, congratulations," Melanie said with a little edge. "I think that's the first time you've called Ted by the right name."

"I know his name is Ted," Brian said, making a dismissive little sound. "I managed to get a college degree from a fairly respectable institution. I just do it 'cause it gets under his skin."

"I have the feeling that you do most of the things that you do to get under other people's skin," Melanie shot back with a little grin, and an idea that maybe she wouldn't have to hate this guy quite so much.

"I'd rather be looked over than overlooked," Brain said offhandedly.

"Hi, guys," Emmett gushed, bursting through the door, charging the table, and shoving himself in next to Brian on his and Michael's side. "I just got a great new job at Torso and I owe it all to Michael."

"To me?" Michael said, pointing at himself.

"Well, you and Ted," Emmett corrected, patting Ted's arm. "I would have told you last night but you never came home."

"Oh, really?" Deb called from the other end of the diner. "What's his name?"

"Brian Kinney," Michael yelled back, giddy with relief from Emmett's ebullient mood.

"That louse?" she yelled back. "I thought I told you to stay away from that no-good, miserable sack of shit."

"He can't help himself," Brain answered in his own defense. "He's so fucking charming and he's hung like a horse."

"My mistake, honey," Deb called back, holding her thumb and forefinger an inch or so apart. "We must be talking about two different Brian Kinneys."

"I'm quittin' now," Brian said, sinking behind his menu.

"So what's the new job?" Michael asked over Brian's head.

"I'm part-time sales and part-time display," Emmett said. "So all total I'm full-time. And it's fashion and merchandising so I'm using my whole associate's degree."

"Both parts." Michael nodded, so pleased that he resisted the urge to make fun, but it was hard.

"Are you people ready to order?" Deb asked, stalking over, no sign of her guest checks, the pen still planted firmly behind her ear.

"Mom, why do you always do this?" Brain said.

"*Moi?*" Deb said, touching her chest with all five fingers of one hand.

"It's true, Ma," Michael said. "Why do you make us order when you know you're just going to bring us what you think we should have?"

"Well, I never," Deb said, taking the pen from behind her ear and beginning to write. "Ted, Em, you boys eating?"

"Just coffee for me," Emmett said. "I've got to get to work in a minute and I had some fruit at the house."

"Liar," Deb said.

"Okay, I had a chocolate Pop-Tarts and a piece of cold pizza, but I really do have to get to work and I'm not hungry," Emmett admitted, hanging his head.

"How about you, Ted?" Deb asked.

"Whatever you say," Ted said, hand raised in surrender, taking a seat beside Melanie on the other side of the booth.

"Coming right up," Deb said, walking away.

"But she didn't take our orders," Melanie said.

"You're family now," Lindsay said. "You'll never order breakfast in this place again."

"What do you think she'll get?" Brian said, speculating. "I've got five dollars on French toast with jam and syrup 'cause she's so skinny."

"I'll take a piece of that," Michael said.

"Pancakes, sausages, and scrambled eggs with fruit," Lindsay said, tapping the table authoritatively.

"Let's see your money," Brian challenged.

"You take a check?" Lindsay asked, batting her eyes.

"Here's a five, honey," Melanie said, pulling out her wallet. "I've got your French toast right here."

"Drinks are on me," Vic called from the door as he wheeled himself in, balancing a three-tiered wedding cake on his knees. "Look, I got an A-plus on my final cake."

"Look's more like a couple of plastic guys in tuxedos to me," Brian said, squinting at the enormous cake as Vic got closer.

"Wedding cakes were the final, and this is mine," Vic said proudly. "I've been perfecting my butter cream rosettes and scallops for weeks."

"And I've got the ten extra pounds to prove it," Deb put in, freshening their coffees and handing Michael a fresh pot.

"Cut it out, Ma," Michael warned.

"God, there's no winning with Bugsy," Deb said, giving Brian's shoulder a playful poke.

"You're telling me," Brain said, nodding.

"It's a gorgeous cake," Emmett said sweetly, rising and going over to Vic. "What are you going to do with it?"

"I thought you weren't hungry?" Deb accused, giving Emmett the eye.

"Well, it seems a shame to let such a fabulous cake go to waste," Emmett said, putting an arm around Vic's shoulders.

"All we need's a wedding," Vic said.

"Michael Novotny," Brian said, dropping to one knee. "Will you be mine forever more?"

"Don't tell Mom, it'll kill her," Michael said, putting the back of his hand against his forehead melodramatically.

"I'll get a cake knife and some plates," Deb said, throwing up her hands.

"Okay then," Vic said, rising with Emmett's help and putting the cake on a nearby table. "Do you, Michael, take this man no matter what other people tell you about him or how big a jerk he can be, until someone shoots him or runs him down in a parking lot and you get all his cash and back issues of *Freshmen*?"

"There's cake involved, right?"

"An A-plus, triple-tiered, French-vanilla cream cake with marzipan and raspberry filling," Vic said, gesturing to his masterpiece.

"Then, yeah."

"And do you, Brian, take this man, admitting how lucky you are and promising to do your best and try not to fuck it up or one of us will surely shoot you or run you down in the parking lot so Michael can at least have your cash and your back issues of *Freshmen*?"

"And some of that cake," Michael put in.

"Oh, yeah," Brian said, turning to face Michael and taking his hand, just under the table. The look that passed between them was lost in the mirth and the merriment of the moment of family and friends playing together, and Emmett was forced to return Michael's troll-doll bouquet even though he "caught it fair and square." But the words that Brian said to Michael were never lost between them, and he reaffirmed them often, though Michael never forgot them. "Do I take this man?" Brain repeated, giving Michael's hand a squeeze. "Always have, always will,"

"I now pronounce you inseparable," Vic said.

"You may now cut that cake," Emmett led the cheer.

Before they were grown men working and playing in Pittsburgh, Brian Kinney and Michael Novotny were high-school friends dealing with bullies, secret crushes, and their emerging sexuality. Step back in time with *Queer as Folk*'s hottest characters in the first two books in this provocative new series.

NEVER TEAR US APART
by Quinn Brockton

Never Tear Us Apart

QUINN BROCKTON

They've been to the prom and signed the yearbooks. Now Brian and Michael are apart for the first time since grade school. Brian's soccer scholarship takes him to Carnegie-Mellon, where he finds that he's a fresh—if not a small—fish in a big new pond. Meanwhile Michael, Deb, and Uncle Vic embark on the annual Novotny family vacation in the Poconos, where Michael makes some "new" friends. As sex becomes more than experimentation for both, Brian and Michael struggle with jealousy, homophobia, the realities of HIV, and finding a place of their own as they find their way back to each other.

EVERY NINE SECONDS
by Joseph Brockton

Every Nine Seconds

JOSEPH BROCKTON

On the eve of Brian's eighteenth birthday, he and his best friend, Michael, celebrate a bond that could link them forever if their future paths don't separate them for good. In a few short weeks, Brian, the seductive soccer star, will leave for college, where he'll be free to explore the adult pursuits in which he's only dabbled in high school. Michael is destined for a more sedate life in community college while living at home with his eccentric mom.

POCKET BOOKS
A Division of Simon & Schuster
A VIACOM COMPANY

Available now from Pocket Books

www.simonsays.com

10450

As many as one in three people living with HIV in the U.S. today... don't know it.

KNOW
HIV ▶ AIDS

[Get Tested. You Can Live with the Results.]
For a free guide on HIV/AIDS and other sexually transmitted diseases, or to be connected to someone who can answer your questions NOW...

CALL TOLL-FREE
1 (866) 344-KNOW

OR VISIT
www.knowhivaids.org